Angel Light, Angel Dark

by

Annette Miller

Angel Haven Romance, Book 5

Angel Light, Angel Dark

COPYRIGHT © 2022 by Annette Miller

Cover Art by *Kristian Norris*

The Wild Rose Press, Inc.
PO Box 708
Adams Basin, NY 14410-0708
Visit us at www.thewildrosepress.com

Publishing History
First Edition, 2022
Trade Paperback ISBN 978-1-5092-4249-8
Digital ISBN 978-1-5092-4250-4

Angel Haven Romance, Book 5
Published in the United States of America

He bit the inside of his cheek. He couldn't get involved with her. The princess and the pauper. He snorted. Would the cosmos really be such a bastard to send him someone he wanted to love and couldn't? He hoped the "Powers That Be" got a good laugh out of this because he didn't find any amusement in it at all.

The moment he saw her, he instantly regretted having looked. He suspected Liv put her in those clothes on purpose. The thin, fleece pants accentuated her curves. The T-shirt she wore outlined her breasts and revealed her interest in him. The urge to hold her ran like liquid fire through his veins. Being in her company gave him a little too much pleasure. The longer she remained in the underground, the more he had to remind himself the consequences of touching her.

He'd left so much behind topside, as her presence continuously reminded him. To see what her future held would send him right back to the dark place in his mind. He wished he could spend one night in her arms. One night to have her hold him and chase away his own personal demons. All he craved was one night to not be alone.

Praise for Annette Miller

"[NIGHT ANGEL] is the first book of Ms. Miller's Angel Haven series, and I am hoping she will come up with a bunch more."

~*Annetta Sweetko, Fresh Fiction Reviews*

Ms. Miller's WWW.CUPID was the 2017 4th place winner in the Short Paranormal Romance, International Digital Awards.

Her AN ANGEL'S HEART was the 2018 finalist in the American Fiction Awards.

Her ANGEL IN SHADOW was the 2020 finalist in the American Fiction Awards

Her PRALINE DREAMS was the 2020 winner in the Short Paranormal Romance, International Digital Awards.

Dedication

Dedicated to my husband, Brian, and my sons, Scot and Alex. You guys made me believe in my dreams.

Books by Annette Miller

Angel Haven Series

  Night Angel
  Bedeviled Angel
  An Angel's Heart
  Angel in Shadow
  Angel Light, Angel Dark

Novellas

  www.cupid
  Praline Dreams
  Macaroons by Moonlight

Prologue

Would the palace, the only home Felissina had ever known, stand against the invaders?

Groans echoed as the building's foundation trembled. Windows rattled in their frames, the glass shimmying from the force of the tremors. An explosion outside the wide, mahogany double doors sent down a rain of dust and debris. Felissina's father pulled her and her mother close to his side and covered their heads with his hands. She sneezed before scratching at the dust under her collar as it drifted down her spine.

The king stood with his back to the pair of simple, elegant, oak thrones. "We shall make our stand here."

Onyx energy swirled around Felissina's shaking fingers. "I am ready, Father. These invaders will not get by us."

"Yes, my girl, they will." He gazed at her. "General Primeau himself gave them access to the palace grounds. He has betrayed us." Her father beckoned to one of the servants hidden in deep shadow at the back of the room. "Your mother and I will hold them here while you make your escape. You have just turned eighteen and are of marriageable age. The usurper will take you as his bride if you do not go now. The task of raising an army and freeing the people of Erlymere now falls to you."

Her voice echoed the trembling in her body. "I can

help defend our home. My skills with a sword are excellent, and my powers increase in strength every day. Let me help you fight." She laid her hand on his arm, fighting back tears. "Please."

"Yes, you have grown proficient with both your powers and weapons. However, you do not have the battle experience to fight these men off. You must do as I command." He held her in a tight embrace for a moment, then pressed the gold medallion etched with the family crest into her hand. "I have prepared for this day as soon as the other provinces began to fall to the usurper's army. You will be sent somewhere safe where you can find the aid we need. This is your royal duty."

Felissina stared at the ground and swallowed the growing lump in her throat. "I understand." She stepped back and wiped her eyes. The servant kept watch down a dark corridor as he motioned to her to hurry. She nodded at him before giving her parents a quick hug. "I love you both, and I shall return when I am able to free our lands."

At the concealed entrance, Felissina paused and turned. The door to the throne room crashed open, and soldiers stormed in. Her mother fired quick blasts of black energy from her hands while her father alternated between his own powers and his short sword. The brief but hard fought battle ended, and her parents were taken prisoner.

She eased the door closer to being completely shut while keeping her gaze on her parents. "I should be at their side."

"You know it isn't possible, Your Highness." The servant tugged her toward safety. "I'm not without sympathy, but we must go now before we are discovered."

"Please. Just one more moment."

She clenched the medallion in her fist, her knuckles white as her grip tightened. A deep ache filled her chest as the troops surrounded her parents and stripped the crowns from their heads. She took a small step toward them when the servant grabbed her sleeve. He put a finger to his lips and shook his head.

The usurper sauntered in, and General Alden Primeau, head of the palace guard, followed at a slower pace. Primeau looked directly at her. He gave a small jerk of his head. Did he mean for her to escape? Would he tell the usurper where she went? The servant tugged at her again, and she turned to follow him, pausing one more time.

The invading leader stopped in front of her parents and smiled. "In spite of what you believe, you will not be executed. It wouldn't do to give the people such fine martyrs. No, you shall be imprisoned, but have no fear. You will be quite comfortable." He stepped closer. "Now. Where is the princess? She and I have an appointment at the church."

The servant shut the door before he grabbed Felissina's sleeve tighter and dragged her along behind him. They hurried through the long tunnels for what felt like forever. Did these dark corridors never end? Moisture coated the walls, and the tunnel narrowed.

More minutes passed, and Felissina bit her lip, swallowing the urge to cry. None of this should be happening. Just last month, she'd had her birthday celebration. Everything had been perfect. She scowled. Until today. The tunnel angled up a slight incline, and they emerged behind a small hedge.

They hesitated at the edge of the palace grounds near the science research center. He pulled her to the small, nondescript building and gave her a gentle push inside. The distant echoes of gunfire and swords clanging still reverberated across the courtyard. Sounds of the battle grew closer, and they ran down the short flight of stairs to the lowest level.

The servant knocked on the steel door three times, and it opened a crack. The door was yanked open, and two hands dragged Felissina inside. Judging from the different machines half built on tables, her father's scientists had kept busy. Dozens of machine parts covered a counter along the wall behind the door. Other workbenches held different chemicals laid out with notepads covered with formulas next to them. In the center of the room, a gray tarp, well-worn and faded, covered a huge object.

The head scientist bowed low, the rest of his staff following his lead. "I am sorry, your highness. We couldn't prepare an adequate defense before the invaders arrived. Our priority now is to get you away from here before you are discovered."

He yanked the tarp to the floor. The huge, octagonal machine reached almost to the ceiling, with a control panel bolted to the side. Above the panel were three tubes with clear chemical compounds in them. Lights flashed in a pattern as it emitted a low hum. The whole machine sat on a platform which covered almost the entire open area.

"This will get you to where you need to go."

She walked around it and stared. "You've built a wormhole generator?"

"Yes. It's not perfect, but it will transport you to

another world in our dimension. Don't be afraid. It will be the same as if you stepped through a doorway. You'll be safe." He handed her a bulky, silver belt. "This is a stabilizer belt, in case there are unforeseen problems wherever you end up."

Echoes of metal as it clanged against metal drifted down the hall, and the small group turned as one. Felissina's grip tightened on the belt as she held it against her chest. The hum grew louder as the machine warmed up. The console lights flashed in rapid order, then became a steady glow.

"It is time, your highness. Be safe and come back soon."

"I will."

The door crashed open, and Felissina dived through the dim light of the gateway as the troops fired. The transport started easily enough. Suddenly, lights swirled haphazardly while lightning flashed and Felissina spun out of control. It shouldn't be like this. The scientist said she would feel like she stepped through a doorway. What had gone wrong in the lab?

****

Light exploded around her as Felissina dropped onto hard ground before curling in a tight ball. By all the gods, it hadn't resembled a doorway at all. Her arms and legs tingled with tiny pinpricks of pain. The strange sensation radiated through her limbs, and her fingers twitched. Pressure built in her chest as pain exploded behind her eyes.

Her heart pounded as she struggled to draw a decent breath. Wherever she landed, either the world or the dimension wasn't compatible with hers. Her fingers shook as she finally managed to hook the stabilizer belt around her waist. The controls were simple enough. Her vision began to blur as she adjusted the settings. She released a shuddering breath as the pain in her body began to subside. She lay back down, fighting the urge to cry.

Soft grass tickled her cheek as a light breeze ruffled her hair. Where had she ended up? The air held a hint of brine, so water must be nearby. Could she have landed in some type of wilderness? She rubbed her head, desperately wanting to make sense of her surroundings. A crowd gathered, staring at her, and a man in a uniform approached. His calm tone soothed her a little, but his words were incomprehensible.

"I do not understand your language." She grabbed his arm. "Please. You must help me."

The uniformed man spoke to what appeared to be his colleague. If they couldn't communicate with her, how would she get back home? Tears held in check for too long flowed freely as she lay back down. Hands lifted her with gentleness onto some type of conveyance.

An atrocious cleanser odor burned her nose as she drew in a deep breath to calm her racing heart. A white blanket was placed over her, and she held it in a tight grip. The rolling bed-like apparatus bounced and shimmied over the rough ground. The doors slammed shut before the faint scream of a siren echoed inside the vehicle.

Had she found a safe haven? Did her current location have the resources and people she needed to save her family and her province of Erlymere? She would know in time. Hopefully sooner rather than later.

Chapter One

Fifteen years later

Why had she ever decided to come out here alone? Maybe she should've ignored the stated instructions and brought one of her teammates. Felissina sighed. She'd been told to come alone or she wouldn't get the information she wanted. Her team needed to know what her contact had discovered.

So here she stood, waiting for someone who made his living selling information. She snorted. Imagine her, Felissina Markhov, princess of Erlymere and world-famous pianist, skulking about in a dark alley. Powers considered normal and second nature in her anti-matter dimension gave her the unique classification of "superhero" here on Earth.

Beating up criminals couldn't be the best thing she could do with her abilities, could it? So, why continue with this line of work? She did it because she owed The Angels' superhero team a debt for taking her in and teaching her how to get by on Earth. Each member of the Angels' team had a different type of "superpower." Until recently, they'd been a step above vigilantes. Now, their hero team was recognized as one of the top teams in the city and acted as liaisons for law enforcement.

She glanced at her watch again. The man should

have arrived by now. Felissina constantly checked the time, her foot tapping against the pavement as her impatience grew. He said he'd meet her at five sharp, and already fifteen minutes had slipped past. The autumn sun had almost set, and her irritation grew as the minutes ticked by and the shadows lengthened. He'd better show soon if he didn't want to be the recipient of her temper. Why did he want to meet tonight of all nights? It was movie night and her turn to pick.

The chill November air pierced her jacket, making her shiver as she jammed her hands in her pockets. Thank goodness she'd decided against her Angel team uniform. She didn't need the attention her superhero identity would garner. She also hadn't figured warmth in the design of the bodysuit. Sure, she could wrap the long cape around herself, but the suit itself had no sleeves, with a high cut around the tops of her thighs. She'd designed it for ease in combat, not for comfort in the cold.

Felissina glanced at the colorful harvest banners hanging from the lampposts. As much as she missed her home dimension, Earth did have some wonderful celebrations. Humans loved to throw holiday parties for almost any occasion. Displays of leaves and flowers in red, gold, orange, and brown were prominently displayed in nearby store windows, surrounding turkeys, pilgrims, and cornucopias.

Another glance at her watch showed ten more minutes had passed by. As she paced, she checked the dark crevices between buildings. Why did she continue to wait? If trouble decided to find her, well, she could handle herself. Had unforeseen circumstances delayed her contact? Could this just be a vicious prank to waste her time? She zipped her jacket all the way up and headed for the street. His time and her patience ran out simultaneously. Time to go home.

"I didn't think you'd fall for this," a deep voice said. "From everything I've learned about you, you've become more suspicious in recent years. I guess it helped that I bribed your contact to call you."

Felissina spun around, and her eyes narrowed. "General Alden Primeau. You've finally tracked me to this dimension after all this time. You don't know how often I've prayed for your death over the past fifteen years."

The burly man stepped from the shadows, his black utility suit allowing him to hide in plain sight. He pushed up the burgundy beret he wore and smiled. "I don't go by Alden Primeau here. I've taken the name Shadowjack, in keeping with my own abilities. I'm pleased to see how well you've adapted here, I really am." He rested his hand on his sidearm. "But you've been away from home for far too long. The king is worried about you."

"My father is king. He gave you his complete trust." She scowled, trying to keep her temper under control. "You repaid his trust with utter betrayal. I wouldn't be here if not for you. You should've stood with us, not against us. How could you let the usurper into our palace? Why would you turn on us?"

"The usurper demanded my allegiance. I'd been given men and told to use them to replace some of the newer guards. A word here, an unlocked door there, and because of me, the kingdom fell." A faraway look came into his eyes for a moment. His gaze snapped back to her face. "You were fortunate to escape. I wasn't given the choice or the opportunity. I wish I could tell you the whole story, but time is short." He closed the distance between them. "You need to come with me now. Your presence is desperately needed in our dimension. I'm not the villain you believe me to be. I'm on your side, your highness, and always have been."

"You'll forgive me if I don't believe one word out of your lying mouth. If you insist upon this course of action, things will end badly for you, trust me. I won't regret one minute of what I'll be forced to do."

Felissina shot a black bolt of energy from her hand, forcing Shadowjack to dodge to his left. With continuous, rapid blasts, she backed him toward the streetlight's amber glow. He kept his wrists up, blocking her attack with his thick, metal gauntlets. No matter. A few more steps and she'd be home free.

Three figures turned the corner and entered the alley. She spared them a quick glance as she continued her assault. Shadowjack seized on the distraction and lunged, his large hand curling around her neck. He shoved her back and slammed her head against the brick wall. Dots of light spotted her vision as sharp pain spiked through her head. Spears of agony rocketed down the length of her spine sending stabs of pain through her arms and legs. Did the cretin plan to split her skull open?

"Forgive me, your highness. I'm sorry I have to use force to gain your cooperation."

His grip on her throat tightened, and her struggles grew weaker as she tried to pry his hands from her neck. If she could get him to ease up, just for a moment, she'd be able to draw a decent breath. Her hair snagged on the bricks as he pulled her forward and smashed her head against the wall again. Any more blows and he'd return a corpse to the usurper. And the three people needed to be warned.

"Run," she croaked out. "You're in danger."

She kicked her leg out and caught Shadowjack on the inside of his thigh. His grip loosened a tiny bit, and she kicked out again. Her ears rang, dulling his curse as he slammed her head against the wall for a third time. Blood trickled down the back of her neck and left a warm, wet trail between her shoulder blades. Black dots converged together into a veil of darkness across her vision. As she slid to the ground, she worried the newcomers would become Shadowjack's next targets.

****

Martin Long stopped and wiped beads of moisture from his forehead. The two women with him turned around when they realized he'd fallen behind. He held a hand up to stop them from talking. He closed his eyes and stood still. After several minutes, he opened his eyes and glanced around them while his friends stared at him.

"Something's wrong. If we don't help, someone could be in serious trouble."

Martin jogged down the street, his friends hurrying right behind him. He turned a corner and stopped short as he watched a large man slam a woman's head into the brick wall multiple times. As she slowly slid to the ground, he took in the woman and the man who stood over her.

"Attacking a defenseless woman in our neighborhood will get you hurt. Now back away from her. She isn't moving and probably has some serious injuries, thanks to you. She needs help."

The man turned and glared at the trio. "What she needs is to come with me. What you need is to mind your own business." He slung the woman over his shoulder, and she moaned. "The princess is my property."

"This is the twenty-first century. No one is anyone's property."

The kidnapper pulled a gun, aiming it at Martin's chest. "You don't get to give me orders. I don't know, nor do I care, who you are. Besides, who'll stop me? You? Your compatriots? The three of you are hardly a match for me. She won't be harmed, but you're a different story. I can't let you stand in my way."

Martin glanced at his friends. "You want to bet?"

Martin reached out with his power. The gun the man held aged in seconds, then dissolved into dust. He angled his head a little toward the woman on his left, keeping his concentration on the man in front of him. "Kaz, get the woman away from this guy. Liv, take out his weapons."

"Done," Kaz replied.

Kaz wove her fingers in the air, and tendrils of pale lavender light shot out. They wrapped around the unconscious woman and yanked her from the man's grasp. Liv summoned a blue bolt of light. As it surrounded the man they fought, it fused most of the metal on his body. The bulky, dull gray, metallic belt around his waist appeared to be the only thing unaffected.

Kaz cradled the woman in her arms. "There's a lot of blood. It's hard for me to tell the extent of the injury."

"Gate the three of you back home and get her checked out," Martin said. "I'll follow along in a minute."

"Are you sure?" Kaz glared at the stranger. "He's dangerous."

He narrowed his eyes. "So am I. Get out of here."

"Come on then, human. Do your best to take me down." Shadowjack picked up a pipe from a trash pile. "Better soldiers than you have tried and all failed."

"I'm sure, but I'm not easy to beat, either." He nodded at the rusted pipe. "Do you really think that will work any better than the gun?"

Martin braced himself as the man charged forward. He raised his hand as the pipe swung close to his head. The pipe crumbled to ash as fast as the high-tech gun and blew away in the slight November breeze.

"I suggest you leave my neighborhood. Now. Don't let me catch you here again."

Shadowjack narrowed his eyes as he frowned. "I will be back, human, and you'll regret your actions when we next meet."

Martin frowned as his adversary stepped into the surrounding darkness and disappeared.

"Yeah, like I've never heard someone tell me the exact same thing before," he mumbled as he headed back home.

Chapter Two

Felissina groaned and raised a hand to her head. Her fingers touched soft gauze while hammers clanged out the Anvil Chorus in her brain. The raw, fiery pain in her throat demanded something cold and wet. Every time she moved, different muscles screamed in protest. She grimaced when she turned her head. If only she could loosen the stiffness in her neck. She stilled when she heard quiet whispers nearby.

"You shouldn't be prying in her things, Martin. What will she think if she wakes up to find you pawing through her wallet?"

"We don't have any choice, Liv. What if she's got amnesia or something? The guy who attacked her really did a number on her head."

"Fine, but I want you to know I am *not* happy with this."

He chuckled. "And I'm okay with your state of unhappiness. I'm not stealing anything. I just want to know who to call to come get her."

She cracked open first one eye, then the other to take in her surroundings. No sour smells assaulted her, so she wasn't in the alley. She didn't recognize the room, and the mattress she lay on was firmer than her own. Okay, so not at Angel Haven either. No bleach smell or telltale beeps reached her, so she couldn't be in the hospital. Could those people have taken her to a place where she couldn't be found?

She tried to push herself up and groaned. The room tilted for a brief moment, and she squeezed her eyes shut as she held the bed in a white-knuckled grip. Opening her eyes and trying to move at the same time had become the epitome of bad ideas. She wouldn't be doing that again any time soon.

"Who are you people, and why are you going through my possessions?" she said in a hoarse whisper. "If you're thieves, you won't find anything of importance." Footsteps approached, and she tried to push herself up higher and the room flipflopped again. "Stay out of my personal items."

"We're not thieves. We helped you escape from the man who attacked you," a woman's voice said.

The firm mattress eased the pain in her back, and she sank down. She sighed. It would do until she returned home. The scent of lavender reached her, and she inhaled deeply and let the calming scent fill her. Someone here liked lavender as much as she did. She tugged the covers up higher and smiled when the scent got stronger.

"Hang on. Let me help you. There's a glass of water on the table next to the bed."

Felissina grimaced as she slowly opened her eyes. An unfamiliar young woman propped up the pillows behind her head. She handed her a small, square glass filled with water. Felissina smiled her thanks as she accepted the assistance to sit up. She swallowed a little, then drained every drop. As she drank, her attention was drawn to the other person in the room.

A tall man with shoulder-length, dark-brown hair leaned against the far wall. His arms were folded across his chest, and he studied her. His gaze pierced her as interest lit his eyes. What could he be planning? Had he saved her from one attacker to give her to someone worse? If the ache in her head would abate, even for a brief moment, she might be able to get some answers. While the current raw fire burned her throat, though, maybe not.

"Thank you," Felissina croaked. "I feel like I swallowed a large fireball."

"You must be pretty powerful to hold your attacker off as long as you did. We weren't sure how badly you were injured." The young woman nodded toward the man against the wall. "The two of us and a friend of ours ran him off and brought you here. You have a slight concussion. Our healing magic took care of most of it, but you'll have to heal the rest the natural way, like everyone else."

"I guess I owe you my thanks." As she glanced around the small room, she fought to keep her gaze from drifting back to the man. "Can you tell me where 'here' is exactly?"

"Our team's headquarters. We live underground, in the tunnels beneath the city. We wanted to get you out of sight as quickly as possible. We weren't sure of the bad guy's abilities, and you needed medical attention." The woman checked the bandage, her touch gentle as she pressed on the edges. "You've got a pretty nasty bump on the back of your head, and the bruises on your neck will be there for at least a few days, a week at most."

"I want to trust you, but I don't know you." Felissina touched her throat and grimaced. A momentary flash of relief coursed through her. If she'd been taken back to Angel Haven after her fight, her team leader would hover over her until she healed completely. "Who is your team? How many members do you have? What are your motives?"

"There'll be time to answer all your questions later. You need to rest." The woman fluffed her pillow. "I'll be back in a little bit to check on you."

"Who are you?"

"Olivia Greene. The guy back there is Martin Long. Get some sleep. I know it's hard for you to believe me right now, but you're safe."

The door shut with a quiet click as the two of them left the room. Felissina settled herself in a more comfortable position and closed her eyes. Could her safety be as assured as the girl Olivia claimed? What about the man with her? Olivia mentioned her friend and healing magic. Did she reside in a lair of wizards? The man who watched her certainly seemed to have a magical quality about him.

Right now, though, she craved rest above all else. Desire to return to Angel Haven warred with curiosity about the man who stood against the wall, watching her. Enough. There were more important matters which demanded her attention. After she returned home, she'd begin her search for Shadowjack. When she found him, there would be hell to pay.

****

Martin glanced at the closed door. "I'm glad we got to her when we did. I'm not sure what would've happened to her without our intervention."

"Me, too." Olivia looked at him, making sure to keep plenty of distance between them. "If your powers hadn't evolved again and we hadn't gone to see Kaz, who knows what he would've done to her. I'd call it a coincidence, but Kaz says those are fictional and not to believe in them. She'd say we were meant to be there."

"I guess there is some relevance to all the hocus-pocus you two continuously spout at me." He grinned when she frowned and placed her hands on her hips. "Keep the lecture to yourself, Liv. You know I'm kidding."

"I know, Martin," Olivia said. "But you'd better not call it hocus-pocus to Kaz. She'd laugh at you first, then zap you in a place which shouldn't ever be zapped."

"Kaz is a good person. Stop making her out to be someone she isn't." He headed down the hallway, Olivia right behind him. "Our patient's driver's license says she's from out in Westchester. We have a contact in her area. I'll give him a call. He should be able to tell me more about her."

Olivia grinned. "We should go topside more often and talk to other people than our usual contacts."

"Good point," he said. "After I call, I'll poke around online and see if I can get some kind of ID on her attacker."

Chapter Three

"I didn't expect to hear from you," Grayson Styles said. He pushed his dark hair out of his eyes as he leaned against the doorway and glanced around the room. "This place hasn't changed a bit. I should've come back sooner. Sorry I didn't keep in touch like I promised. Too many memories."

"I get it. Our home hasn't changed in about a hundred and fifty years." Martin took a step back as his mouth curved up in a half smile. "I didn't want to call you. I know you're not fond of the underground, but I didn't have a choice. You've become a bridge between us and your new topside neighborhood. We rescued a woman named Felissina Markhov last night. We might need your help to get her home."

Grayson nodded. "I can do you one better. Felissina is part of the Angels' hero team. She went to meet one of their contacts last night and never made it back. Her team leader, who just happens to be the new Mrs. Styles, worried about her constantly. The whole team wanted to form a search party for her."

"I bet. We had to put her in the personal area instead the medical section. Liv's got some patients down there right now waiting to be transferred to Kaz's clinic." Martin led Grayson down the hall to the private bedrooms. "What made her think she should go out without at least one team member to watch her back?"

"Who knows?" They walked in silence for a few minutes as Grayson stayed a few feet behind Martin. "Felissina is overly headstrong and doesn't like to be known as weak or needing help. She always seems to feel like she has to continually prove herself. I guess it's how she was raised."

Martin nodded. "I'm glad Kaz decided to come back with us. She's usually too busy to leave her clinic for long. She and Olivia got her back here quickly and used some spells to heal the cut on the back of her head. The slight concussion and lump are different stories." He glanced at his hands. "There's no way I could've have brought her by myself."

"It's a big positive having witches for healers," Grayson said and winked. "And friends. Kaz discover what's up with your powers yet?"

"No, not after the recent surge. Now it appears I can age any object in a matter of seconds." Martin sighed and gazed upward. "I don't believe she'll ever figure out what's wrong with my abilities. It's becoming harder for her to keep up with how fast they keep changing. She's not as all-powerful as she likes to think she is."

Grayson laughed. "If you can say that to her face, I'll be happy to bring you flowers in the hospital. That sentiment would go over like a lead balloon. Let's go visit Ms. Markhov."

Martin kept silent the rest of the way to Felissina's room. He hadn't mentioned to anyone about the specters he'd sensed following him in recent days. He'd catch movement out of the corner of his eye. When he'd turn, there wouldn't be anyone there. He didn't need to be haunted by entities that didn't have the decency to at least tell him why they were there.

Every time one particular specter appeared, he ended up drenched in moisture. Water would run down his face, sticking his clothes to his body. And now a strange mist had started to swirl around him at odd times. Did he now attract ghosts, or had he committed an evil act in a former life and karma had decided to make him pay for it? Kaz should be told about this. She might have some weird ghost repellant spell.

Martin knocked on the bedroom door. He entered and stopped short. Felissina sat propped up on several pillows while she sipped water. Her gaze registered no surprise to see him there. What did Olivia tell her about him? Should he ask, and did he really want to know? He opened his mouth to talk to her, but the words never emerged. His breath caught in his throat as he stared at her.

Bright, emerald-green eyes stared at him from an angular face. High cheekbones complemented full lips, now curved up in a small smile. Her shoulder-length hair wasn't just any blonde, but a deep honey gold, a color a lot of women would kill to be able to duplicate. The baggy nightgown Olivia dressed her in hid the rest of her charms, and he breathed a mental sigh of relief. He didn't think he could take the knowledge of how perfect the rest of her would be.

"Do you have something to say to me or can't you speak?" she said. "I can see someone else behind you. If you're not going to say or do anything, I'd appreciate it if you'd step aside and let them enter."

Martin cleared his throat as he moved out of the doorway. "I didn't know if you'd be awake. I brought a mutual friend to come see you. I figured he'd know where you live. I thought we might need his help to get you home. Turns out, he already knows your address."

"I see," she said, her eyes sparkling with quiet amusement. "Why didn't you just ask me? I would've told you all you needed to know."

He shrugged. "Kaz and Olivia diagnosed you with a slight concussion. You could've ended up with some form of amnesia. Sorry I poked through your wallet." He stepped off to one side. "Anyway, a friend of yours is here."

"Feli?" Grayson said as he entered the room. "What the hell happened to you? And why didn't you take someone with you? We've told you how dangerous it is to go on any kind of mission alone."

"I thought I only had to meet with an informant. I didn't know I'd be set up for a vicious attack by a known traitor from my home dimension." She glared at him. "Do I need to remind you *again* not to speak to me like I'm a child?"

"No, sorry." He pulled the chair closer to the bed. "Your friends got worried when you didn't come home. When I got the call from Martin, I hoped luck would be on our side." He grinned. "And here we are."

"I'll leave you two to talk. If you need me, I'll be in the kitchen." Martin turned to Felissina. "Did you want some food?"

"If you've got some soup, I believe it would be the best possible remedy right now, thank you."

"We do. I'll heat it up."

Martin hurried to the kitchen. He grabbed one of the smaller containers with a single serving of soup in it from the freezer. As the thick broth simmered, he thought about the encounter with her attacker. The man called her a princess. As far as Martin knew, princesses didn't lurk about in alleys. However, Grayson called her a superhero, and they did lurk in alleys. While he stood alone for a few minutes, he allowed her to fill his thoughts.

He could picture those bright, emerald eyes and her impossibly golden hair. He'd never seen any woman so beautiful. She had a certain aura about her which tickled the back of his mind. The image of her being attacked had slammed into him, clear as day. No way would he tell Olivia and Kaz. They still couldn't figure out why his powers changed on an almost daily basis.

Time to stop these thoughts before he gave himself a headache. He got a soda from the refrigerator. He grabbed deli meat, mustard, and two kaiser rolls and threw them on the counter. He rummaged in the silverware drawer and pulled out a butter knife, pausing when he heard movement behind him. He glanced over his shoulder and smiled.

"Hey, Liv. I wanted to come see you after I ate. Our patient would like some soup."

Olivia stood a good foot and a half shorter than him. She'd dropped out of nursing school when her magic started to become harder to control. She got "volunteered" to be the underground's medical person when she first came. Her gamer side showed when she'd laughed and said, "Someone has to be the cleric." He'd come to rely on her sense of humor more often than not.

"I'd hoped she'd want some food." Olivia grabbed a soda, staying a good distance away from him. "I'm glad we got to her in time. What do you think the guy who attacked her meant when he called her a princess?"

"I've given his comment a lot of thought." He ate his sandwich, taking his time to answer. "Somehow, I think she is a princess. She certainly has the air of the upper class. When do you think she'll be able to go back home? With the way my powers have evolved, someone who doesn't know about me could pose a problem or could possibly be in danger."

"I know." Olivia paused. "I don't think she should leave for at least a few days. I'd like for the lump to go down a little more. Kaz said she has a slight concussion and not to move her so much. We listen to the woman with more experience than me. I also want to be sure she's not dizzy or feels faint when she stands."

"I agree." Martin jerked his thumb toward the ceiling. "With the walking armory up there gunning for her, she needs not to be so shaky." He glanced at Olivia. "If he attacks when we take her out, it won't end well for her."

"Or us." Olivia tapped her fingers on the table. "I hope she doesn't object too much."

"I have a pretty good suspicion she'll probably object. We can't call this place the Ritz." Martin leaned against the counter while he ate his second sandwich. "Grayson says she's a member of the Angels."

"I knew he'd recognize her. He knows everyone." Olivia stared at the table. "You don't mind if she stays longer, do you?"

He shrugged. "If this is where she needs to be, I'll have to be okay with it."

"Martin, I saw how you looked at her. I could almost feel the electricity flow between you two." Olivia turned the soda can in a slow circle. "You felt some kind of emotional connection, didn't you?"

"And here I thought I hid my feelings so well. She's the most beautiful woman I've ever seen." He straightened up the kitchen, not wanting to look at his friend. "And there's no way I could ever touch her. You know, people always say our powers are a gift. My 'gift' seems more like a curse or some kind of sick cosmic joke. You don't know how many times a day I wish I was just a plain, ordinary person. No gifts, no powers, nothing."

"I know. I'm so sorry."

He turned and stared at his friend, seeing the all too familiar look he hated. "Stop. You don't need to pity me. I've made peace with this strange power I possess. She'll go home soon, our routine here will get back to normal, and the rest of the team will come out of their rooms. I'll be all right."

He placed a bowl of soup and some crackers on a tray and left the kitchen.

****

Felissina woke and saw another glass of water on the table. As she drank it, she realized another person sat in the room. She stared at Olivia, taking in her appearance. Her long, dark-brown hair had the richness of mahogany. Her features were as plain as her clothes, but Felissina thought Olivia could be very pretty, given the chance. She only needed a little makeup and possibly a better wardrobe. Such a small change would make the young woman stunning.

"Hello, Olivia. I'm happy to see you again," Felissina said, keeping her thoughts to herself.

"Back at you. If you don't mind, I need to check your wound and see how it's healing so far."

Felissina hesitated, then nodded. "If not for

Grayson's presence, I would've fought to get away."

Olivia put her medical supplies on the table. "And none of us would've blamed you in the least." She worked in silence for a few minutes. "The wound itself is closed and almost healed. The bump may take a day or two more to go down. Your voice sounds better, too."

"The soreness has eased a lot since I first came here. It's a relief to hear good news about my injury."

"Grayson let your team know you're all right while you were eating. He had started to leave but stayed a little longer." Olivia stood. "He wants to talk to you for a few more minutes. Are you up for it?"

"Yes." Felissina adjusted the covers when she left, and Grayson walked in. "Please tell the team I'm very sorry for all of this. I didn't mean to make them worry."

He laughed and pulled the chair next to the bed. "Apologies already conveyed. Next time, will you take some backup with you? We've told you this many, many times."

"By all the gods. Everyone acts as though I can't take care of myself. I'm the daughter of a warrior king. I've learned from the best trainers, including Kristin, my team leader and your wife."

"Uh huh." He gestured to the room. "However, I think this situation says it all. Kristin had your car taken back to Angel Haven. Do you remember what happened?"

"Of course. The former general of my father's palace guards, Alden Primeau, attacked me. He told me he's taken the name Shadowjack here. As I began to lose consciousness, I saw some people enter the alley where he ambushed me."

"Those people were Martin, Olivia, and Kaz, all friends of mine. They found you and sent your attacker on his not-so-merry way. They brought you here." He winked. "Isn't it better to have magic heal you instead of Kristin poking you every hour of the day?"

"Yes, but don't tell her I said so." She smoothed the covers. "Are all the people here magic users?"

"No, just Olivia and Kaz. The team here has, I guess you'd say 'normal' powers, like you and the other myriad of superheroes in this city."

Felissina looked around at the sparse furnishings and felt the chill bleed through the rough, brick wall. An area rug with bright red, blue, and green geometric designs covered the floor. It didn't look very thick, but it was still pretty. No pictures hung on the walls. The furniture looked neat, but worn. Visible scratches could be seen on the few wood pieces.

"Can't I return to Angel Haven today?"

"Not today. Be nice." Grayson patted her hand. "The team here doesn't have much because they don't need much. I know this isn't exactly what you're used to, but for now, you'll have to make do."

"I suppose," she mumbled. She laid a hand over her mouth, stifling a yawn. "When I woke earlier, I glimpsed a man in here with Olivia. Then he came back with you. Who is he? And who exactly is this team everyone keeps mentioning?"

"His name is Martin Long." Grayson nodded. "He's the temporary leader of this team. The team here is called the Underground. They hide themselves away when a new person shows up. Once you leave, they'll come out. Some of them have odd appearances and some have unpredictable powers. They don't want to scare or hurt you."

She picked at the blanket, forcing her eyes to stay open. "I see. What else can you tell me about Martin Long?"

He stood and put the chair back. "All I can really say is you can trust him. I'm headed back topside. I've got my own assignments to complete. They'll let me know when you're able to come home." He walked to the door and turned. "And Feli? Don't zap anyone, okay?"

She frowned slightly. "As you wish."

Chapter Four

"Would you care to explain again how she escaped?" Dr. Anita Haines' eyes narrowed. "You told me no one got away from you once you caught them."

Shadowjack examined his beret and brushed off a few dust specks. "Even the best of us can have an off day."

He forced himself to refrain from rolling his eyes as he watched her pace. The telepath could be considered beautiful with her blonde hair and long legs. "I know you think you can intimidate me, like you could a 'normal' person, but you can't. I'm not even close to normal."

She stopped and glared at him. "I could rip you apart telekinetically before you could bat an eyelash. Don't push me."

"Nice to see you've decided to show your true colors at last. I believe complete candor is always best, especially in these types of arrangements."

"Really?" She folded her arms. "How perfectly naïve of you."

"I knew all those smiles and calm determination you showed when we first met were just a front." He held his hand up, stopping her retort. "I was, and still am, grateful for your help when I first arrived on Earth. I was impressed when I found out you were Dr. Anita Haines, the head researcher of HelixCorp. Imagine my surprise when I discovered the exalted scientist was actually the psionic criminal, Vertigo. You've built quite a reputation for yourself, in the lab and on the battlefield. Of course, the more I got to know you, the more I've come to realize you're no better than the usurper I left behind."

"The fact you think I care about anything you say is laughable. Just prove to me I haven't made a mistake hiring you."

He tugged his beret down on his head. "You haven't. I told you that at the beginning of this mission. You still haven't explained why you want my princess brought here."

Her scowl deepened as she ignored his comment. "You've been paid, in advance, to deliver the Angel CT to me, sooner rather than later. If you can't do the job, tell me now and I'll hire someone more competent."

"I've warned you not to question my abilities." He rose to his full height to tower over Anita, not surprised when she didn't back down. "You can call her CT, or superhero, or Angel, I don't care which. To me, she is Princess Felissina Markhov of the province of Erlymere, and under my protection. If I didn't need your resources, I wouldn't be here now. I remind you once again. You aren't to harm her in any way. She is of royal blood."

"I promise you, she'll leave here unmarked." She moved closer to Shadowjack. "Unless she decides to be uncooperative. Then it may present a small problem."

He folded his arms and glared at her. "As a telepath, I wonder why you need her here at all. Can't you mind scan and get her location?"

"Because she's from an anti-matter dimension, her

psychic signature is hard to read. It's easier to deal with her when she's close by. Now, find her and bring her here."

Shadowjack sauntered to the door and turned. "If you can't read her and she's been here for over a decade, this explains why you can't contact me with your telepathy. You can't read me either." When her eyes narrowed, he smiled. "Don't worry, doctor. You've paid for my services. You're safe."

As he left the office, his smile faded. "For now," he murmured.

****

Anita stared at the closed door, happy she'd decided to have him slated for experimentation. As soon as he delivered CT to her, Shadowjack would find himself as one of her subjects. She smirked at the thought of destroying his smug confidence. She sat at her desk and opened a spiral notebook. All she had to do was find out what made him tick.

She jotted down notes on what she knew about Shadowjack. He had strength, but she could overcome that attribute easily enough. She listed his height at over six feet, sandy blond hair, and too much attitude. The wide, silver belt he wore obviously contained his life support. It wouldn't do to tamper with it until she was ready to or he gave her a reason. If he had any powers, he hadn't demonstrated them yet. Check on paranormal abilities, she wrote in the margin.

A soft knock roused her from her thoughts. "Come in."

A thin man with a lab coat at least two sizes too large hanging from his shoulders entered. He hurried straight over and stopped in front of her desk. "Dr.

Haines, your new test subject has been brought in. I believe this girl is one you've wanted for quite some time. She has no family or team affiliation. No one will search for her. She won't be missed by anyone."

She thumbed through the file her assistant handed her. "The psionic who projects a sonic attack directly into the mind?"

"Yes, ma'am."

"Wonderful. I'll be down to the lab in a moment. Mr. Trust will want to be notified right away."

Her assistant gave a slight bow and walked out of her office as she reached for the phone. Now, if Shadowjack would be as competent as he claimed, things would go her way.

****

Felissina lay in bed, glad the pain in her head had dropped from a sharp ache to a dull throb. The room no longer spun when she glanced around. Once again, she sent up a prayer of thanks for her enhanced healing factor. The same man who stared at her earlier sat in the chair, his gaze on a paperback in his hands. The sparse furniture and the condition of the room were immediately forgotten.

How could he not have commanded her full attention right away when he brought Grayson in earlier? His shoulder-length, wavy, black-brown hair had streaks of silver, even though he didn't look old enough to go gray. Short, scruffy stubble covered his cheeks and made his angular face look narrow and thin. His shoulders were broader than the average human, the muscles in his arms visible under the short sleeves of his T-shirt.

But his hands caught her attention. White scars

crisscrossed over his knuckles, and a burning desire to ask how he got them roared through her. Large hands with long fingers cradled the book he held, treating the small item as if it were a priceless heirloom. What kind of man could he be to treasure such a simple thing? And would those wonderful hands hold her with as much tenderness?

He looked up and a small part of her, whether it was her heart, her soul, or her mind, recognized him. The sense she knew him, had known him, for many years on a deep, primal level raced across her nerves. Pale, gray-green eyes held a hint of sadness. His life couldn't be so hard, could it? Then he smiled, and the sadness evaporated as though it never existed.

"How are you feeling?" he asked.

She shivered at the deep, melodic tones of his voice. His words rolled through her and caressed her nerves to send tiny tremors up her spine. She tried to speak, but the words refused to come out. She cleared her throat and tried again. "A little better, thank you. I still get tired too easily, though."

He nodded toward the table next to the bed. "I refilled your water glass, in case you needed more." His small half smile drew her gaze to his mouth. "From the sound of your voice, I think it's a fair assumption you do."

Her heart began to skip beats the longer she watched him. Words failed her. She should say something, give him any kind of response. Her mind went blank as she tried to make herself give him some type of answer. He raised his eyebrows, and she realized he waited patiently for her response.

"I think you're right." She sipped the water, giving

herself time to come up with something coherent to say. "I must thank you and your friends again for your timely intervention." She rubbed her throat. "I can't wait for this soreness to ease."

"It should clear up in a day or two, along with the bruises. You already sound better than you did. You healed a lot faster than I thought. Liv thinks you should stay a little longer, though, to give yourself more time to rest."

"Who's Liv?"

"Sorry. I meant Olivia, our medical person. I slip sometimes and use her nickname around new people. Most times, I call her Liv. She checked your bandage a little while ago."

Felissina nodded once and even such a small movement started the ache all over again, spiking for a brief moment, before fading. "I'm glad Grayson came here. He told me you can be trusted." She lay back, imagining the pillow as his shoulder. "If you hadn't come along when you did, my attacker may have accomplished his goal."

"Whatever he wanted, it couldn't have been good. We weren't sure of his identity, but we knew we'd better stop him." He inched the chair a little closer to the bed. "Who is he? Where's he from? Any idea as to why he wanted to take you prisoner? The more you can tell me, the more prepared I can be if I meet up with him again."

"In my home dimension, his name is General Alden Primeau. He told me he goes by Shadowjack here on Earth." She stifled a yawn, already worn out just from the few minutes of talking. "I don't know why he'd show up after so much time has passed."

"And your dimension is…"

"I'm from an anti-matter dimension." She covered another yawn, amazed at how tired she became from just a short conversation. "You live in a matter dimension. There are similarities between our homes, but many more differences. I've tried to find a way to return to my home for the past fifteen years."

"So I guess the old line of 'you're not from around here' applies."

"Quite so." Felissina struggled to keep her eyes open. If she could stay awake for a few more minutes, he'd stay and talk more with her. "I've told you a little bit about me. Can you tell me something about yourself now?"

He gripped the paperback a little tighter. "That's a story for another day. You need your rest." He stood and walked over to the door and hesitated. "Liv will be back later to check on you."

She laid a hand over her mouth, hiding her third yawn, wishing the fatigue would go away. "All right."

What did he mean? Could his secrets be so terrible to make him brush off her request so quickly? Martin's reluctance to talk about himself ignited her curiosity and sparked her imagination. He must have an interesting story to tell. It would be hard, but if she got him to open up it would be worth the trouble.

"I wish you'd come back instead," she murmured.

She heard the door click shut and let her eyelids close. Would she have her familiar dream of home or of a stranger with an unexpectedly tight grip on her heart?

****

"How's she doing?" Olivia asked.

Martin shrugged as he pulled the door shut.

35

"Better. She's sleeping right now. We had a brief conversation." He hesitated. "She wanted to know about me."

"And what did you tell her?"

"Nothing." Martin shook his head. "It's better if she never knows the truth. This power of mine is a damn curse. I can handle the rough parts, but not the way it changes all the time. If I can't get my powers to stabilize…"

"I get it, but you can't stay shut away forever."

"And I'm going to repeat myself and say you've repeated yourself." Martin straightened up. "Trust me. I'm okay with the isolation. I'd appreciate it if you keep my past to yourself."

"You know Kaz and I will keep it all quiet unless you give us the go ahead."

He walked around Olivia. "I've got to go to the computer lab. This Shadowjack clown has to have some deep reason for wanting to kidnap her. You know, other than the fact he called her a princess. I think I'll check with some people I know and see what they've heard."

"Good idea." Olivia hesitated. "Should you try to call Kaz? Someone may have come through The Center who's heard a rumor or two. There's a possibility Felissina might know his reasons. When she wakes up, ask her."

"She already said she doesn't have a clue about his recent appearance, but I'll ask her again," Martin said.

If he talked to her, it would give him a little more time in her company. Even if he could never know how her skin felt under his hands, he could at least look at her. If he asked her for more information about Shadowjack and her dimension, he could be with her.

For now, conversation would have to be enough.

****

That night, Martin tossed and turned in his sleep, kicking off the covers. He dreamed again of the colorless land he'd seen before. He stood in one spot, afraid to move, afraid to stay still. Voices murmured quietly in his ear, telling him he had finally come home. His knew his home was Boston and the gray, washed-out landscape looked nothing like the familiar buildings of his childhood.

When the voices increased in volume, he put his hands over his ears, desperate to shut them out. Silver mist crawled over his body, solidifying into what looked like a type of armor. Legions of spirits floated closer to him, and he lashed out. A sword appeared in his hand, and he swung in a wide arc, keeping the specters at bay.

As they rushed toward him, his eyes flew open. He sat up, wiping sweat from his forehead. His chest heaved as he sucked air into his lungs and rubbed his eyes. That had to be the worst nightmare yet. When would these dreams end?

And why did he feel compelled to go back to the strange land with its ghostly inhabitants?

Chapter Five

"Why are people always up in everyone's business until I need them to be?" Martin grumbled.

Shadowjack certainly lived up to his code name. He seemed to be the embodiment of shadow. Didn't anyone else have any contact with this guy? From the small amount of intel he'd received, he'd have to say no. To be fair, the higher profile topside teams were kept busy with bigger problems. He supposed lesser-known teams, like his, had to take care of the smaller issues. Tracking some scumbag mercenary hit the bottom rung on the topside teams' priority ladder when it came to fighting crime and corruption.

Movement in his peripheral vision caught his attention. He stared straight ahead and hoped the specter would come closer so he could identify it. "Who are you? Why do you keep following me?"

A small, cool breeze flowed over him, and a thin sheen of moisture beaded on his forehead. He couldn't stand it any longer. He jumped to his feet and faced the figure as the door opened. Liv waved at him and smiled. He sat with a hard thump and watched as the specter dissipated, a cool mist left in its wake. Well, so much for getting answers right now.

"Damn," he muttered.

"What? Did I do something wrong or interrupt you in the middle of something important?"

"No. I'm just frustrated with different aspects of my life right now."

"Oh." She leaned against the frame, making sure she'd stayed more on the hallway side of the door. "Did you ferret out any interesting information?"

"Nope. Not even a tiny bit of the boring kind of information." He tossed the pen on the desk. "I called George before I got on the computer, and his information panned out. No one's even heard about this guy."

"Could someone have hired this Shadowjack person to grab her?"

Martin swiveled the chair to look at her. "I've considered the possibility. George said rumor has it Benedict Trust is the one calling the shots. None of us needed to hear such wonderful news. If Trust is involved, you know his favorite scientist, Anita Haines, isn't far behind. And he can throw money at this guy until Felissina is picked up. If Shadowjack is from Felissina's home dimension, as she claims, how did Haines get in touch with him?"

Olivia shrugged. "In her alter ego as Vertigo, her influence runs very deep in this town. One of her spies could have told her and then brought him to her."

"It would explain a lot." He turned back to the computer screen. "Except how he got here."

"I suspect he came through a wormhole, like Felissina did. Remember the big explosion a couple of months back?" When he nodded, she continued. "Need I say more?"

"How come he didn't get hurt? He should've had some kind of injury, no matter how small." Martin rubbed his chin. "Can wormholes cause explosions big enough to wipe out a hundred feet of trees in every direction?"

"I guess so. Grayson told me Felissina explained when a wormhole is opened, it's like blowing up a balloon. A generator makes it bigger and bigger until it's large enough for a person to fit through. When it reaches the right size, it pops, like a small explosion." Olivia grinned. "But the pop shouldn't have been quite so dramatic."

"Huh. It's not like it is in movies, is it."

"Not even close." She folded her arms and leaned against the doorframe. "You have any thoughts?"

"Maybe it was so much bigger because she and Shadowjack come from an anti-matter dimension. Since our dimension is matter, the two don't coincide and therefore, boom. Did her arrival cause an explosion as big as his?"

She nodded toward the computer. "Oh, yeah. Look it up. It happened about fifteen years ago. I've got to run. I need to call Grayson and give him an update on Felissina's condition. I'll see you later."

Martin watched her leave and glanced at the computer. He shouldn't look for the article. Other leads needed to be checked out. He'd had some bad ideas before, but knowing Felissina's history would top the list. Once he started down this path, he wouldn't stop until he knew all he could. He entered his topic into the search bar and hit enter before he changed his mind.

First things first. He needed to know the definition of an anti-matter dimension. "Please don't be all scientific jargon or theoretical mumbo jumbo."

When the definition loaded, he gave a heavy sigh of resignation. Of course luck wouldn't be on his side.

The scientific doubletalk stated "anti-matter is defined as a material composed of anti-particles (or partners) of the corresponding particles of ordinary matter."

Yeah, right. The familiar urge to bang his head on the desk ran through him. "Thanks very much, internet gods. And Webster, your definition didn't help either."

On to the woman who held his interest. He found the article and pulled it up. Fifteen years ago, a large explosion lit up the middle of the city. When the smoke cleared, a young girl lay on the ground, curled on her side, a wide silver belt around her waist. No one could identify the language she spoke. She'd been whisked away and taken to an unknown location.

Somehow, she ended up with the Angels. Martin guessed the "Powers That Be" didn't want a strange, alien girl lost in the city. He rubbed his chin. Somehow, she adapted to their dimension and learned the language. But how? What happened?

Martin stood and stalked from the computer room. It had happened, just as he feared. He'd started to learn about her, and now he wanted to know more. Time to go topside and see what kind of information he could dig up on Shadowjack.

****

"No new info since the last time we talked?" Martin asked. "George, as Kaz's righthand man, you should know something. You have the most extensive network of anyone around. I'm not sure how you find out as much as you do, but I'm grateful you can. Are you sure there's nothing you can tell me?"

"Sorry. You should be glad I discovered as much as I did." He lowered his voice. "The best lead I got turned out to be what I told you about Benedict Trust.

My sources are sure he's the money behind the operation. Until I get some kind of confirmation, though, you're flying blind."

"It wouldn't be the first time." Martin glanced at the end of the alley. "Trust is the biggest and most powerful of scumbags in this city. He's got his fingers in a lot of pies, some legal, but a lot more illegal. You have to wonder why he wants the Angel and why now all of a sudden."

"I don't work with suppositions, only facts. But if he wanted her dead, he wouldn't have hired Shadowjack to get up close and personal. I don't think I want to know what he wants from her. Whatever it is, it won't be good."

Martin shuddered and rubbed his hands together, trying to ward off an internal chill. "If you hear anything else, let me know."

"You know I will." George waited a moment, then asked, "Any more of those weird dreams or visions? Kaz told me to ask."

"Not in the last week. Let her know, the last time I had one, I saw this strange land. Vague shapes were everywhere. I feel like I hear a summons from there. It doesn't scare me, but it feels familiar, like it's calling me home. I'm also sensing spectral gazes on me. Every time I catch movement out of the corner of my eye, I end up covered in a thick mist. It could give her a good place to start."

"It might. See you later, Martin. I got to get back to The Center."

"Take care, George."

Martin watched as George hurried away on whatever errand Kaz sent him on this time. What should his next move be? He could ask the topside hero teams for help, but they all had too much on their plates to worry about one halted kidnapping. Once again, it fell to him to figure out what Shadowjack wanted with Felissina.

****

Shadowjack leaned against the wall, his arms folded across his chest. "Are you sure this is accurate?"

The grimy informant nodded once. "Yeah. I don't know the one woman's name, but I do know she's currently with a team who lives underground. The second in command down there is a guy called Martin Long. They stay out of sight because they all got freaky powers or looks.

"I know the other person, though. It sounds like a woman who goes by Kaz. She's got a clinic somewhere in the city. No one can find it unless they're invited. Rumor says she moves it around by magic to keep it hidden and has a lot of power. Her righthand man is a short guy. He always wears dark or drab colors. Unless you're actively looking for him, he's easy to miss."

"Interesting." Shadowjack tapped his fist against his thigh. "You've given me a good lead, for a change. Can you let me know if you see him again?"

The man shrugged. "I can try. No one ever sees him come or go. When he's on one of Kaz's errands, it's like he hides himself so he can't be seen."

He handed the man some bills. "Do your best."

"Yes, sir."

As his informant left, Shadowjack pushed away from the wall. Martin Long. Such a common name for the man who attacked him. As soon as he could, he'd meet with Martin Long, try to discover his motives. As much as he regretted it, he'd then take Felissina to Anita and activate the wormhole generator. They'd be out of this backward dimension and back home soon after.

He laid his hand on a single panel on the bulky, gray belt around his waist. The way back sat hidden under his fingers right now. He could leave whenever he wanted. He and the scientists had worked day and night to fix the machine. He toyed with the idea of going back to tell the usurper Felissina hadn't survived. No one would know she still lived. He squeezed his eyes shut and frowned. No. He'd hurt her parents badly enough already.

However, the fat pig of a king would never marry her. Shadowjack would make sure of it. The thought of those sausage fingers on her flesh made his own skin crawl. With his cooperation forced, he'd had no choice but to betray the royal family's trust in him. He still considered the princess under his protection. As long as he lived, she'd be safe. He'd do all in his power to stop the usurper's marriage to her.

When he felt sure no one watched him, he stepped into the shadows and disappeared.

Chapter Six

Anita stared at her newest subject, but her focus turned inward. Nostalgia began to consume her as she dwelt on her past. The girl on the other side of the glass screamed when her assistant injected the improved serum into her arm.

"Well, here I am again, Dad," she whispered. "I'm back in charge of research at HelixCorp. It was touch and go there for a while, but I managed to convince Trust he needed me." She frowned. "Damn heroes always get in my way. Why can't they just leave me alone and let me do my work in peace?"

She gave a small snort. "I know you wouldn't approve of my recent methods, but they seem to be the only way I can get the results demanded of me. Wouldn't it be something if one day I could lead HelixCorp?" She laughed quietly. "Don't worry, Dad. It's just a pipe dream. Benedict Trust can have it and all of its political red tape. I'm happy in the lab."

A lab tech walked up behind her. "Dr. Haines, here's the report on the new subject and the three we picked up last week. The results look promising."

She took the folder and flipped through the pages. "You're right. Two of them might be ready for the second phase. This time, I won't be rushed. Draw more blood, run the advanced diagnostics, and up the serum's dosage. Monitor them closely for the next several days to see if they exhibit any unusual symptoms. I want to be informed about any changes, no matter how small."

"Yes, ma'am. I'll make sure the team knows."

He walked away, and she hurried back to her office. Time to let Benedict Trust know the progress on their various experiments. Her phone vibrated before she could pick it up, and she frowned when she glanced at the caller ID. Shadowjack. He'd better have good news.

"What is it?" she snapped.

"I talked to one of my informants. He has an idea who the people are who helped the princess escape. I have a few more leads to check out, then I'll be in to make my report."

"It's about time you made some decent progress. I'll see you soon."

With his phone call, her day got better. She hit the auto-dial and looked forward to her report to Mr. Trust. This Thanksgiving, she'd give thanks and, for the first time in years, would mean it.

****

Shadowjack stared at the woman in front of him. One of his contacts told him she might know more information. Another correct lead. Humans turned on each other faster than two starving dogs over a bone. She knew Martin Long. He'd helped to save her, but when he refused her offer of physical payment, she'd been offended. Very offended. This world did have a wonderful quote about a woman scorned.

"So, how do I find this underground team?"

She shrugged. "I don't know. They show up when someone's in trouble. They stay out of the spotlight as much as they can." She rubbed her upper arms. "Bunch of weirdos if you ask me."

He reached in his pocket and pulled out wad of bills. "You said Martin Long came to your aid. Did anyone else accompany him?"

"Some girl with brown hair." The prostitute snorted. "I didn't give her a second glance. He did most of the work. She just stood there, waving her hands in the air."

Could Martin Long's other companion be a magic user the same as the woman, Kaz? The possibility of witches seemed to grow with every person he spoke to. The women with Long, when they'd ambushed him, had demonstrated powers. The fact this woman didn't see anything proved she was less than ordinary, with no powers or any other kind of ability.

"Anyone else?"

She shrugged. "Yeah. A woman with red hair was with him, too. I got a real bad vibe from her."

She just described Kaz, whom his other informant mentioned. He handed over a few of the bills to her. "Thank you for your help."

She moved closer to him. "If there's any other way you want to say thanks, look for me. You can find me around here this time of day."

Shadowjack watched her walk away and admired the sway of her hips. However, admiration was all he allowed himself. Right now, there was work to be done. Martin Long and his companions needed to be found. Would he be able to grab all three of them simultaneously or would he have to pick up the witches by themselves?

If they stayed true to heroic form, taking one companion would make the others come to him.

Felissina would hear of it, then would come out of hiding to effect a rescue. After leaving her sanctuary, she wouldn't be a problem to grab. He'd take her to Anita, let the telepath get whatever information she wanted, then they'd take a quick trip through the wormhole to their dimension.

He stared at the small scanner he pulled from his belt. "Now, how to find a woman who may or may not have magical abilities? I don't think it's possible to recalibrate such a low-tech device to scan for magic."

The way his informant talked about Kaz, the woman had some serious power. He'd need to take special precautions with her. The time had come to talk to his network of informants and see what they knew. Stepping into the shadows surrounding him, he teleported to an impoverished neighborhood.

The rundown apartment building provided cover for him, should he have to make a hasty escape. Residents scurried in and out, keeping their gazes down or straight ahead. Human rats trying to hide from the world. More than an hour had passed when a small man hurried in. He thanked the gods he'd been staring at the front of the building. This could be the man his contact told him about.

His clothes and demeanor made him easy to overlook. Reddish-brown hair peeked out from under the flat cap jammed down on his head. He stood at the most five feet tall. He wore a brown shirt, dark blue pants, and a deep green jacket. He didn't look around, just kept his face forward, his stride strong as he walked with purpose. People lounged on the steps of the building, and he dodged around those who refused to move.

The little man clutched a bag to his chest and ran up the stairs, taking them two at a time. Shadowjack checked the time and waited. Fifteen minutes later, the little man came back down without the bag and hurried to the street. With luck, this man would lead him straight to the magic user. He pushed away from the comfort of the shadows and followed him.

He glided through the darkness climbing the walls, staying behind the man for several blocks. The man stopped before a brick wall and passed his hand in front of it. The bricks faded and a door appeared. He knocked three times and held up a paper resembling a large playing card. The door opened and he slipped inside. When the door clicked shut, the bricks reappeared.

Shadowjack rubbed his chin. "It appears it will be far more difficult to see the witch than I planned. She should definitely come out to me."

He backed into the shadows and faded in an instant.

****

Martin stood inside the entrance to his team's underground home. Why didn't anyone have anything to tell him? Even the tiniest shard of information would've helped. Shadowjack may want to find out who they were. If he did and decided to come for them, could Martin protect those in his care?

"As much as I want to keep Felissina with me, my team has to come first. It would be selfish to ask her to stay when it would keep my people in hiding. Why can't there be a middle ground? Why do I always have to choose between the rock and the hard place?" He sighed and stared at the ceiling. "And now I'm back to talking to myself. Terrific."

The long main tunnel stretched out before him. As he trudged down the familiar route, he ran his fingers along the rough, stone wall. Life threw him so many odd twists and turns. As he touched the walls, he lived their "memories" and never grew tired of their stories. Knowledge of the past filled him, and he took a deep breath, trying to calm his turbulent emotions.

Martin told Olivia he'd found peace with what he could do, but had he? Humans weren't meant to live without physicality with other humans. He'd taken those connections for granted all his life. As time dragged on, the absence of touching someone opened a wider gap in his heart. Over the past few years, he'd turned more and more into an extreme isolationist.

A light shone in Olivia's office. He straightened his shoulders, forced a smile on his face, and walked in. If Liv saw his defeated expression, she'd worry about him more. Just because he'd turned into a hot mess didn't mean everyone around him should be, too.

Olivia looked up from some paperwork. "I wondered when you'd get back. What did you learn?"

"Not a whole lot." He jerked his head toward the area where Felissina recovered. "When do you think she should leave?"

"Not for another couple of days yet. There's still a lump on her head, and she's been in bed for a few days. She needs a little more time to regain her strength."

Martin sagged down on a chair. "Makes sense. I thought so, too. She might be weaker than she's used to. She's got a rapid healing factor, but it doesn't mean she's recovered all of her strength yet."

"Kaz could use a transport spell like she did when we brought her here," Olivia said slowly. "However, I don't want her moved too much until I'm confident she'll be okay. A portal can jar a person pretty hard sometimes, especially if they aren't used to it."

"True. Is she any better?"

"Getting better every day. I've got to get my med kit and change the bandage on her head."

Martin stood and walked toward the hallway. "I'll ask her again if she has some idea why Shadowjack would show up here after all these years to take her down. Maybe she's thought of a piece of information we haven't considered yet."

Olivia smiled. "You go ahead. I'll be along in a minute."

Her knowing smile told him he didn't fool her for a second. She knew he wanted to be with Felissina, and it became harder and harder to resist the rising desire.

Chapter Seven

"You have no idea at all?" Martin said, as he paced the same path. "I realize I've asked this before, but could you have missed some detail? Some small, unrelated thing?"

"I'm sorry. The wormhole generator in my dimension must have been repaired and my location traced." Felissina gazed at him as he walked back and forth. Tingles of pleasure tickled the small of her back and other, more intimate places, as she watched him move. "His body hasn't yet adapted to this dimension. He still wears the stabilizer belt. I would've thought the scientists would have found a way to make it less bulky."

He stopped and turned to her. "Don't you still wear one of those belts?"

"Yes. People expect to see me wearing it, but I don't need it any longer. The belt functions as a part of my Angel team uniform now, nothing more. I wasn't wearing it when you found me, was I?"

He thought about it for a minute. "No, you weren't. I'm surprised at myself for not realizing it sooner."

If only he would gaze at her all the time. She'd never seen such pale eyes in all the years she'd lived on Earth. She couldn't call the gray-green one color. The two colors appeared to be intertwined with each other. Why did he have to question her about such banalities?

She wanted an explanation of the desire stirring deep within her. The strange and yet familiar connection between them cried out to be explored.

"So, if I pull his belt off, could it disrupt him?"

She tugged at the covers. He always kept a fair distance between them. What could be his reason for staying away from her? "I'm afraid it doesn't work in such precise fashion. It would be like someone here losing oxygen. He'd die a slow, painful death." She paused. "I don't believe he has adapted enough to do without the belt for a period of time."

"Didn't you notice the huge explosion a few months back? Is that when he came through? I would've thought you and your team would have investigated."

She sighed. "The other hero teams checked it out before us and proclaimed it to be some sort of natural fluke. I told them it reminded me of when I arrived on this world, but they said not to worry. They'd take care of any potential invader, if evidence came to light."

Martin shook his head. "It appears it isn't only the resident supervillains who suffer from overconfidence." He paced again and glanced her way more often. "Do you think he wants to hurt you?"

"I don't believe so. I'm sure the usurper king in my dimension offered him a reward for my return. He meant for me to be his bride after the defeat of my parents. I'm sure the usurper hasn't given up on those particular plans."

"Shadowjack said as much when we fought him. He did call you a princess. Who are you in your dimension?"

She sat up straighter in the bed. "I am Princess

Felissina Markhov of Erlymere. The usurper took over our province and imprisoned my family. I was able to escape, and the scientists created a wormhole generator to save me. I hadn't intended to end up in this dimension. I should've gone to a compatible planet where I could raise an army to fight and free our province. The generator must have malfunctioned somehow, and I ended up here."

"You don't have any other ideas? It must have malfunctioned?" His mouth quirked as he fought not to smile. "I thought you'd have a better explanation. It's like you said, 'here, a miracle happened.' "

She chuckled. "I suppose it does sound a little foolish when you put it in those terms. But unless I know what caused the disruption, I can't give you a better explanation."

Olivia walked in, a tray balanced on one arm. "What did I miss? What's so funny?"

"You didn't miss anything." Martin walked to the door. "I'll let you take care of Felissina's head."

Felissina heard him laugh quietly, muttering about miracles under his breath as he left.

****

Olivia removed the gauze and cleaned the wound. "Looks like you two have hit it off."

Heat rose to Felissina's cheeks. "I believe we have. I like Martin very much."

"I'm pretty sure he likes you, too. He's a lot happier since you've come here. I haven't heard him laugh in a long time." Olivia continued to work in silence for a few minutes. "I can tell you want to keep him close all the time. It's in the way you look at him, but Felissina, don't push him too hard. He's dealt with a lot in his life."

"I'm not sure I know what you mean. What can I do to help?"

"Not much. Just remember to give him space when he needs it."

After another couple of minutes, Olivia sat back and grinned. "Like most of the topside superheroes, you have an accelerated healing actor. I didn't need my magic this time at all. The wound is closed but there's still a small bump. You should be able to go home in another day or two."

"I'm glad to hear it. I'm sure my friends are worried about me."

Olivia stood and gathered her supplies. "I'm sure they are. Maybe if you feel better later, I'll walk you around our home. It'll help get rid of some of the weakness."

"A walk sounds nice."

Olivia picked up her tray. "Would you care for a light meal?" When Felissina nodded, she smiled. "I'll bring you some dinner as soon as it's ready."

After Olivia left, Felissina stretched in the bed. She should be happy she'd be back at Angel Haven soon. She frowned at the odd melancholy which came out of nowhere to hold her heart in a tight grip. She'd only been here for a couple of days. Why did leaving this place and these people make her reluctant to go back to her own home?

She loved the view from her window at Angel Haven as it overlooked the in-ground pool. The bright, mosaic tiles inlaid in the concrete patio sparkled in the sunlight. There were large flower pots with colorful blooms and two four-foot high rocky fountains at the corners. She proclaimed it to be her most favorite place on the entire estate.

As much as she wanted to stay, she wanted to leave. The stale air in these underground passages congealed in her lungs. At least it did when Martin wasn't with her. She relived the memories of when she followed the servant through dark tunnels and of the gunfire as it echoed around her. The sound of the soldiers' booted footsteps followed her in her dreams almost every night. She shouldn't still be haunted by these memories. The last nightmare occurred the week before Shadowjack attacked and Martin found her.

Since she'd been with Martin and his team, the nightmares had lessened. In fact, she hadn't had any since she'd been brought here. She smiled, positive Martin's presence gave her the sudden peace of mind she'd sought for a long time. If he would get close enough for her to touch his hand, she felt certain physical contact with him would dismiss all of her inner demons.

****

Martin jumped and dragged in a deep breath. He placed a hand over his wildly thumping heart and glared at his friend.

"Kaz, you need to quit with the surprise pop-in whenever you feel like it." He jerked a thumb at the empty wand holster clipped to the outside of her right boot. "You're not armed today? What's the occasion?"

A tall woman with coppery red hair grinned, her bright, blue eyes sparkling with humor. Today, she wore a royal blue silk shirt, black leather vest with laces up the front, black jeans, and knee high, black, leather boots. She carried a medium sized cardboard box with labels scratched out in black marker.

"You should expect this from me by now." She put the box on the table and shoved it back a little from the edge. "And I don't go armed all the time, smartass. I needed to drop off some stuff for Liv. It arrived a little while ago. We made plans to meet later and discuss what's next for her to learn."

Martin turned back to the computer and stared at the screen. "What if one time you appear too close to me? What would happen if I accidently touched you?"

Kaz hopped up on the table next to the box. "One of us would get a hell of a surprise."

"I can't believe we're friends," he muttered. "What else do you want? You never hang around this long after a delivery."

"Of course we're friends. You love me and you know it." She laughed when he shook his head. "I also wanted to check on you. I wanted to make sure you're still alive and stuff."

He swiveled the chair around and rolled his eyes. "Cut the crap. If you have something to say, say it."

She half shrugged and rolled her eyes. "Fine. Have it your way. I need you to come by The Center soon. I want to try another type of scan to see if I can determine your origin. We already discovered you aren't totally human."

He sighed. Not another scan. "The last one took me weeks to get over the pinpricks in my hands. I've started to think this is hopeless. You said your contacts in the fairy realm figured out I'm not from there."

"True," she said as she swung her legs back and forth. "But there are many other realms and dimensions to be explored." She leaned forward. "Sweetie, I can scan you until frigging doomsday if I want."

Terrific. "You're the witchy magic person here," he snorted. "I hope you understand all of this."

Kaz jumped off the table and winked. "Hey. Get it right. I'm a *professional* 'healer who uses magic' person. Of course I understand this stuff." She traced a circle in the air, snapped her fingers, and a portal appeared. "I have to get back. I've got to take care of my own patients. Oh, and Martin? You call me a 'witchy person' again and my wand will have a new holster. You get me?"

"Got it."

The portal faded away, and Martin fought the urge to bang his head on the desk.

Chapter Eight

"Ow! Damn, Kaz." Martin rubbed his chest and scowled. "You said this one wouldn't hurt as much."

She laid down her wand on the exam table near Martin's leg. "Did you even hear the exact words I said? I told you it *might* not hurt." She walked to the sink and washed her hands. "I don't know why your reaction to the scan I did would cause you so much pain. This is one of the easiest ones I can do. It's supposed to give out calming vibes while it works, not light you up like a Christmas tree."

"Please tell me you found out what my powers are without having to ever do that again."

Kaz smiled and leaned against the sink counter. "Maybe. Your abilities aren't normal 'superpowers.' If anything about those kinds of abilities can be labeled normal."

"Well, you already said I'm not completely human." Martin stood and grabbed his jacket. "So maybe I'm part alien?"

"I don't think so. Whatever you are, you're not from some outer galaxy. I would've discovered alien physiology six scans ago."

If he could, he'd shake the answers out of her. However, he'd never do it because he wasn't into pushing what little luck he had. There needed to be a stronger word than "witch" to describe the forces under her control. He wanted to stay on her good side. Her bad side could be, well, bad.

"Kaz, we've been friends for years, and you know I never worry about your temper or your power. However, at times like this, if I could touch you, I'd probably strangle you."

She winked at him. "Promises, promises. This scan did show me something I can't figure out. You've got a strange kind of makeup. It's like a combination of human DNA and something…else."

"Can you skip the cryptic messages and get to the point?"

"Sorry. Side effect of my chosen magical profession. I think it's a union rule." She shrugged. "I just can't decipher what you are. I don't know how to make it any plainer." She held up a hand when he opened his mouth. "All it means is I haven't found the right scan to identify your origin. And if you give up and get depressed, I'll hit you with such a spell you won't know your ass from a hole in the ground."

"Your bedside manner needs more than a little work. Like truckloads of work."

She laughed. "You're not the first person to say so. Okay. Let me get serious for a minute. Your power is sort of familiar, but I can't quite place it. It's like a childhood memory I can't pull to the front of my mind."

Martin stared at the floor in silence for several minutes, then raised his gaze to his friend. "I'm not human at all, am I?"

"Like I said earlier, part of you might be. I wish I could give you the answers you want, but for now you'll have to wait until I do more research." She pushed off the sink to stand in front of him. "Can you be patient a little longer?"

"I don't have a choice, do I?"

She shook her head. "Nope. I need to check into this spooky land you constantly see. There's got to be a clue in there somewhere. Some of my contacts in the fairy realm may be able to give me some kind of help."

"Thanks, Kaz. You don't know how much I appreciate this. You put up with a lot from me."

"What are friends for, buddy?"

Martin shrugged into his jacket. "I guess I'll head home. Let me know if you hear any new info on this particular problem."

****

Anita studied her new subject's blood sample under the microscope as her lab assistant waited for instructions. She'd tweaked the formula. The serum seemed to be working the way it should in the beginning. Now, it looked like there could be a significant problem. She jotted down notes on the tablet. Taking one more look through the lens, she frowned. Something just didn't look right.

"So far, the girl's power increased, but her physical health began to decline," she said, flipping between charts. "Measures need to be taken to ensure her survival. She might be allergic to one or more of the components in the formula."

"If true, it would be unfortunate," her assistant said. "We'd need to dispose of her, and a new replacement subject would need to be found as soon as possible."

"You're right. In the meantime, see what you can do to keep her stable. I'd rather not start over if it's not necessary. Give her a complete physical. Take at least four more vials of blood. Run more tests, and make sure nothing changed from when she was first brought in. Determine if she has any underlying health issues we didn't catch earlier. I want to know every detail."

"Yes, ma'am," he said.

The door to her office banged open, and Shadowjack sauntered in. An ache started in her jaw, and she rubbed the side of her neck, trying to relieve the tension. "From the look on your face, I assume you have good news for me?"

"I believe so." He leaned back in the chair and propped his feet up on her desk. "I mentioned before I had a line on who helped the princess escape."

She telekinetically shoved his feet to the floor. "Yes, you did. What have you learned?"

"Her rescuers are part of an underground team. If she's with them, she'll have to emerge sometime. I've employed a number of contacts throughout the city. When she appears, I'll know."

Anita closed the folder she'd been studying. "What of the other person you mentioned?"

"It's a woman, and she might prove to be a problem. She's rumored to be one of this world's magic users. If my sources are to be believed, she's got a lot of power at her disposal. She could be hard to take out."

"Do you think you might be able to bring her to me? So far, I've experimented on people whose abilities were of the 'naturally evolved' variety. Someone who uses magic would give me a proper challenge. Having her here would let me see exactly what gives her the ability to wield magic. It would expand the algorithms I need to continue improving my formula."

He shrugged. "I'll see what I can do, but it might cost you extra."

She dismissed his comment with a wave of her hand. "Money isn't a problem. All you have to do is deliver what you promise."

"Don't worry. You'll get everyone you want."

Anita narrowed her eyes as he walked out. "Make sure I do," she murmured as he left her office.

She flipped through the girl's folder, pausing when a new thought hit her. What if her current project used magic and not regular superpowers? Never having run into it before, she'd never developed any tests for it. She made several notes in the girl's records.

Her assistant stood by her desk, speaking quietly into his phone. The call ended, and he walked to stand in front of her desk. "Dr. Haines, the girl's condition has worsened. What are your orders?"

"Damn. We can't lose her. Stop all injections at once and try to purge her system." She hesitated. "Her powers might have magic at their base. If so, it might be the problem."

"It's a contingency we didn't plan on." His gaze turned thoughtful. "I don't know what type of test we could run. We'd need someone who uses magic to detect magic."

She walked around the desk. "See who you can find. I don't want to proceed with her until I know the base of her powers."

"Yes, ma'am." He stopped and frowned, his brow creasing. "I may know someone."

"Wonderful." She walked over to him and laid her hand on his shoulder and smiled. "You and the rest of the team are the only ones who've never let me down. Ask whoever it is to come see me. Make sure they know they'll be well compensated for their time and expertise."

"I will. Thank you, Dr. Haines."

After he left, Anita tapped the file. If the girl's powers were indeed magic, she might not be able to do the transfer of powers to Benedict like he wanted. Would he consider it another failure on her part? If he did, she didn't want to consider the consequences. The man needed to stop being such a pompous glory hound and tying her hands with red tape more often than not. She snatched up the file and headed down to the lab.

Her grip tightened on the folder as she considered she may have to let the girl go. Let her go? No. To spare someone so insignificant could be considered a sign of weakness. Her mother had told her so many times after her father died. She'd let Benedict Trust make the call and carry out his orders. She mustn't be weak, or she'd never get what she wanted.

And what she wanted, was everything.

****

"Are you ready?" Olivia called after she knocked.

Felissina smoothed down the borrowed T-shirt and fleece lounge pants. The light supper she'd eaten worked wonders. Afterward, she'd taken a hot shower, then donned the clean clothes Olivia left out for her.

"Yes. After all the recent rest, I'm anxious to move around."

"Great. I'll give you the nickel tour, if you're up to it."

Felissina nodded once. "It sounds wonderful. I feel more like myself every day."

Olivia pointed to the room next to Felissina's. "Over here is Martin's room. We wanted to put you closer to the medical section, but I have to leave those rooms available for emergencies, and some of them were already in use." They turned down a long, narrow hallway. "This is the way to where we do most of our work."

Felissina tried to listen, but her mind wandered back to the closed door behind them. He'd been right next to her the whole time she recuperated. They'd been so close. With the odd magnetic connection between them, could he be the reason her dreams weren't as bad? She forced her attention back as Olivia pointed out the living quarters of her team.

"You've often mentioned your team, but I haven't seen anyone else around. Are they afraid of me? I've never had people go out of their way to avoid me before."

Olivia shrugged. "Some of our members have strange or fearsome appearances. Others have dangerous powers. They make themselves scarce when someone new arrives. If you're here long enough, they may come out and introduce themselves to you."

Felissina nodded. "It must be hard for the people of the underground to know they aren't accepted by those who live, what term did you use, topside?"

"When a new person comes here, the team does have it hard at first. After the new person has been here for a bit, they realize they're among their own kind, and everyone's lives smooth out."

Felissina understood completely. She'd been an outcast when she first arrived on Earth. She mentally shook herself, pushing the memories down. She tried to pay attention to Olivia's tour, but her mind wandered to questions surrounding this outcast team. She smiled a little. And the man who currently led them.

Chapter Nine

Felissina poked her head into a room and discovered yet another closet. "You have a lot of storage space down here."

"It's a lot more than we need," Olivia said. "We figure if we get new members, some of these storage areas can be turned into some pretty decent sized rooms."

Felissina listened at some of the doors. "I can hear movement. Are these rooms where some of your team members live?" When Olivia confirmed her suspicions, she laid her hand against the wood. "I wish they'd come out and say hello. I hope I can meet them someday, but only when they're comfortable enough with my presence here.

"They just need a little time to know you. They want to make sure you won't be scared of how they look or what they can do."

"You should meet some of my teammates' husbands. I don't believe they could scare or shock me. I think I'd get along rather well with the team here."

Olivia stopped in front of a room where the door stood wide open. There were two desks pushed together so they faced each other. On each one sat a computer. A counter lined one wall where two more units sat connected to their own printers. A desk sat against the other wall with a laptop and printer. The chair's seat faced the door. Maps of the city and other tunnels hung behind thin panes of clear acrylic. White paint covered the walls in uneven splotches, revealing the concrete cinder blocks underneath in places. Cracked, gray tile, some with pieces broken off the corners, covered the floor.

Olivia stood in the doorway. "We call this the computer room, for obvious reasons. The closest I get is the doorway. The electronics and metals don't play well with my power. Take a look around."

Felissina walked in and shook her head as she examined the computers and printers. Some of them looked cobbled together from parts made decades earlier. She punched a few keys and frowned at the old programs loaded on the screens. Every unit had a landline plugged into it. How could this team begin to keep up with current events with machines as old as these?

"These aren't even close to what this world claims to be top of the line," Felissina said. "I can upgrade these to make them more efficient or replace the entire lot. The more I look at these antiques, the more I believe replacements would be the best way to go."

"Thanks, but new equipment isn't in our budget. Our leader has limited funds, and we try not to create extra expenses."

Felissina turned to her. "Olivia, I haven't asked you for any money. I'll take care of all the costs."

"You don't have to." Olivia stared at how many machines occupied the room. "There would be a lot to upgrade or replace. It would be expensive."

She smiled. "It would be a small repayment for the care you've given me."

"Well, then I guess I should say thank you. My friends call me Liv."

Felissina frowned. "Are nicknames a common practice on this world? My friends have designated me 'Feli.' It took me a long time to get used to the shortening of my name."

"Nicknames are more common than you'd think. They're seen as a type of endearment from those who care about you."

"Oh. I suppose it makes a certain amount of sense."

They continued down several hallways as Olivia pointed out the kitchen, the small living area, and the various bedrooms. Down yet another corridor, Olivia opened a door. Inside looked like a doctor's office, only there wasn't any metal in evidence. A ceramic sink with a granite countertop sat nestled in the far corner.

"From the look on your face, I can tell you want to know about this room. I'm the medical person here. I attended nursing school until my powers took a bizarre turn. Turns out, I'm a witch. Metal has a strange effect on my magic. Large amounts tend to make it go crazy. Kaz took over my training, and my control is a lot better than it used to be."

"I wondered about your power," Felissina said. "You don't have an unusual appearance. Is your power the reason why you've chosen to live here?"

"Yeah. Kaz makes sure she sends me glass or plastic containers. I don't want to take any unnecessary chances. Not down here where we have limited escape routes."

"You have a very generous and thoughtful mentor. I'd like to meet her."

"I think you'd like her." Olivia shrugged. "She's

got this whole tough persona she shows to people, but she's got a good heart. You still don't want to get on her bad side, though. Especially if she's out of coffee."

"I understand," Felissina said. "Some of my teammates have the same addiction. When Ariadne, the alien on my team, first joined with the Angels, she'd discovered coffee. Now she can't live without it. Who knew you couldn't get coffee in other galaxies?"

A portal opened, and a woman with long, red hair stepped through. Her knee-high black boots were covered in dust, and she smacked more from her black jeans. Her purple, silk shirt had been torn at the shoulder, and blood spatter covered her tan, leather vest like red freckles.

Olivia smiled. "We were just talking about you."

"I thought so. My ears were burning." She held her hand out to Felissina. "I'm Kaz. I helped rescue you. Liv and Martin couldn't have done it without my help. Trust me. Nice to see you up and around."

"Felissina. I'm happy to make your acquaintance. I'm glad you were there to help rescue me." She shook her hand, her gaze riveted on the blood droplets on Kaz's clothes. "Forgive me, but why are you covered in blood spatter?"

Kaz glanced down and shrugged. "A situation turned bad, and the idiots I'd been forced to work with made it worse. I warned them their dumbass plan wouldn't work. And they'd better pray to every deity they can think of this blood comes out." She sighed. "I'm so glad this is the last time I have to deal with them. Nice to meet you, Feli. Liv, when you get a second, I need the list you promised to send. I've got to get back to The Center. If I can help in any way, holler and I'll come right back."

They watched Kaz open a portal and walk through. After a few minutes, Felissina blew out a breath. "She has a lot of personality, doesn't she? What's The Center?"

Olivia laughed. "She certainly does. The Center is her medical clinic. She treats all sorts of people there, from magic users and superheroes to normal humans. Let's move on."

"She's a fascinating person. I hope I'll be able to get to know her better."

"She pops in here a lot, so I'm sure you'll have ample opportunities."

They turned down another hallway, and Olivia stopped before a closed door. "This is our fitness room. With all the equipment in there, it's off limits to me. Martin should be almost done with his workout. Would you ask him to finish your tour? I've got to call Kaz with the list of items she needs for The Center."

"Of course."

Felissina stepped inside and shut the door. Her attention was instantly drawn to the far corner where the weights were located. Martin looked to be in the middle of a hard workout. He wore a T-shirt with the sleeves cut off and jean shorts. Her eyes grew wide as she watched him do squats, a barbell loaded with weights across his shoulders. No man should look so delicious while working so hard.

When he squatted down, the muscles in his legs tightened, then relaxed when he slowly straightened up. His biceps bulged with the effort of holding the barbell steady. Felissina swallowed hard, her gaze never leaving his body. Down and up. Down and up. She wanted to say something but couldn't break the spell of watching him. Perspiration beaded on her forehead. She'd been chilly, but now a raging heat started a slow burn in her belly.

The fleece pants, which had felt so comfortable when she first put them on, trapped the fire as it built inside her. The shirt she wore rubbed against her breasts. The slow heat inside her exploded to flaming boil. If only his hands created the hot desire in her and not the clothes she wore. Visions of different uses for this room filled her mind, and the flames rose higher. How she wanted him to touch her.

"Have I disturbed you?" she said when she could make herself form words.

He set the weights down and grabbed a towel off the bench and wiped it across his neck. "No. Some of my teammates left a few minutes ago. I wanted to get in a few more reps before I headed to the shower."

She stared at him, unable to articulate what she longed to say. His hair was plastered to his forehead and no pain clouded his eyes. What she wouldn't give, right then, to have him hold her. The fact a thin sheen of sweat coated his body made no difference. Heat rose to her cheeks as she thought about the water cascading over him in the shower. By the gods, where did these wanton thoughts come from?

"Did you want something?" he said.

You have no idea. "No, no. Olivia took me on a tour of your home. She needed to contact Kaz and wanted to know if you could continue showing me around."

He nodded. "She did mention she might have to hand you over to me. I'd like to finish your tour. So what do you think?"

Her mouth instantly became drier than Death Valley. "What do I think?" she stammered.

"About where we live." He gestured to the room. "What do you think?"

"Oh. It's a nice layout. I offered to upgrade your computers. I told Olivia I'll take care of all the cost."

"You don't have to."

"I'd like to." She walked a little closer to him and sat on one of the weight benches. "It would be a gift for the good care you've given me while I recovered."

"I see. So it wouldn't be because you're a princess and you think we can't afford to do it ourselves."

He moved to stand over her, and she glanced up at him. His shadow gave her the sensation of being wrapped in a large, velvet blanket. Her soul cried out for him, and the same sense of recognition shone in his eyes as well. An ache started deep in her heart, making her want him to ease it.

She swallowed and worked to force her words out. "I didn't think any such thing. I simply want to help you the way you helped me."

"I'm kidding." He smiled, and her heart stutter-stepped in her chest. "Don't you ever get teased at home?"

"Of course," she said with a huff. "My teammates have a strange addiction to teasing and practical jokes. I remind them all the time to leave me out of their hijinks."

"Hijinks?" His smile grew wider while he raised an eyebrow. "I didn't think people used old fashioned words like that any longer."

"Humans don't, but I do." She lifted her hand, and

he stumbled back. "I used to speak much more formally when I first arrived on Earth. I don't anymore, but every so often, I slip back into my old speech patterns." His distance from her made her hesitate. "You don't have to continue to show me around if you don't want."

"It's not a problem. I'd like to finish your tour. I'm done anyway. Like I said, I need to go take a shower."

When she moved a little closer to him, he backed away the same amount of steps. "Don't you wish to be near me?" she asked.

"I like being near you," he said in a low voice. "Because of the nature of my power, I can't have any physical contact with people."

"Oh." She moved away a little. "I'm sorry. You must feel so alone."

"I used to, but I'm okay with it now. I've lived with the isolation for a lot of years. Shall we?"

He opened the door and followed her out to the hallway. His warmth spread across her shoulders, and she wanted to wrap herself in it. Her emotions had a newsflash for her. Martin Long had firmly entrenched himself in her blood. She'd never get over him. Not ever.

****

Why would Liv drop off Felissina at the workout room when she knew he wouldn't be done for another ten minutes? Martin worked out at the same time every day. When Felissina came in and shut the door, her presence slammed into his senses.

The scent of soap and shampoo drifted to him on the breeze from the vents around the room. Her warmth slid across the floor to wrap itself around his legs and work its way up his body. Even if she were invisible, he would've known when she walked in. Ever since they'd rescued her, he'd picked up a sixth sense whenever Felissina came anywhere near him.

When he and his friends found her on the ground and Shadowjack standing over her, his protective instincts kicked into overdrive. He could almost hear her in his mind call out for help. As he walked next to her now, the same instincts were there, bubbling beneath the surface. Right now, his problem was wanting to hold her and not being able to have her in his arms.

She stamped her foot and folded her arms. "How do you find your way down here? I'm so turned around."

"You need to get used to the layout." He chuckled. "Let's stop in the computer room. I can draw you a map. It'll help you get your bearings when I'm busy elsewhere."

He bit the inside of his cheek. He couldn't get involved with her. The princess and the pauper. He snorted. Would the cosmos really be such a bastard as to send him someone he wanted to love and couldn't? He hoped the "Powers That Be" got a good laugh out of this because he didn't find any amusement in it at all.

The moment he saw her, he instantly regretted having looked. He suspected Liv put her in those clothes on purpose. The thin, fleece pants accentuated her curves. The T-shirt she wore outlined her breasts and revealed her interest in him. The urge to hold her ran like liquid fire through his veins. Being in her company gave him a little too much pleasure. The longer she remained in the underground, the more he had to remind himself the consequences of touching her.

He'd left so much behind topside, as her presence continuously reminded him. To see what her future held would send him right back to the dark place in his mind. He wished he could spend one night in her arms. One night to have her hold him and chase away his own personal demons. All he craved was one night to not be alone.

Chapter Ten

Martin sat in the chair by Felissina's bed. "Liv thinks you should be able to go home tomorrow."

"So soon?" She frowned as she jerked upright. "I don't think I'm strong enough to make the trip yet."

He gave her a small smile. "I'm sure Liv would be okay if you want to take some extra time. You know, just to be sure."

"Yes." She moved nearer to where he sat. "I want to be sure I won't have any complications or setbacks."

He inched a little closer. "It's probably better if you take a little more time. I mean, I don't want you to relapse."

He cringed. That lame line was the best he could come up with on the spur of the moment? The last time he'd been this tongue tied was in middle school. It hadn't worked out well then, either.

She leaned toward him a little bit. "I do have to go home soon, though. I'm the featured performer at a holiday charity event the week before Christmas. The event organizers said my presence increases donations."

He pulled a folded flyer out of his back pocket. "I know. I found this on the event's website. Your name sounded familiar, so I looked it up. You didn't say you were a celebrity concert pianist as well as the daughter of a king *and* a superhero." He paused. "I wish I could be there to hear you play."

"Does my status make you uncomfortable? Events like this seem trivial compared to when I'm with you." She gazed up at him. "I know we've only known each other for a few days, but I'd like you to be there. I can get you in, if you think you'd like to come. I should be able to secure a private area so you can avoid people."

"I'm not quite ready to hang with the public at large yet." He tapped the flyer. "This looks like a very high-profile public. Actors, politicians, local corporate heads. Quite a dignified audience will attend to hear you." He stood. "I'll let you get some rest. I'll be back later."

She picked up the flyer. Her picture with her name underneath in bright, blue letters stared back at her. It showed the brightness of her eyes and the deep, golden blonde of her hair. She thought her small smile made her look warm and personable. What did Martin see when he looked at this picture? Did he see the woman she wanted him to see or the princess she thought intimidated him? She feared it might be the latter.

****

Shadowjack watched the one entrance to the underground he knew about. His patience could be endless as long as he achieved a positive result. One of his informants approached and stopped a good ten feet from him. He sighed and gestured him closer with an impatient wave of his hand. Did no one in this backward dimension have the spine to just approach and speak their mind? This small man was just another reminder of everything he'd left behind to retrieve the princess.

"What is it?"

"I've heard the Angel will be taken home within

the next few days. You should be able to make your move then."

Finally. If he timed it right, he should be able to grab Felissina when her guard would be down. They'd go see Anita Haines, and then he could take them home. He frowned. If he could take the doctor out of the equation, matters would be greatly simplified. Holding onto Felissina while activating the recall signal before his plans were discovered would be difficult at best.

"Do you know which exit they'll use when she leaves?"

The informant pointed in the direction of Shadowjack's gaze. "Their main entrance is behind those dumpsters. We expect them to use their other entrance a few streets over. It's the one with the best camouflage. I stationed people at their other known exits as well."

"Very good." Shadowjack handed him a few twenties. "If this plays out the way I want, there could be a bonus for you."

The man's eyes lit with a mercenary gleam. "You're too generous," he said as he backed away.

"Vermin," Shadowjack muttered.

He may as well go back to his hotel. No point in waiting if she wouldn't appear today. As he walked to his car, he pulled out his cell phone. Time to let Anita know what the plan would be.

"Tell me you have the Angel," she snapped when she answered.

"I'll have her in your office in the next day or two, the end of the week at the latest." He twisted the key in the ignition. "Remember what I said before. You aren't to harm her in any way. She needs to be returned to our home dimension as healthy as she is right now."

"I've told you she'll leave here basically in one piece. Don't make me repeat myself."

Shadowjack smiled. "I won't. I wanted to make sure you remembered."

He threw the phone on the seat when she hung up on him. "You know, Dr. Haines or Vertigo, whichever you prefer. For a telepath, your reactions are completely predictable."

He considered possible scenarios as he drove back to his hotel. He'd have to be quick. Someone would come to meet her and take her home. Once she went back behind the gates of Angel Haven, it would close to impossible to get her out. Her suspicious nature had gone on high alert, so the ruse he used before wouldn't work again.

Well, he'd made spur of the moment plans in the past, so he could do it again. Whether she called herself Felissina, the Angel CT, or princess, she would come with him. It would be his chance to tell her the truth behind his betrayal. He didn't want her forgiveness. He wanted her to understand his reasons. Life could never be called good or evil, black or white. There were always other, ambiguous factors at play, and those were what ruled all life.

****

Olivia gave Martin a smile when he asked if she thought Felissina should leave now. "A few more days couldn't hurt." Olivia looked up from her supplies. "I'm glad she agreed to stay longer, too."

"I had a feeling you'd see right through me. What'd you do? Read my aura or something equally magical?"

"Nothing like that. We've been friends for several years. I could tell you want her to stay." She closed the cabinet door after storing the last of her supplies. "I wish the team would come out and meet her. I think they'd get along."

Martin leaned against the exam table and folded his arms. "I know they would. I'll have a talk with them, even though I don't think it will do much good." He paused. "Should she stay until we get this Shadowjack guy stopped? It doesn't matter how careful we are. If he wants her badly enough, he'll find a way to grab her. The team can scatter for now if you think she should stay."

Olivia's chuckle stopped him. "It's not what I think, but what you think. I've noticed small changes in you, Martin. You're not as stressed as usual."

Martin kept his gaze on the floor. "I'd like to make sure she's safe when she leaves here. I don't know if I'll, I mean we'll, ever see her again. It'd be nice to know we did our best." At her small smile, he admitted aloud what they both knew. "Fine. There's a connection between us drawing me to her. As much as I'd like to know what it is, I don't think it's possible to pursue it."

"I get it. I'm surprised you think you guys have a special link. She's not really your type. The wealthy, upper class is your Achilles' heel. They have been since you lived in Boston."

"I don't believe she's like those women." He glanced over his shoulder. "My instincts tell me she's a little more down to earth."

"As a member of the Angels' team, she'd have to be. There's always a chance she might be the one for you." She nodded toward the doorway. "Go fix dinner.

I'll be along in a little while."

He left Olivia with her new batch of medical supplies and headed to the kitchen. Again, he ran fingers across the wall while he walked, reliving the stories he knew by heart. The past filled his mind, and he closed his eyes as he reveled in the sensation. He didn't know how to describe what he felt to anyone, even if he wanted to. He could hold onto these private images and keep them all to himself. Selfish? Maybe a little.

Movement out of the corner of his eye grabbed his attention. He kept his hand on the wall as his steps slowed. He stared straight ahead, wanting the figure to stay. "Please, tell me who you are. Why are you always around me?"

"You have been lost to us for so many years," it whispered. "We have now found you. Come back to where you belong. You have been sorely missed. Your presence is desired in your own realm."

He wiped beads of water from his forehead, then dragged his hand across his jeans. "I don't understand. Where do I come from? Who am I?"

The figure faded, and he blinked several times to clear his vision to find himself outside Felissina's door. How did he end up here? He didn't think he'd moved, but the evidence said otherwise. His T-shirt stuck to his back, and his clothes were damp, as if he'd come in from a light rain. Every time this particular specter appeared, he ended up soaked.

He needed to confer with Kaz and soon. Where did all this moisture come from? Was it connected to the specter or to him? Reporting sudden blackouts and conversations with ghosts to his friend would give her fits. Her frustration with him made her batch of patience run out quicker than usual. He grinned. For as long as he knew her, Kaz's patience had never set at a high level.

The doorknob turned and he jumped back. Felissina stood there, the short, almost see-through nightgown she wore coming to the tops of her thighs. The soft light behind her outlined the fullness of her figure. Full bust, wide hips, taut stomach, and toned arms and legs. Did she wear any underwear under the short gown? What he wouldn't give to find out.

Martin took a few steps back when she smiled at him. An overwhelming temptation to hold her made his arms shake. He jammed his hands in his pants pockets, forcing down the ache to feel her skin.

"I wanted to thank all of you again for the assistance you gave me," she said, her gaze on his face.

"You're welcome. Liv thinks it's a good idea for you to stay a little longer," he mumbled. "Can I get you anything? Are you hungry? I'm getting ready to fix some dinner."

"I am," she said softly. "But not for food." She stepped back and opened the door wider. "Please come in."

He took a deep breath and stepped into the room, pushing the door closed with a quiet click. "I can't do this, be with you. My power doesn't let me have physical contact with anyone. This can't go any further. I can't let there be any physicality between us."

"You're wrong. I feel a strong pull toward you. I've seen the same attraction in you."

"Oh yeah? And how do you 'see' an attraction?"

She sat on the edge of the bed. "It's the way you

look at me. It's your consideration of my feelings and fear for my safety. There are many ways to see attraction." She patted a spot next to her. "Sit with me."

He hesitated, then did as she asked. "You could have your pick of any man out there. Why would you want someone as messed up as I am?"

"I don't believe you're as 'messed up' as you claim." She gazed at him. "Yes, I could have my pick of any man. The problem is, I know the type of men who always try, without success, to impress me. With you, it's like I've known you for years, instead of the few days I've been here. You feel it, too. I see it in your eyes whenever you look at me. The heart knows what's best. I, for one, tend to listen to mine."

"Quite a fanciful view for someone who's royalty. Aren't you supposed to be more practical and levelheaded?"

"Not at all. Fairy tales often have princesses and kings at the center of the story. All of them follow their hearts' instincts. Though I've been fortunate to never be a damsel in distress." She smiled. "Except, of course, for the circumstances which brought me here."

"Of course. Except for one small incident," Martin said. "Who knows? Maybe someday you'll rescue me."

"It's a possibility." She leaned closer to him, and he trembled. "Does my proximity bother you?"

He nodded. "Yes, because we can't finish what we start here. Felissina, you don't know how much I want to touch you, to hold you." He closed his eyes. "And I can't."

"We can always pretend." She held her hand a few inches from his head. "I would start with my hands in your hair."

He lifted his hand to her cheek and stopped an inch above it. The warmth of her skin felt drawn to his palm, sending warm tingles through his nerves. Her hand came close to his face and sent vibrations shuddering through him.

"I'd cup your cheek before I kissed you," he said, his voice quiet.

"As you did, I'd wrap my arms around you and pull you close." Her fingers danced above his arm. She nodded at him. "I'd begin to undress you, then trace the planes of your chest."

Goosebumps popped up on his skin, making the fine hairs on his arms stand at attention. He swallowed hard and removed his clothes. "I'd return the favor, wanting to see all of you."

She stood and pulled the short nightgown over her head. She loved the admiration she saw in his eyes as she let it drop from her fingers. One garment remained. She hooked her thumbs in the waistband and lowered her panties and stepped out of them.

"What would be next?" she asked.

"When you were naked, I'd lay you back on the bed. I'd want to feel how soft your skin is and do whatever I could to make you want me."

She walked over to the bed and lay down. "You couldn't make me want you any more than I do now. I'd make very little room for you so our bodies could have as much contact as possible."

She nodded, and he followed her, kneeling by the side of the bed. "By all the gods in my dimension, you're beautiful. Wide shoulders," she said as her fingers danced in the air over them. "Broad chest, arms most men would kill for, and no sign of any part of you not defined." She smiled as her gaze drifted to another part of him. "And I can see how much you want me."

"Not as beautiful as you," he said. He held his hand above her breasts and said, "I'd lay my hand here. I'd want to feel your heartbeat as we began to get to know each other intimately." He let his touch float above her body as his gaze drifted over her.

"Then what would you do?" she asked in a breathy voice.

His gaze roamed over her. "I'd kiss you again and smooth your hair back. You have the most incredible eyes I've ever seen. I'd want to see them as I began to explore every inch of you. You'd beg me to give you release, but I'd want to draw it out."

"I, too, would tease you until you did as I bade. When you'd get close, I'd kiss you, wanting not even your words to escape me." She winked. "As a princess, my commands have to be obeyed."

"Obey is kind of a heavy-duty word, but I think I'd be okay with it." He took a huge gulp of air and tried to calm his shaking hands as they hovered inches above her body. "When our hearts returned to normal, I'd start it all over again. This time, I'd want more than hands on you."

She spread her legs, just enough to give him a peek. "I would open up myself and let you take all of me." She gave a languid, catlike stretch to raise her chest up. "Then, I believe we wouldn't get any rest for the remainder of our time together."

"I think you're right. After a brief break, I'd start all over again, kissing you here." He pointed to her mouth. "Then here and here," he said, letting his hand come close to her breasts. "I'd run my hand down your body until I got here." His hand stopped above where she ached for him the most. "I'd watch your eyes the whole time, and then we'd come together. This time, we'd stay joined until I decided to let you go."

"I'd like that very much." She gazed at him. "Your eyes have changed. They are mostly green now instead of gray and green."

"Maybe I just want to be joined to you in more ways than one."

They stayed undressed in each other's presence for a long time, talking about what they could do if things were different. As more time passed, the appreciation of his body shone brighter in her eyes. He never thought someone as wonderful as Felissina could ever want him this much. He'd give everything he owned to make what they'd said a physical reality.

Looked like Liv would be fixing dinner tonight after all. He had more important things holding his attention at the present time.

Chapter Eleven

Could he have gotten a much-needed break? Shadowjack stared at the man with dark hair as he emerged from an abandoned building. He recognized him as the one who rescued the princess. His informant had said his name was Martin Long. What special qualities about the man drew Felissina to him? As far as he could tell, Martin Long was ordinary to the point of bland.

But Martin did possess a dangerous power, so maybe not quite so ordinary after all. The man was as human as the rest of the beings here, though. He had no right to keep the princess hidden. If he wouldn't cooperate with Shadowjack's request, he'd be forced to proceed with elimination. Then Felissina would have to come with him.

He considered that particular option as he followed Martin down the street. No. He'd never indiscriminately murdered anyone and wasn't about to start now. Such drastic action should only be taken if there were no other recourse open to him. If he could find another way, he'd take it. He prayed to his gods an alternative way could be found.

He glanced around the city. The longer he remained on Earth, the more he feared he would be stuck here for longer than he anticipated. He cursed his princess's stubbornness. If she'd only curb her temper and just listen to him. He smiled. She hadn't listened to anyone since she'd turned ten years old.

Shadowjack stared and stayed in the shadows as Long started off down the street. He laid his hand on the large gun on his hip and hesitated. With Martin's strange power, his approach would need to be cautious. Martin had reduced different items to dust in mere seconds. What could he do to a man? He shoved those concerns to the back of his mind. No need to worry about what he couldn't control.

His prey turned the corner and dodged down another dark street. Shadowjack picked up his pace as he hurried after him. Martin had to be convinced of the need for Felissina to go home. He could tell Martin why. It wasn't any kind of great or state secret. Whether the human believed him or not didn't matter. Felissina's royal duty called her to return.

"What do you want?" Martin demanded.

Shadowjack stumbled back. He'd been so caught up in his thoughts he didn't notice when Martin turned to face him. "Maybe I'm lost and wanted directions from you. Would you believe me?"

"No. You've followed me for the past ten minutes. You need to back off."

Shadowjack stepped closer to him and noted Martin backed up the same number of steps. "You have someone I want. Return the princess, and you'll never see me again."

"The princess stays with me." Martin raised his hand. "Do you need a reminder of what I can do?"

Shadowjack backed away. "Not at all. You may disagree, but it's time for her to go back to her dimension. She must return, the sooner, the better. Her people need her leadership and guidance. Please tell her I mean her no harm. My only purpose here is to take her home."

Then he vanished into the darkness which surrounded him.

****

Martin stared at the spot where Shadowjack had stood seconds before. He appeared to become one with the shadows he'd backed into. Why did his entire current life revolve around shadows, ghosts, and some downright creepy situations? From the spectral figures, to the land he dreamt about, and now this guy. Maybe he'd been inspired to pay Kaz a visit.

The passage Martin hurried into dead-ended at a brick wall. He looked around and made sure no one entered the alley behind him. He knocked on the bricks three times and showed the large card to whoever answered the door. The brick wall vanished, and a large, oak door banded with iron appeared. Martin edged his way inside as it opened with a slow, deliberate groan.

"Is Kaz around?" he asked the doorkeeper.

An ogre towered over him, leaned close, and looked down his long nose. His deep frown turned mere wrinkles on his face into caverns. Black eyes glared from under bushy, black eyebrows. The low light glistened off his dull, gray skin, and twinkled off the double-bladed axe on his back.

"Did you make an appointment?" he growled.

"Do I ever make an appointment? Come on, Larry. Get out of the way. This is important."

The ogre snorted. "One day, Martin, you will suffer for your insolence."

"You say the same threat every time I show up, and yet, here I am." The two grinned at each other, then laughed. "How're the wife and kids?" Martin asked.

"As well as can be expected." Larry jerked his thumb to the corridor behind him. "Go on. You don't have any bad situations right now, do you?"

"Yep, by the bushel full, but nothing I can't handle with a little bit of luck. I have some questions I hope she can answer."

Martin hurried down to Kaz's office. He rapped on the door and walked inside. Kaz sat at her desk and frowned at papers scattered across the top. Her wand sparked and jumped every time she slammed her fist down. Maybe he hadn't picked a good time after all.

"Problems?"

She glanced up. "I can sum it up in two words. Frigging vampires."

"Uh oh. You never scowl hard at paperwork unless it's bad or the Conclave wants to know what you did this time." He leaned on her desk. "Please tell me you didn't attack another one of The Family."

"In this instance, I'm blameless. And I'll thank you to keep your assumptions to yourself in the future." She shoved the papers into a messy pile. "You accidentally, on purpose, attack one uppity, condescending vampire woman, and all of a sudden you're labeled the bad guy." She frowned at him. "Why are you here anyway?"

"Shadows. Everything around me, even the guy hunting Felissina, is somehow involved with shadows. I'm beginning to sense more and more spirits around me. Could it be a coincidence?"

Her mood changed in a blink of an eye. "There are

no coincidences in magic. That particular lesson got drummed into me when I was a kid. Most often at the business end of a ruler. Let's do another scan. Some force has attracted specters toward you."

"Let's hope it's not bad. My life is complicated enough."

****

Anita walked into her office, and her good mood vanished as soon as she saw Shadowjack. "What do you want this time?"

"I'm here to make my report. I made contact with the man who aided the princess. Even though he's a rather ordinary man, his powers are impressive."

Her fingers curled into tight fists, and blood welled around her nails. "One of these times when you come here, I would appreciate your delivery of someone you were assigned to pick up. Not more empty promises and vague observations. What're this man's powers, and why do I care?"

A smug smile crossed his face as he sat in one of the chairs. "How about a man who can disintegrate any object with a wave of his hand."

"Unexpected and unusual." She leaned against her desk. "Can you take him?"

Shadowjack shrugged. "I'm not sure. I know you have safeguards in place in the lab, but I'm not sure even those would be enough. He looks ordinary, but I believe there's more to him and his abilities than what shows on the surface. It might be better to find some way to neutralize him. He could pose serious problems to your plan."

"Try to take him." She spoke on her phone for a few minutes then turned back to him. "My techs tell me we do have an item which might work. You'll have a brief window of time to administer it. If you can't stop him, proceed with elimination. I can't take any chances with my current project or Mr. Trust's plans."

"I'll see if I can make this happen."

As soon Shadowjack walked out, her assistant poked his head in her office. "Dr. Haines? I have a gentleman here to see you."

"Bring him in."

A tall, thin man glided in. His tailored clothes fit his lanky frame with absolute precision. The blood-red shirt and indigo-blue suit highlighted his olive skin. His straight, long, black hair lay on his shoulders like a coiled serpent. He stood before her desk, looking down his pointed nose at her. His black eyes shone like coal dipped in ice. Arrogance drifted from him, as well as an expensive cologne.

"I am Ra-Vel." He gestured to her assistant. "This man tells me you have need of my skills."

"It's possible. What are your skills?" she asked.

He waved his arms in a wide arc, and a glittery green web of sigils and runes appeared in three interlocking circles. "Magic, dear lady. I hear you need magical assistance."

"Yes, I do." She walked to the door. "Come with me."

Anita led the way to her lab, trying hard to keep from trembling. The hair on the back of her neck prickled as Ra-Vel walked close behind. A mercurial, dark quality oozed and flowed around him. Could this association be a good idea? Maybe, maybe not, but she'd hit a dead end with her current subject. She hated to admit it, even to herself, but she needed his help.

Hopefully, he'd figure out why her new acquisition couldn't process the serum. After he helped her with this problem, she could be done with him. She glanced over her shoulder and shivered when he moved closer. She almost smiled. Considering some of the actions she'd done in her past, it said a lot about his mere presence.

She opened the door to the observation room and walked over to the large window. "In the exam room is a girl who has a unique ability. Her body had an unfortunate adverse reaction to the serum I devised to increase her power. There's the possibility her abilities might be magic based."

A cold smile curved his thin lips. Anita half expected to see a forked tongue dart out as he stared at the girl. "I see. There is a simple scan I can do to check for magic in her." He turned his black eyes to Anita. "What's in it for me?"

She refused to take a step back and crossed her arms. "It depends. What do you want?"

"I would like help with my own problem."

Anita stared at her current subject to avoid looking at the mage. "Oh? Do tell."

"There's a woman in this city who runs a type of secret clinic. If possible, I'd like her removed from the picture."

"I see. How do you think I can help you with this?"

He leaned close, and his serpentine smile grew wider. "Let me bring her here. Then she'll be gone, and you'll have a new subject." He straightened and tugged at his jacket sleeves. "In the meantime, I'll do what I can for you."

"If you succeed in bringing her here, I can make

sure she stays out of your way."

He opened the door next to the window and walked inside. Anita watched as the girl shrank from him and tried to move away. It appeared she wasn't the only one who wanted no part of Ra-Vel. He summoned the strange green light again, and it flowed around the girl before it delved into her mouth. In moments, Ra-Vel completed the scan and headed back to the observation room.

"Well?" she asked. "Is her power magic based?"

"Yes. I believe it is." He paused and smoothed the front of his jacket. "I performed a preliminary test this time. If you want to know more, I'll need to gather a few items and do a more in-depth scan."

"No, thank you. You've given me the answer I sought. I'll have to tweak the formula now to allow for magic. I must admit, it's not an area familiar to me."

"I'll be glad to lend my expertise and assistance, if you like."

Anita frowned at the thought of continued close contact with Ra-Vel. There weren't many people she feared, but this man was one of them. Better to keep on his good side for now. She could end their partnership whenever she chose. Not even Benedict Trust, with all his threats and thugs, worried her. Unfortunately, she needed this dark mage.

She rubbed her arms, as if completing such an action would give her some kind of barrier against him. She'd keep their time together brief. She did a quick scan, and he didn't even notice her psychic presence in his mind. Good to know. If he got too out of hand, her powers could take him down.

"Fine. Come back in two days. I want to give her

Annette Miller

time to recover."

He gave her a slight incline of his head as he backed toward the door. "I look forward to our association." He raised her hand to his lips. "Maybe we shall become closer."

She read his mind and knew exactly what he meant. The magic user could dream on with those particular ideas. As soon as he exited the exam room, she breathed a sigh of relief and rubbed her hand on her pants. The miasma of magic which surrounded him dissipated when he left. No wonder people mistrusted magic users.

Ra-Vel may be a powerful mage, but her area of expertise was psionic ability, research, and experimentation. She'd be happy to leave magic and all it entailed to others better suited to deal with its strange workings.

Chapter Twelve

Felissina paced in her temporary room. Why did she continue to put off her return to Angel Haven? Because Martin's presence quieted the turmoil in her soul. She wanted to be able to make love to him. He hadn't been uncomfortable when he stood naked in front of her, and she'd never been shy. Would he want to do the non-touch love making session again? Her body gave her a definite yes when she considered it. Maybe she'd reach out and grab him, his power be damned.

She stared at her hands. Hands that had trembled as she struggled not to touch him. She'd seen him shake as he battled to keep his hands to himself, too. His concern for her safety made her heart beat faster whenever he came near. Despite no physical contact, she felt close to him, closer than anyone since her arrival on Earth. Their strange and wonderful connection touched her soul in a way no other man ever would.

She stared at the bed. Would she ever feel his weight press her into the softness of her mattress? The thought of it made her squirm. Why couldn't he put aside his fears for a brief moment so they could touch? By all the gods of her dimension, she needed relief from the physical and emotional torture he put her through on an almost constant basis. His physical reaction to her told her how much he wanted her.

Didn't he know what he did to her emotions?

She contemplated her return to Angel Haven the day after tomorrow. The clothes Olivia loaned her were okay, but she wanted her own clothes. A knock jarred her out of her thoughts.

She smiled when Olivia walked in. "Thanks again for all your help."

Olivia grinned. "We were glad to do it. Are you thinking about when you go home?"

"Yes. It's convenient Grayson has ties to your team. It helps not having to explain to a new person where I've been or why. Was he a member long?"

Olivia shrugged. "He'd been here for around ten years or so before I came. It could've been longer. I'm not really sure. I was here a few years before Martin. Grayson left a couple of years after Martin joined the team. From what I understand, he was hiding from some people who were hunting him."

"I guess I need to get the full story from him." Felissina picked up her jacket and stared at it. "Martin doesn't want me to go, does he? I mean, I can already picture him arguing against me leaving."

Liv sat in the chair near the wall. "He worries about everyone. He takes his responsibilities as team leader seriously. He's also pretty sensible, well, most of the time. I'm glad he found you, Feli. You're perfect for him. He needs you."

"I need him, too. It's necessary I go home to get some personal things, but at the same time, I don't want to leave. I've never been so torn in two before." Felissina turned to face Olivia. "I'm considering moving to the underground permanently. I'm already missing being here, and I haven't even left yet."

"I get it," Olivia said. "Magic helps me to understand auras and a lot of emotions. I could sense your connection to him the moment we brought you here. Don't worry. As soon as you come back, everything will sort itself out. To tell you the truth, I think you belong here with us."

Felissina sighed. "I just hope Shadowjack sees it our way and decides to give up on trying to grab me."

"You never know. He just might at that." Olivia stood. "Well, I've got to get back to my office. Paperwork waits for no man, woman, hero, or witch. You going to see Martin now?"

"Yes. He should be almost done with his workout. I'm headed to the weight room. I need to spend more time with him before I leave."

Felissina entered the gym, and Martin stood in the far corner in all of his powerful glory. She could watch him all day. The too tight clothes she wore began to rub her intimate areas in all the wrong, and yet right, ways. She walked over to him and sat on a nearby weight bench.

His back was ramrod straight and his body rigid. His chest heaved as his breath came in shallow bursts. He stared at the wall, his lips moving in silent conversation, a weight in each hand. Should she interrupt? He appeared to concentrate or listen to some force she couldn't see. They were the only two people in there. Did he have a type of telepathy?

He blinked and shook his head. When he caught sight of her, he smiled. Felissina breathed an internal sigh of relief. What happened to him? What did he see and hear?

"I like your outfit. You look good in it," he said.

She stood and tugged the hem of the shirt to pull it even tighter against her breasts. She'd been right not to put a bra on. "I picked it out for you. I wanted to know if you'd like to come back with me to my room for a little while. I'm sure part of you does."

"You're right." He stood as close as he could without contact. "I hate the fact I can't touch you."

"I feel the same." She raised her hands to his face, leaving barely an inch between his warm skin and her suddenly sweaty palms. "Maybe someday you will. I can't wait for that particular day."

"You aren't the only one."

She led the way to her room, his presence soothing the nervousness wanting to claim her. Once inside, she shut the door and locked it. "I don't want us to be disturbed. I'd like us to try a new way to be together. I've never done this before, so you'll have to guide me."

"Okay. How can I help?"

She dropped her clothes on the floor and settled herself on the bed. "I'm not the only one who needs to be undressed." She waited until he'd stripped and knelt next to her. "Tell me how to get some relief from this terrible desire for you. I need you to show me what to do."

"Are you asking me to teach you what I think you're asking me to teach you?" he said slowly.

"Yes. If we can't give each other physical release, we'll have to find another way." She smiled and lay back on the bed. "This is the oddest request I've ever asked of someone. Yet no one but you can teach me such a personal and intimate act."

He began to fidget, telling her she wasn't the only

one this nervous. She nodded at him as he took his place, kneeling beside the bed.

"Shall we begin?"

He swallowed hard. "I guess so."

****

"So she hasn't made her expected appearance yet?" Anita said through clenched teeth. If this level of frustration kept up, she'd need to cap every tooth in her mouth.

"Not yet. I've stationed spies at their suspected exit location. They'll keep watch and call me when she appears." Shadowjack crossed his ankles and leaned back in the chair. "This is a delicate situation. If I miss this time, I won't have another chance. We have to be patient."

"Patience has never been Benedict Trust's best quality." She stood over him. "Or mine."

Anita paced. If Trust knew the problems this mercenary gave her, he wouldn't demand results on an almost daily basis. At least she'd been able to turn over some more supers for him to drain in his quest for increased psychic powers. Which had probably been the one thing keeping her from her own cell at HelixCorp.

"I'm on a tight schedule. Mr. Trust has demanded results. If I can't supply them, there will be consequences." She glared at him. "Who do you think will save you if I'm not in the picture? Mr. Trust may gut you for fun."

"I'll deliver, don't worry. It may take a few more days. End of the week, guaranteed, even if I have to go into their underground lair and drag her out by her hair. How's your association with the magic user progressing? Are you two getting along?"

She rubbed her arms. Just thinking about the mage made her want to shower. "Well enough to complete my work. How I feel about him makes no difference, as long as I get the results I want. He asked me to help him find your powerful witch. Can you work with him to accomplish this?"

"I can work with almost anyone. Have you talked to him about it?"

"Not yet." She paused. "I wanted to make sure of your compliance before it became a solid plan."

Shadowjack stood and headed for the door. "Send him my way. Like I told you before, you'll have everyone you want soon enough."

As soon as the door shut behind him, her eyes narrowed. "Yes, I will, and you may not like it when I do."

She reached for the phone and called Ra-Vel. His continued presence made the once tiny pinpricks of fear grow a little larger every day. Unfortunately, he'd become a vital piece of her project. They were close to perfection of the serum for Mr. Trust. The psionic girl showed no dangerous side effects after the initial injection. As long as Anita and her team took it slowly and gave her smaller doses, they should be able to increase her power and then complete the transfer.

She smiled. Soon, she'd have the Angel and Shadowjack at HelixCorp, and Mr. Trust's faith in her would be restored. She stared at a photo of an older gentleman, his lips curved in a gentle smile. She hated keeping it hidden in a locked desk drawer. This was the one personal item no one at HelixCorp or in her lab knew about. It was a secret she meant to keep.

"I'm on the right track now, Dad." She smiled.

"Soon, I'll have everything we worked so hard for. It won't be long before it all comes together."

She walked over to the cabinet stocked with different, expensive liquors. She ignored all those and reached in the small refrigerator and pulled out a bottle of wine. The holiday season would be here before she knew it, but she deserved a small celebration now.

Chapter Thirteen

"I should only be gone for a couple of days at most," Felissina said. "I need to get some of my own clothes. There's a strong possibility I may not want to leave when I come back. Since there's no piano here, I also need to practice for my concert. The date will be here before I know it."

"I understand, but I still don't think it's safe for you to leave right now." Martin closed his eyes and took a deep breath. "I'll call Grayson and tell him to bring you some of your stuff. My topside contacts tell me Shadowjack's got people at all of our entrances. I won't let you put yourself in danger."

"You're very sweet, but I don't trust Grayson to gather what I really need. I know you're concerned about me, but this can't be put off any longer. I must return to Angel Haven." She smiled to reassure him. "Don't worry. I'm not without my own defenses. When Grayson comes, he'll keep me safe. I'll be fine."

Martin stood inches from her. "Those are what are known as famous last words." His hands clenched, and he frowned a little. "I can't even hold you before you go."

She laid her hand above his cheek. "I'll call Grayson and have him pick me up in the morning. This will give us tonight."

Someone cleared their throat behind them, and they

turned. Kaz stood there, a wide grin on her face. "If I knew the words, I'd sing 'Isn't It Romantic.' "

"What do you want, Kaz?" Martin said, annoyance creeping into his voice.

"I came to get you for another scan. Some important people in the fairy realm gave me an artifact which could help me determine what the hell you are."

"I'll be there tomorrow," he said. "Today is booked solid."

Kaz grinned. "So I heard. Feli, will you excuse us for a minute?"

"Of course. I'll go call Grayson."

Felissina headed for the computer room. It would've been easier to call home if she could get a cell signal out. Since she didn't have the option, the landline in the computer room became her link to the topside world.

****

"Okay. What's this great, new, magical doo-dad you want to poke me with now?" Martin said.

"And you say I have a crappy attitude." Kaz snorted. "I've been loaned a very special item. I'm iffy about its use, and I'm not sure how or even if it will work. If I break it, let's just say, the elves will destroy me so bad, my ancestors and my descendants will feel it at the same time."

"What is it?" When she hesitated, Martin frowned. "Kaz, for all the hassle I give you, you know you have my complete trust. We've been friends for way too many years. I know you wouldn't do or try any kind of magic which might hurt me. What is it?"

"If I use this particular item, there's a chance it could permanently damage you. I could get sent to

Dukar Prison just for having it in my possession. But I'm desperate. We've tried all the elements, compounds, and magic sensory devices I have in The Center." She lowered her voice. "It's an artifact of dark magic."

Martin stared hard at her. "Are you sure you want to do this?"

"No, but it's come down to no choice. Martin, with how often your powers change, we need to know what we're up against."

"Not enough for you to jeopardize yourself. You're my best friend. If it's this dangerous, you could be seriously hurt."

She smiled. "I notice you didn't mention yourself in your little statement."

"Because you're more important than I am. This city needs you, not me."

"Hey, buddy. Did you ever think I might need you? You give me a much-needed dose of reality when events get too weird, even for me." She straightened her shoulders. "So, come by the clinic tomorrow and we'll see what we can see. Deal?"

He nodded. "I'll be there. We'll do your funky magic scan and maybe, just maybe, we'll both come out okay."

"Later."

Kaz opened a portal and disappeared in an instant. Felissina came back in the room as the portal faded away. "You look upset. Is Kaz well? Should I know what she said?"

"No, it isn't serious. Kaz needs me to come to her clinic for another kind of scan. It's one she's not too familiar with and wanted to give me a heads up."

"I see." Her gaze turned wary. "What else did she say?"

He shifted from foot to foot. "Did you get in touch with Grayson?" he said, ignoring her question.

"He said to meet him by your third entrance at ten tomorrow morning. He says it's better camouflaged than some of the others."

"Yes, it is." He held his hand just above her cheek, absorbing the warmth radiating from her skin. "You will come back, won't you?"

"Of course. We're connected on a level deeper than anything I've ever experienced before. We must explore it more as well as other personal matters."

He remembered their afternoon. If he didn't get these powers under control soon, he'd go crazy. While he watched Felissina and let her watch him as they relieved their individual sexual tensions almost made him rush to her. In a weak moment, he reached for her before he remembered the dire consequences of the power he'd lived with for far too many years.

Damn.

****

That night in Felissina's room, Martin sat in the single chair and watched as she got her few items together. "Are you sure you'll be all right?"

"Yes. I'll be fine." She checked the pockets in her jacket and determined all her possessions were still there. "Martin, I want to ask you again. Please tell me about yourself."

"I guess I should, before you go. When I touch someone," he said slowly, reluctant to reveal his shame, "I see, in my mind, that person die. A darkness covers them while a misty white fog circles them. I get a heavy, sick feeling in my stomach. I don't get any details, like how or when; I just know they'll die. No barrier can stop the visions of the future. As much as I want a deeper relationship with you, I can't take the chance. I don't want to see that darkness cover you. I don't think I could take it."

He watched her face for any kind of reaction but only saw neutrality in her expression. Her gaze held no pity and no sympathy, just calm contemplation of what he'd revealed. The seconds stretched out into long minutes before she spoke.

"You have a terrible power, Martin," she said, her voice quiet. "Have you been able to control it?"

He shook his head. "No. It triggers at any touch. Kaz has tried to find the origin of this ability, but so far, no luck. The bad part is, when my powers change, it's like they evolve into more dangerous versions. The one power I can control is the ability to rapidly age items. I can make them decay and crumble in seconds."

"Is this her reason for wanting you to be scanned often?"

"Yes." He sat back and rubbed his eyes. "There's a chance the more my powers change, the more probable it is they could get stronger or even worse. She tests me constantly because she doesn't trust me to tell her when a new event crops up."

"I don't think so. From what I've learned about her from you and Olivia, I believe she has your best interests at heart. You're friends. I don't think she'd do anything to harm you." She hesitated. "When did you discover this power?"

"Let me give you a little bit of history on the Martin Long story." He stared at the floor, the need to avoid the look on her face greater than his courage. "I grew up a weird kid in a normal house. No one else in my family had these or any abilities. They all talked about my wonderful power. I thought so, too. Back then, I could only read the past of objects.

"The trippy stuff started in high school. The other kids called me a freak and, to a degree, I guess they were right. The past called to me. I sensed so much history inside the school and the other buildings around the campus. I didn't have a lot of friends but, with the stories I learned, it didn't bother me. Some days, I would walk down the hallways and run my hand along the wall. When I do, it's like when someone speed reads. I see the past, and it stays with me. Later, I go through the stories a little slower."

He got up and paced, still avoiding her gaze. "Fast forward to my college years. I went into archeology. My power made it easy, and I enjoyed my work. I didn't go out into the field. I wanted a research position, inside, where I wouldn't get sunburned or eaten alive by bugs."

She smiled. "You must have been fascinated by what you learned through your abilities."

"Oh yeah, and I still am. I see, in my mind, what happened to the object in its past. The older the item, the more history I see. There's a rush of emotion. I can almost sense how it felt to live then." He glanced at her. "But I digress. When I graduated, I got hired by a prominent Boston museum. I worked in the artifact room. I dated objects and wrote their histories down."

Felissina scooted closer to the edge of the bed. "What happened next?"

"The other shoe dropped. A wealthy patron

donated a lot of relics. I started to date them and discovered they were fake. I brought this to the attention of the director. He wanted to know how I learned the truth. I couldn't tell him about my power. I lied and said the collection didn't match with my data. So, rather than losing the patron's incredibly large monetary and artifact donation, he fired me. He told me if I ever tried to go public, he'd ruin me."

"What a terrible man." She jumped up and slammed her fist into her palm. "I think I need to find this person and teach him the right way to treat an honest, good man."

He smiled at her reaction. "It's been a long time. Let it go."

"What did you do afterward?"

"All the museums in the area blackballed me." He started to pace again, and she moved away. "I found a small carnival at the park. I told the man in charge my sad, sordid tale of woe and he hired me. I used my power in my act and told people the history of different items they'd give me. I met Kaz at the carny. We hit it off right away, but not in the romantic sense. We clicked as friends. She's still never told me why, with all her power, she worked there."

He swallowed hard and sat for a moment. His body trembled, and he jumped up to pace again as he stared at the floor. His hands shook, and he jammed them in his pants pockets. Muscles in his neck tensed and stood out. Memories flooded his mind. The terror and hopelessness of the next part crammed into his chest, constricting his lungs and making his heart pound. He swiped at the sweat beading on his forehead.

He stopped and bowed his head, rolling his

shoulders to loosen the tension building at the base of his skull. He licked his lips and fought to keep the tremors from his voice. Maybe if he cleared his throat. As he spoke again, his voice softened as he forced the words out. He'd relived this moment so many times. Familiar tears burned behind his eyes. He should've been faster. He should've made people listen to him. He should've tried to do more.

"One day, I brushed against a woman's hand. She and her son were on their way to the airport. I saw a devastating plane crash. I saw her and her son die. Through their eyes, I saw everyone else die. The darkness around them was so heavy, I felt like it wanted to consume me. I guess I scared them because they ran off. I got to the airport as fast as I could. I found their flight and ran toward it. I blew through security and tried to stop people from getting on the plane."

When he looked at her, the tears he couldn't shed shone in her eyes. She hurt for him. He saw no pity, only sadness for all he'd been through. Her hand lifted toward him for a moment before she lowered it to her lap.

"The more people who touched me, the more death I saw. TSA agents locked me in a room. The plane took off. One of the engines exploded minutes later. It crashed at the end of the runway and killed everyone on board.

"I know security questioned me, but I don't remember any of it. They told me all I would say is 'I tried' over and over. I refused to tell them how to contact my family, or my name. After they determined I had nothing to do with the crash, the authorities sent me to a sanatorium. I wouldn't let anyone touch me. The one orderly who did, I told him there was death in his future. He didn't believe me. His car got hit head on by a drunk driver, and he died at the scene."

"Martin, what happened to your hands? Your knuckles are covered with scars."

He held his hands up and looked at them. "This is what happens when you can't stand looking at your own reflection. Every mirror, every window, and every single surface where I could see myself, I smashed. I kept seeing that woman and her son. I couldn't stand looking at myself. So I punched through everything showing me my greatest failure. Me."

"I'm so sorry you felt lost."

He shrugged. "I came to terms with the fact I did all I could. It took a long time. I stayed at the hospital for a little over a year. When the year passed, the doctors had no other treatment for me. So my doctor signed the discharge papers and he released me. I couldn't go home."

"Why not? Didn't your family want you back?"

He looked at her. "My mom's a hugger. I couldn't have her anywhere near me. I made my way here to New York City. I had earned enough money to buy one particular item. So, I did and took it with me to a deserted section of the subway. Liv found me there. She sat with me for a long time, and we talked. She brought me here, and I've been with this team ever since."

"Martin, what did you buy?"

He took her next door to his room. "Come with me. I'll show you."

He glanced at her, then opened the nightstand drawer. Her reaction had been the same as everyone else. She stared at the gun nestled on an old towel, silent and ominous, as it glowed in the lamplight. Grayson's shock had surprised him. He'd caught Kaz off guard when he showed her. None on his team knew about it. Only the people he trusted most.

"Liv stopped my suicide. She and Kaz talked me through the bad times and helped me keep my sanity when it began to slip away. This thing is a solid reminder to never descend to such a low level again."

"Oh, Martin. I wish I could hold you right now."

He glanced at her, giving her a sad smile. "I wish you could, too."

Chapter Fourteen

Shadowjack stood in the nearby shadows and checked the time. Felissina should appear at any moment. A car pulled up, and a tall man got out to lean against the door. His stance looked casual to an untrained observer. To him, the man's body language told a different story.

The way he continuously scanned the area, the way his fingers occasionally twitched. This was a man used to action, used to keeping his senses on high alert. From the way his jacket bulged, he carried a large gun. Felissina had surrounded herself with too many protectors. Not only did he have to deal with them and the princess's hardheadedness, but also his temporary employer.

Why did the damn recall signal have to be so strong in Anita's lab? If it worked anywhere, he could grab her now and they could go home. Damn her and damn this backward dimension with their primitive science. If the technology here were more advanced, Felissina could've been recalled without his presence.

However, plans seldom worked out in favor of the heroic side, no matter what dimension in which resided. So he'd wait and plan before he'd take them both home. He reached into a side pocket and pulled out a device to amplify sound. Earth did have some useful tech after all. He put it in his ear, marveling at how such a small thing could give such clear sound. When Felissina appeared, he would hear every word exchanged between her and Long. Then, his plans would fall into place.

****

Martin opened the door which led to the street. He didn't want her to go. He'd seen flashes of darkness around her if she left now. He knew she wouldn't change her mind, but he had to ask one more time. He held his hand up, signaling Grayson to wait for another moment.

"Are you sure you need to go today?"

"Yes," she said. "I'll be back in two days. I'm determined to help you control your power. I'll work with Kaz and Olivia until we discover an answer."

"You know, if I could kiss you right now, I would." He opened the door a little more. "It looks clear, and Grayson's out by the car. You have the number here. If you need me, call and I'll be there before you hang up the phone."

"I know you will. I won't be away a second longer than necessary."

"Two days will feel a lot longer without you here."

Martin took a deep breath and checked the area. Grayson nodded as he straightened up, then walked over. Felissina squeezed out, and Grayson hurried her over to the car. They got in, and Felissina waved as they pulled out. Martin watched until their car disappeared into the traffic before he turned back to go home.

The tunnels felt empty without her presence. Even the stories he knew by heart from the walls didn't ease the loneliness gnawing at his soul. He stopped as a thought struck him. He strode toward Olivia's lab and opened the door, relieved to see her in there.

"Call Kaz with your communication spell."

"What, I don't even get a 'please' out of you?" When he frowned, she gave a slight shrug. "Okay."

She retrieved a crystal bowl and a small, plastic vial from a lower cabinet and placed both on her desk. She carried a pitcher half filled with water and poured a small amount into the bowl. Two drops from the vial followed as Olivia murmured a short incantation. Thin, blue mist wafted up, and Kaz's voice drifted out.

"What's up, Liv?"

"Martin needs to speak with you." She motioned him forward.

"Speak and be heard, oh pal of mine. What's the haps?"

Martin took a deep breath. "I'm afraid what I'm about to tell you may be a serious complication, but here goes. I have a strong suspicion Felissina and I are soulmates."

Kaz's laughter rang out of the mist. "Sweetie, it's not a complication. It's great news."

"How can it be?" He paced in front of the bowl. "Creatures from the fairy and magic realms have soulmates and I'm not from there. As of right now, I'm not from anywhere. Tell me what to do."

"Okay, I'll concede the fairy point. You might be from another area of the fairy realm we haven't explored yet. When you come over, maybe we can find an answer."

"What about the weird spectral figures I see constantly following me?"

"Tell them to come with you. Maybe they'll be

useful," Kaz said, then hung up.

Martin looked at Olivia, who couldn't keep the grin from her face. "Great. What's so funny?"

"You and Kaz. She's all fire and bluster, and you've got to be one of the mellowest people I know. You guys are perfect friends."

He thought about what she said. Yeah, he guessed they were.

****

So Felissina planned to return in two days to the underground. Shadowjack would have more than enough time to plan how to take her to Anita. The telepath should be happy with this news. Then maybe she'd shut up and quit badgering him about his competence.

Time to stake out Angel Haven. The time to take her would be after she left the grounds and the gates were closed. If he did it right, he would deliver the princess with minimal collateral damage. Every day brought him closer to the return to their home dimension. He strode to the car Anita gave him to use. Ra-Vel waited for him at a nearby restaurant. Plans needed to be laid.

Shadowjack drove to the address Ra-Vel gave him. Anita had made some valid points about strength in numbers to solidify his agreement to work with the mage. He stowed his gun under the driver's seat before he entered the restaurant. The waitress led him to a back table where the magic user waited. After he placed his drink order, Ra-Vel spoke.

"The woman you seek is a very powerful witch named Kaz." Ra-Vel sipped his water. "She's friends with the people from the underground team. There is a man there called Martin Long. He's second in command when he needs to be. I couldn't get any information on what his power is, but it's believed to be dangerous."

Shadowjack nodded once. "I know of Martin Long. We've met several times. I don't want to eliminate him, but I may have no choice. His interference has caused more problems than expected."

"Sounds like a reasonable solution." Ra-Vel leaned forward. "There's another person who's in the way. I believe the brown-haired girl you mentioned is Kaz's apprentice. I'd like to be rid of both of them, if possible."

"The women you're talking about helped to rescue the princess at our first encounter. I have no quarrel with either of them as long as they stay out of the way. What's your connection to this Kaz woman?"

Ra-Vel paused as the waitress brought their food, and he smiled at her as he waved her away. "Kaz and I are, to put it simply, rivals. She wants to help people. I don't. I've tried to sabotage her whenever I could. After I help Anita adjust her formula, Kaz will be a prime subject. If it's at all possible, hold off on Long's elimination. The eminent Dr. Anita Haines may have plans for him."

"I'll try, but I make no guarantees."

"I ask you to practice a little patience, if you can," Ra-Vel said.

They ate in silence and paid their bill. Shadowjack opened the car door and stared at Ra-Vel over the roof. "Do you need a ride somewhere?"

"No. I have some business here in town. Make your plans for your princess."

Ra-Vel disappeared before Shadowjack could ask what he meant. It seemed there were many players in this convoluted game. He got in the car and turned the key. First, he'd grab Felissina when she returned to the underground. After he accomplished this part of his mission, the next would be to get them both home. He'd force her to listen to his explanation of the fateful day when their province fell. She would believe him, whether she wanted to or not.

****

Felissina rushed by her teammates without her usual greeting and ran up to her room. She slammed the door shut and leaned her head against it. How could she pass by her friends without acknowledging them? The others at Angel Haven may have some perspective on Martin's problems. She should've stayed and told them. At the same time, if she did, she felt it would have been a betrayal of his trust. So few people knew what he could do, and he'd kept it quiet for many years.

Right now, all her concentration centered on the deep ache in her chest as it throbbed in time to her heartbeat. Each mile had cut into her the more distance grew between Martin and herself. Innumerable scars continued to be carved on her soul as the hum of the tires ticked away another piece of her heart. She fell backward on her bed and stared at the ceiling. She should be glad to be home. She shouldn't miss living in tunnels under the earth so much when she hadn't even been gone an hour yet.

Felissina turned and stared at her room. The furniture, the carpet, the curtains, all she owned looked so gaudy and unnecessary. If she stayed, she'd have to redecorate soon. Unfamiliar claustrophobia clawed at her chest while she took in every detail. The heavy, dark curtains, the deep, mahogany furniture made the spacious room feel small and confined.

She bounced several times on her bed. How could she have slept on a mattress so soft? No wonder her back bothered her more often than not. While she recovered in the underground, the ache in the small of her back disappeared. Somehow, the firmer mattress she'd slept on fixed the one pain her healing factor ignored. She'd miss her bed in the underground while she resided in Angel Haven.

She kicked at the plush rug. "Who needs carpet so thick you can't see your toes?"

The area rug in her room in the underground felt nice on her feet. The colorful design was easy on the eyes and restful, unlike the garish green she'd chosen for her room here. She couldn't believe she'd spent so much money on what she now considered to be hideous decorations.

"How could I have wasted so much money on…this?" she said, opening her arms wide as she turned in a slow circle. "I must have been delusional."

She stalked to her closet and flung open the double doors. "By all the gods, why do I own so many pairs of shoes? I have more outfits in here than I can wear in a lifetime." She studied the massive amount of clothes. "Of course, the formal gowns are important. But the rest of these can go."

She grabbed an armload off the bar and threw the clothes on the bed. Time to purge a little. There were many charities who would love to receive designer clothes. She could also take them to various shelters around the city. Most of the shoes and purses she would sell online, then donate the money. She could always take some of the items to the underground team.

A knock startled her. She opened her door and saw Grayson lean against the doorframe. "Hello, Grayson."

"The others said you ran by them and didn't say hello. Are you okay?" He looked to the bed where the pile of clothes grew higher the deeper she delved into her closet. "Do you plan to move out?"

"Please convey my apologies to the team. I came back to get a few personal items and some clothes. When I came in here, I saw this room for the first time with clear vision." She sat on the edge of the bed and stared at the floor. "Grayson, I fear I'm the spoiled, stuck-up snob everyone thinks I am."

Grayson sat next to her and patted her hand. "I don't think that's true. You have a high-class background. No one blames you for being who you are. From what Kristin tells me, you've grown a lot since you've been here."

"I don't feel as if I've grown at all." She kicked at the thick carpet. "If I had, I wouldn't have spent so much money on this awful extravagance."

"You can't see it, but the rest of us can. The time you spent with Martin and Liv and Kaz has cemented what you already are. You're a kind, caring person." He squeezed her hand. "I think you'll be a great ruler when you get back to your own dimension."

"Which is a whole other matter," she said. "I've ached to go home for such a long time. I still want to go home, but the urgency isn't as strong as it used to be. It fell to me to find troops to free my province." She walked to the window and looked out. "I have an obligation to do what I can for my people. As much as I want to stay on Earth, I need to return to my home dimension. My responsibility to Erlymere can be as much of a burden as Martin's powers."

"He told you?"

She nodded once. "Yes. Last night. We talked as I prepared to come back here. Would you like to hear a strange secret?"

"Feli, what's wrong?"

She snatched a tissue from the box on her night table. "As soon as I arrived here, it felt different. Angel Haven no longer feels like home. I don't wish to be here any longer than necessary. I've wanted to come back ever since Martin rescued me, and now, I feel like a stranger here."

Grayson walked over and pulled her into a tight hug. "It's not strange. You're in love, girl. This doesn't feel like home to you anymore because you don't want to be here. You want to be with Martin in the underground."

Felissina thought about what he said. Yes, the love bug had bitten her, hard. "The movies I've watched with my friends paint love in a different light. Why don't any of them mention how much it hurts to be separated from the man in a person's life?" She wiped her eyes and laid her head on Grayson's shoulder. "I must say, love hurts quite a bit."

"It can, but it's while you aren't with each other." He took her hand and pulled her toward the door. "Let's go talk to a certain human/gargoyle hybrid. I think you need to learn what soulmates are."

She wiped her eyes and smiled. "You're also from the realm of magic. Can't you tell me what I need to know?"

Grayson laughed. "Hey. I'm a sniper, a covert agent, a harpy, and a liaison between two law enforcement agencies. I don't do touchy feely. The resident guardian of the fairy realm takes care of those things. He's supposed to be sensitive."

"And you aren't?"

"Nope."

She smiled. "I believe I'll let Kristin know. She may be of a different mind."

He gave her a gentle push out the door. "Do you want to go or not?"

"Yes, I do."

Felissina followed Grayson downstairs, grateful for his company. If not for his teasing, she may have burst into tears.

Chapter Fifteen

Ra-Vel laid his wand down on the table. Magic pulsed through the gnarled, dark wood as the glow around it faded. "The girl's power has fairy magic at its base."

"The new formula I designed seems to work." Anita stared at the girl before she glanced at Ra-Vel. "Does it need to be changed again to compensate for the kind of magic she possesses?"

He stroked his chin. "I'm not sure. Her power isn't magic per se, but it has magic at its core."

Anita glared at him as her hands clenched into tight fists. "Would you care to explain yourself? Is she magic or not?"

Ra-Vel walked over to the girl on the exam table and laid his hand on her forehead. "One of her parents could be a creature from the fairy realm. Maybe some type of siren or weaker class of banshee. I'll have to check my sources there. I can have an answer for you by sometime next week. I suggest you concentrate on your other projects until then."

"Fine. I do have a lot to keep me occupied until I hear from you." She glanced at the clock. "I have to go. I'm expecting a phone call."

Anita hurried back to her office. Benedict Trust would phone any time for an update on how the different experiments progressed. He wanted to get his first injection of "superpowers" by the end of the following week. She'd told him time and time again his deadline wasn't doable. She sighed. Her boss needed to learn the value of patience before she lost hers. She opened the door to her office, and the man himself sat behind her desk.

She schooled her expression to hide her increasing annoyance. "Mr. Trust. I didn't expect to see you this soon."

He rose, giving the appearance he unfolded himself rather than doing something as mundane as standing. Gray highlighted his dark brown hair at the temples. He smoothed unseen wrinkles from the designer suit he wore and stalked over to her.

"I wanted to see, in person, how your experiments progressed. Your reports are so vague they're next to useless. Don't make me remind you again the consequences of failure. Tell me something concrete before you're replaced. Prove to me you're good enough to handle something of this magnitude."

The muscles in her neck tightened as she bit back the retort almost escaping her mouth. "Would you like to see how the new acquisition has adapted to the improved serum?" She handed him the folder she'd brought with her. "I thought we might not be able to use her, but my new assistant has proved invaluable with his work on the formula."

He flipped the folder shut and handed it back to her. "Take me to this miracle worker."

Anita led Trust back the way she'd just come. Ra-Vel still worked in the lab. He took a little too much pleasure in the fear of the girl on the table. She gestured for him to join her. "Mr. Trust, I'd like to introduce you to Ra-Vel, one of the city's more powerful mages. He's shown me how to tweak the formula. With his help, I should have your first injection ready by your deadline."

"Mr. Trust, it's an honor to meet you, sir," Ra-Vel said, giving a deep bow. "Dr. Haines has been an absolute delight to work with. Her level of dedication knows no bounds. There is no problem she lets stand in her way. I admire her a great deal."

"She's one of our best," Trust said, the tone of his voice indicating otherwise.

Ra-Vel inclined his head slightly. "I would like to talk to you later about borrowing her to help me with one of my own projects."

"Take her," Trust said. "After this is done, I don't think I'll have any other projects for which she needs to be here. She's all yours. Send her back whenever you like."

The tight lid Anita clamped on her growing rage did nothing to stop her hands from shaking. How dare Trust treat her like this? After all she'd sacrificed for this man and his company. She knew what Ra-Vel wanted. She'd read his mind and seen the depravity there. She'd be damned if she let the magic user anywhere near her.

****

The early morning light cast a warm glow in the courtyard of St. Michael's church. Martin took a deep breath and let it out slowly as he raised his face to the sun. Not many people knew this place existed. If only it could stay this way. He didn't ever want to share it. He shook his head. There he went, being selfish again.

One look, and a person knew the gardens weren't

planned by a professional landscaper. Randomly planted types and colors made it better somehow. Its imperfection and peaceful solitude helped him sort out his thoughts and emotions on many occasions. Right now, he needed more than his thoughts collected. His emotions churned like a hurricane in his chest. Could his heart be blown in fifteen different directions at the same time? It sure felt like it.

"All of my friends need to be warned. Yet I've decided to sit in this quiet courtyard, and why not?" He leaned on his knees, rubbing his eyes. "I have a mission to stop the bad guys, and all I want to do is ponder the meaning of my life. I have the most useless abilities of the entire hero community. Sure, I can turn anything to dust in seconds, but seeing people die and reading the past of objects? What a waste." He straightened up and stretched his back. "And again, I'm talking to myself."

Movement to his left grabbed his attention. He jumped to his feet and took several cautious steps over to the figure. A large rhododendron shrouded the corner where it stood in deep shadow. As Martin drew closer, a gaunt hand reached toward him. He drew back, not wanting to take a chance on physical contact, even with a specter. Again, moisture beaded on his face and clothes. He wiped at his forehead as he stared at the figure.

"You must come with me," it whispered. "You must come home."

"I don't understand. Earth is my home."

"Your true home is far beyond this world," the specter pleaded. "The master misses you. You have always been his favorite."

"Tell me who I am," Martin pleaded. "Please. I

have to know. You talk like you know me. Tell me who I am, where I'm from. If you have the answers, you have to tell me."

A heavy sadness surged through him, threatening to drown him as the figure fled.

"Just great. The one ghost, or whatever that thing is, who knows me runs instead of giving me answers."

He blinked as the bright November sun hit his eyes. Did a cloud pass over the sun or over him? As he remained rooted to the spot, he noticed silver mist swirl around his ankles and begin to climb its way up his legs. He should be freaked out, but it gave him a level of comfort he hadn't felt since, well, since Felissina stood near him.

Enough. Time to get off his rear end and go see Kaz. She expected him at The Center today anyway. He knew he had to tell her about this recent encounter and the weird mist. How could the strange specter know him? He'd never lived anywhere but Earth, had he? To be answerable to someone called a "master" sounded unpleasant to say the least.

He tilted his head back and stared at the sky. "Why me, karma? Couldn't you pick on someone else? What did I ever do to you?"

Here were some more topics for conversation. What was with all the water? Why would mist cover him suddenly? Did it come from him or the specters? The original small amount of questions had grown into a startling, large mountain. He had a sneaking suspicion as soon as he knew his origins, every question he had would be answered. Which led to another question. Would he like the answers he'd receive?

He hurried through the streets to the entrance to

Kaz's clinic. He waved his hand in front of the brick wall, then knocked on the door when it appeared. He flashed his access card at the entrance and ran down the hallways after he called out a quick hello to the ogre.

"Kaz, are you around?" he yelled.

She stepped out of her office. "Hey. Keep it down. This is a hospital." She rolled her eyes. "Sort of. Get in here and tell me what your current problem is this time." She glanced at her phone. "And you're early."

Martin hurried into her office and flopped on the couch. "I think I've taken the final step toward insanity."

"And you call me overly dramatic," she snorted. "What's got you tied up in knots now?"

"Ghosts."

She frowned a little. "Uh huh. Not what I expected you to say. Who's haunting you? It's not my specialty, but I can make a few calls."

"You know about the spirits, specters, ghosts, or whatever you want to call them I keep seeing out of the corner of my eye. I told George to tell you about them."

"He did. I wanted to get in touch with you about this development." She studied him. "So what spooked you today?"

"I went to the courtyard at St. Michael's to try to figure out my next course of action. I saw a ghost in the corner. I walked over to it, and it didn't disappear. It wanted me to go with it. It practically demanded I go. It said I needed to go home. It told me I'm the master's favorite. Favorite what? Who's the master? When it disappeared, some weird mist covered me. Kaz, what the heck am I? What realm actually has a claim on me?"

She walked over to a bookcase and studied the spines as she mumbled to herself. She yanked out a small, thin tome and walked back over to Martin. "I've tried to work on what your visions mean. This book represents all known research about the spectral realm. Yeah, I know. It's not a lot. If what I've started to suspect is true, you have some unique origins."

"Do you mean I'm dead?" He poked his side and frowned. "I don't feel dead."

She shrugged. "I'm not sure. Let's do another scan. Now, since I know where to start, I think I know what to do with you."

"There's more," he said as they walked down the hallway to an exam room.

She stopped and turned. "By all the elders of magic, what now?"

"When we first rescued Felissina, I saw her in my mind. I saw her as clearly as if I stood right in front of her. I knew she'd been attacked and needed me." He gave a heavy sigh. "What's made my life so complicated this week?"

"You want your life to be easy? Keep dreaming, pal. Don't worry about this change. Every step with your powers seems to be a natural progression." When he didn't follow her, she stopped again. "Now what?"

"I think I've started to have visions. They began with the rescue of Feli, but now I see things all the time. They appear more in dreams than when I'm awake." He glanced at Kaz. "Tell me you can get rid of these powers."

She barked out a laugh. "Are you serious? No can do, good buddy. Trust me. I got this. Come on." When they continued down the hall, she winked at him. "Let me tell you about when I still traveled the adventurer's road. My party at the time needed to stay on this family ranch of wizards. You think your week's been bad? Compared to what I went through then, you've had it easy."

Martin let her talk. She'd told this story before, but he wouldn't stop her. She liked to tell it, and he didn't mind. As far as he knew, Kaz didn't have many close friends and neither did he. He was proud she counted him as one of the privileged few. He'd be happy to listen to whatever she had to say.

In the room, he sat on the exam table and watched as she opened a hidden safe. She took out a black wand case, inlaid with silver leaves. She removed an onyx wand and held it with reverence. The braided, wooden wand with a small, intricate knot on the end almost vibrated as she held it.

Martin drew away from it before he could stop himself. "I know you wouldn't own something this dark. Your wand is made of rosewood and sends out a pulse to soothe and calm. This one is repulsive. I don't want to be anywhere near it. Who does it belong to?"

"You're right. This isn't my wand, and I don't ever want it to be my wand. This is the Wand of Oros. It belonged to a mage who ended up being more demon than human. The elven lords smuggled it to me. The more your power evolves, the bigger ripples it sends through the supernatural world. The elves, the High Elves in particular, want to know what you are. Everyone in all the realms wants to know how to help you, so they sent me this. It's very powerful, and it should give us the answers we want."

"This is what could send you to Dukar? Are you

sure about this?" When she didn't answer, Martin took a deep breath. "I'm ready."

"You might be, but I'm not sure about me. It takes a lot of energy to use this. Its magic is forbidden. It taps into darker elements, but I'm out of ideas. I don't have what we need to find answers." She paused and stared at the black wand in her hands. "If the Conclave senses its usage, we're both doomed."

Martin held the edge of the bed in a white knuckled grip. "I trust you, Kaz. Let's do this."

She dimmed the lights and wove the wand in an intricate pattern. As she spoke a strange incantation, silver light outlined the edge of the wand, and the onyx pulsed with power. Martin closed his eyes against the light as it grew brighter.

He didn't know what would come next, but he did know he didn't want to see it when it finally happened.

Chapter Sixteen

Felissina played a familiar classical piece from Bach. As her fingers danced over the piano keys, she remembered the almost touch above Martin's skin the first time they stood before each other naked. He'd taken her breath away with his perfection. He'd discounted her praise, but he would always be perfect in her eyes.

"Could this be how Kristin and the rest see their husbands?" she said quietly. "Do they also think no one else compares to the men in their lives? They told me they suspect I've found my own soulmate. Could they be right?"

Her thoughts consumed her, and she stumbled over a complicated passage in the music. She stared at the sheet music, replaying the part slowly without error. How she wanted Martin to hear her play. There must be a way to control his power so he could be among people again. A frown creased her brow. Did she have the right to take him away from where he belonged?

"What if he belongs with me and not in the underground?" she murmured.

"What if you belong in the underground with him and not here?" Grayson said behind her.

She laid her hands in her lap and stared at him. "That possibility has consumed me quite a bit lately. I'm so confused by all these emotions. I don't know what's right for me or him."

"Welcome to love, princess."

"It's much more complicated in real life than in the movies." She closed the lid over the keys and leaned on it. "Grayson, I want to go back to the underground as soon as possible. Would you take me?"

"Can't right now. I have to go talk to my boss and file a report. I'll take you tomorrow at first light. All right?"

"I guess so. At least that will give me time to pack what I need."

He headed for the door and turned around. "Feli, do you plan to come back to Angel Haven?"

"I'm not sure. This is my home and has been for many years. Martin's home is where I want to be now. This is a difficult decision, and I want to make the right choice."

"I get it. I've been in this exact spot you're at right now. I'll see you in the morning." He winked at her. "When I met Kristin, a friend told me we were like orange juice and champagne. I think his description fits you and Martin, too."

"What do you mean?"

He kissed the top of her head. "It means just because the two of you come from, literally, two different worlds, doesn't mean you aren't meant to be together."

Felissina stared at the door after he left. His words made a lot of sense. She closed the music and stored it in the piano bench before she meandered to her room. She'd lied to her friend. She'd already made her mind up. If Martin wanted her to stay, then stay she would, and she'd never leave him again.

****

A portal opened, and Martin and Kaz stepped back into the underground. Smoke wafted from Martin's hair and clothes. Kaz's fingers were bright red, and small, white blisters covered the tips.

Olivia hurried over to them. "Are you two all right? Were you attacked?"

"We're fine." Kaz gave her a nonchalant wave. "A scan spell went a little haywire. I'm pretty sure we can rule out that procedure and any other like it."

"Haywire?" Martin shouted. "Kaz, you blew me up!"

"What? I don't believe it." Olivia looked back and forth between the two of them. "Is there a reason you blew up Martin?"

"It turned out to be a very small explosion, barely worth mentioning. It just happened. I didn't know that particular scan would have such a bad backlash. We've had a temporary setback," Kaz said as she blew on her fingers. "Do you have any of Gizel's salve left? These burns hurt like the dickens."

Olivia hurried out of the room as silver mist swirled around Martin, turning darker the angrier he became. "This isn't a temporary setback. This is a major disaster. The wand you used almost took your hands off. Your fingers got scorched. If even dark magic can't help me, what's left?"

"I've had it with you, Martin." Kaz scowled as her eyes narrowed to slits. "I've done my level best to help you, and all you do is bitch and complain about whatever I've tried. I'm sorry I ever said I'd try to find the answer to your problems. I'm almost as crazy as you now!"

Olivia hurried in and pressed a cup into Kaz's hands. "Try some of this. It will help." She waited while Kaz took a huge sip. "Better?"

"Ah, coffee." Kaz's shoulders sagged as her tension evaporated almost instantly. "I love your warm hugs."

Martin looked at Olivia. "When did you get coffee?"

"While you two were having your tantrum. I made a fresh pot earlier after I sorted some papers." Olivia pulled a small tube from her pants pocket. "Here's the salve. I summoned it from my lab the same time I 'summoned' the coffee for you."

"I'm sorry, Kaz," Martin said. The mist around him faded, then vanished. "I'm worried about you and everyone else. I'm frustrated, and now weird, dead people want to talk to me."

"I guess I'm sorry, too," Kaz said. "I shouldn't snap at you because I can't figure out your problem. We're all a little on edge these days, what with Felissina, our resident princess, Angel superhero, and whatever else she is, hunted by some psycho mercenary."

"Do you think Shadowjack will come after us?" Olivia asked.

Martin glanced a tendril of smoke wafting up from his shoulder and patted it out. "I think his main objective is taking Feli, but we'd be foolish not to consider it."

"I can and will defend myself if necessary," Kaz said. "The big question is, who else does he work with on this?"

"Who knows at this point? I might have been better

off in the sanatorium," Martin grumbled.

Kaz cleared her throat. "And on that note, I'm out. I'll do some more research. If I find out any new information, I'll be in touch."

"Yeah, bye," Martin said absently. "I've got my own leads to check out."

****

"We meet again, Martin Long."

He whirled around as Shadowjack appeared behind him. As Martin backed away, he eyed the mercenary's hand resting on the gun strapped to his hip. "You, again? What do you want this time, and make it quick. I have places I need to be."

Shadowjack smiled, but it didn't reach his dark eyes. "Same as before. I need the princess Felissina to come with me. I need to make her aware of certain factors arising in her province. The king has not given up on his plan to have her as his bride."

"She says her father is king."

Shadowjack stared at the ground, then glanced back up. "Her father is king, but now a usurper sits on the throne of Erlymere. Tell her to abandon this attachment to you and convince her to come with me." He stepped closer to Martin. "She can't remain here while her people are suffering. They desperately need her leadership."

Martin stared at the mercenary and narrowed his eyes. "You don't talk like the cold-hearted betrayer she makes you out to be. What's your game? Why do you think I'll be able to convince her to leave?"

"For some reason, she listens to you." Shadowjack stepped closer, making Martin back up the same number of steps. "I've been partnered with a man who can hurt someone close to you. You're friends with a witch healer called Kaz. Do you wish for her to get injured because you're too stubborn to honor a simple request?"

"Kaz is all fight and won't be taken easily," Martin said, his voice low. "I don't think there's anyone who can take her down. Go back to your own dimension. Felissina won't ever go with you, and I couldn't make her, even if I wanted to. If you stay, there's a strong possibility you'll get hurt."

"I've taken care of myself longer than you know. Please." Shadowjack held his hands out. "Tell the princess she can no longer stay with you. If you do, I'll make sure the mage Ra-Vel never gets near your friend, Kaz. He thinks he can use his power to intimidate me, but as I've said before, there is very little I fear."

"Who else are you willing to hurt to get your way?"

Shadowjack shook his head. "If you're worried about your team, don't be. I have no interest in them, just my princess."

"I know the name Ra-Vel from a recent rant from Kaz. She told me the two of them have been rivals for years," Martin said. "This Ra-Vel person can try to take her, but she'll have no problem defending herself."

"I don't want to take stronger action against you, but I will if forced."

"I'll tell Felissina what you said, but I won't make her leave." He and Felissina had to be soulmates. The signs were too numerous to ignore. But did it give him the right to keep her from her responsibilities in her own dimension? "If she wants to stay, I'll abide by that decision. If she chooses to leave with you, I'll respect her wishes. I'll expect you to give her the same consideration."

"I can't promise you that, human. I'll give you some time to think about it," Shadowjack said. "Remember, though. If she stays and the usurper continues to abuse her homeland, the fault will be yours alone."

Martin watched him walk away. He knew Shadowjack would find him when he wanted him. He no longer worried about the man's motives. As he'd stated multiple times, he wanted to take Felissina back to their dimension. Time to get in touch with Kaz and give her an update. After all, she told him there were still more scans she could do. No time like the present.

Martin hurried through the streets and spied the new entrance to The Center at last. He understood the need to move the doorway, but it could be damned inconvenient at times. Movement to his left stopped him. He didn't have time for any messages from strange, spectral figures.

"What do you want?" he asked. As the spirit drifted closer, it brought the familiar sensation of water tickling his face. "Stay away from me."

"You need to come with me, Traveler," it whispered. "The master grows impatient for your return."

"Who is the master?" The silver mist started to form again. "Why does he want me back so much?"

A bony hand reached out and grabbed his wrist. Martin tried to jerk his arm back, but the entity held tight. Instead of the usual visions of darkness and weird white fogs, no scenes came to him. Bone chilling cold penetrated his skin, freezing his muscles as blood pounded through his veins and throbbed in his temples.

"Let go!"

Martin reached out with his power, and the silver mist shot forward and enveloped the specter, making it fade away. He stared at his hands, and his heart sped up until he thought it would burst. Did he just banish a specter? And the mist, so far, had only flowed around him. He'd never used it offensively or to defend himself. Could it be another powerful weapon in his already bizarre arsenal?

He couldn't visit Kaz now, even though he knew he should. He wanted to go home and never leave again.

Chapter Seventeen

Morning sunlight bathed Felissina in a warm glow as she stood in the foyer with her suitcase by her feet. The grandfather clock's chimes echoed through the house, and she gave it an impatient glare. If Grayson didn't hurry, she'd go up and drag him down the stairs. Martin's proximity would ease the growing ache in her chest. She needed his nearness, to hear his voice, to be with him no matter what.

She'd have to make one more return trip to get her formalwear. The rest of her possessions would be moved later. She let her gaze travel around her home. It was hard to believe she wouldn't come back here to live. She glanced at the small bag. After the closet purge, she didn't have much left. Elation filled her, making it hard to stand still. For the first time in many years, freedom and lightness lifted her heart higher than it had ever been before.

"I guess you're ready to go?" Grayson asked when he came down.

She nodded. "I was ready before the sun rose. I can't wait to get back to the underground. I've spoken with all my friends, and I no longer have any doubts about my relationship with Martin. The way I feel right now, I'm certain we must be soulmates."

"You've come to the conclusion the rest of us figured out as soon as you came back here." He picked up her bag, and they walked out to his car. "I thought you'd want to leave as soon as possible, so I parked out front. I called Martin and told him you'd be back around ten today. I think you're going to be a little early. I'm pretty sure he won't mind."

"Thank you, Grayson." She kissed his cheek. "You've been a great to help to me. Did you tell Kristin I planned to leave?"

"Didn't have to. She suspected you'd fly out of the nest. She just wants you to be happy."

As they pulled out of the grounds, the ache in Felissina's chest eased. At the end of the trip, her soulmate waited for her. Every mile brought her closer to him. If she closed her eyes, she sensed she could hear his heartbeat, even at this distance. They drove in silence for a few minutes before Grayson took a turn too sharp.

"What's wrong?" she asked.

"We picked up a tail. I have a suspicion who's back there." The car leapt forward as he stomped on the accelerator. "I hope I can lose him."

Fear wrapped itself around her, banishing the hope and anticipation of a few minutes before. "Shadowjack. He's as tenacious as a terrier." She turned in her seat and glared at the car behind them. "I doubt he'll give up before he accomplishes his mission. Do the best you can."

She held on to the door's armrest while Grayson tried every trick he knew to lose their pursuer. The surrounding neighborhoods went from large, almost mansions, to more sedate homes. If anyone could lose their pursuer and keep her safe, Grayson could. As they sped down a deserted side road, a bright light flashed, and they spun a hundred and eighty degrees. The car crashed into a telephone pole. Their journey came to an abrupt, body jerking end.

Grayson sagged in his seat as blood oozed from a deep cut on his forehead. The red smear on the steering wheel testified to him cracking his head in spite of the airbag lying limp in his lap.

She shook his shoulder. "Grayson, can you hear me?"

Her door was yanked open, breaking the lock, and a large hand covered her mouth. A blade flashed in the sunlight and cut through her seatbelt. Large hands pulled her out and slammed her against the side of the car.

"I told you, your highness, you would come with me," Shadowjack said. "Whether you liked it or not. Don't worry. You won't be harmed. I'll be there to protect you."

She glanced at Grayson before her eyes narrowed and black energy formed around her hands. "I don't think you'll take me anywhere, mercenary."

"Are you sure you want to do this?" He aimed his gun toward Grayson. "Don't make me have to hurt him any more than necessary."

Felissina pulled her energy back and surrendered. Grayson could be seriously injured. She forced herself to stand still, acquiescing to Shadowjack's demands. Her body trembled, the only outward sign of her rage. He covered her mouth and nose with a cloth soaked in a foul-smelling liquid. Within mere seconds, she sagged against his body. By all the gods, what would happen to her now?

****

Felissina groaned and rolled over. She blinked several times to clear her vision and sat up. Fog clouded her mind, and her mouth felt stuffed with cotton. What happened? Grayson had started to drive her back to Martin when they'd been attacked. She jumped to her feet. Grayson! His injuries might be severe. Could he be a prisoner also? She ran to the door and pulled on it, wrenching her shoulder. She rolled her eyes, not surprised to find it locked tight.

She took a few minutes to study her surroundings. The white room contained one small, metal bed. Someone changed her into a hospital gown and took her shoes. Her feet were going numb as the cold from the concrete floor seeped into her soles. No obvious closet meant her clothes were probably gone for good.

She shivered and wrapped her arms around her waist as she stood in the middle of the room. The more she moved around, the quicker the haze in her mind dissipated. Right now she had other, more important matters to consider besides escape. Like what else did her captors do to her while she lay unconscious? The door banged open, and a bright, white light filled the room.

"I didn't harm you at all. Not yet, anyway," a woman's voice said. "You were brought here to participate in my experiment. After I collect some data from you, you'll be taken home."

Felissina shielded her eyes against the harsh light. "I demand you show yourself. Tell me who you are, right this minute."

Anita walked into the room and glared at her. "I'd advise you to watch your tone with me, Angel. You won't be here long. Shadowjack brought you to me. As soon as I'm done with you, he's promised to take you to your home dimension and get you out of my life."

"Vertigo. I should've known you were behind this." Black energy coalesced around Felissina's hands. "I don't believe you. I think you have some other plan in mind for me. You have to realize I'll fight you every step of the way. As soon as I'm missed, my team will come looking for me."

"I only use my code name when I'm in the field." Anita used her telekinesis and shut down Felissina's energy flow. "And your team won't find you. You don't know your location, so you can't tell them through your pathetic mind link. This room has no discernable features, so you can't give them any sort of clue. Trust me, CT. You're here until I let you go."

Anita waved in a couple of techs. "Blindfold her and take her to the exam room. We may as well get started right away. Tell Shadowjack and Ra-Vel to meet me in my office."

Felissina backed away from the two men approaching her. She swung at the man on her right and missed. She stumbled away, her legs hitting the bed. The other man pinned her arms to her sides. His partner tied a blindfold around her eyes before dragging her down the hallway. What waited for her at the end and how damaged would she be when Vertigo finished with her?

****

"What do you mean 'you lost her'? How?" Martin shouted into the phone. "Didn't you check the area before you left?"

"Of course I did, and stop shouting. I've already got a serious headache knocking against my skull."

Grayson sighed. "Shadowjack took her. Surveillance systems didn't pick him up, so he had to be hidden nearby. Maybe he's got some kind of invisibility device. We turned a corner, and he was just there. His energy weapon totaled my car. He grabbed Felissina while my head became intimate with the steering wheel."

Martin ran a hand through his hair. All his fears had been realized. He never should have let her leave. Now Shadowjack had taken her who knows where. Grayson didn't deserve his temper. Fear for Felissina had kicked his good sense to the curb. He leaned on the desk to halt the tremors threatening to consume him.

"I'm sorry. I've seen him blend into shadows and disappear. If he doesn't want to be seen, you won't see him. Are you sure you're okay?"

"I'll live." Grayson snorted. "I've been banged up worse than this when I spar with Kristin and the rest of the Angels. Any idea on where he could have taken her?"

"Probably to Anita Haines, whom we all know as Vertigo, the psycho telepath. I wish I knew where she's hiding right now. I'll check with some of my people and get back to you." Martin paused. "Thanks for all you did to try and keep her safe."

"You're welcome. While you talk to your contacts, I'll talk to mine. I hope someone found out some new info by now."

Martin barked out a short laugh. "I doubt it. I haven't had any good information since the initial attack on her."

"You never know. If push comes to shove, I can always call in some friends to get people to talk. Later,

Martin."

Martin hung up and grabbed his jacket. With Thanksgiving gone by and December just beginning, the air turned colder every day. He never figured out why the cold didn't affect him, but he got stares from people when he went topside without a coat. Talk about being more self-conscious than usual.

He hurried through the streets and kept close to the store fronts as he looked for George. He spied him as the little man turned a corner, and he quickened his pace to catch him.

"George, wait up," he called.

"Oh, hey, Martin. What can I do for you?"

"Felissina was taken even after all our precautions. Tell me you've heard who took her and where she could possibly be."

George shook his head. "Not a peep. Unrest has begun to brew in the magical realms. Strange spirits have appeared in odd places. Kaz thinks they might be on the lookout for you."

Martin scrubbed at his face. "I don't need this right now. Tell her to banish them with a spell and start searching for Felissina. She's got to be neck deep in trouble."

"I don't tell Kaz how to do her job. I give her polite suggestions. I know she'll do what she can to find her." George cocked his head. "I can't sense Felissina anywhere. Either she's blocked or…"

"Stop right there. We'll find her, and she'll be okay."

"Of course she will. Good luck, Martin. If I hear anything, you'll be the first to know."

Martin nodded. "Thanks."

As he watched George hurry away, movement out of the corner of his eye grabbed his attention. A filmy, cloaked figure hovered at the corner of the building. He edged his way over and took care not to drive it away. The figure held out a bony hand to him and gestured him closer.

"I don't have time for any weird messages from whoever the master is. Unless you're here to help, leave me alone."

The figure bowed its head and faded into the darkness behind him. "As you wish, Traveler. But do not delay your return to our realm much longer. The master grows impatient."

At least someone listened to him. Martin made his way back to the underground. A couple of questions started to nag at him. Question number one. Why did the specters continue to mention a master? Question number two. Now the specter called him Traveler? Question number three. Where would Shadowjack take Felissina, and how did he get the drop on Grayson? As the quote went, something was rotten in Denmark, and he determined to find out what it could be.

****

"Martin, George told me Felissina has been taken," Kaz said when she appeared in the computer room. "How can I help?"

He turned from the monitor screen. "You and Liv do your magic tracker spells. I don't know if you'll be able to find her, but you have to try."

Olivia stopped in the doorway. "I've only heard vague reports of Shadowjack and nothing concrete," she said. "No one ever notices him. He's hard to pin down."

"So I've been told. George said Benedict Trust is the most probable suspect behind all the attacks on her. If he's involved, so is Anita Haines, his pet telepath." He turned back to the computer. "So, where is Haines now?"

"Easy," Olivia said. "She's back at HelixCorp. She's been reinstated as head of research."

"Well, bad news all around," Kaz said. "We all know her research ends with her subject in a hole, six feet deep and covered in lilies."

Martin's lungs constricted, and his heart froze. The thought of Felissina with Anita Haines and HelixCorp chilled his spine, tightening every muscle in his body. Nervous cold penetrated bones and muscles he'd forgotten he had. Time was now of the essence, as the saying went. Dr. Anita Haines had a well-known reputation for complete focus on her experiments. The longer she kept Felissina prisoner, the more the danger around her increased.

"You're not helping, Kaz," he said, his voice trembling. "Shadowjack wouldn't have taken her somewhere with a lot of people, so not the big building constantly on the news. Where's the closest small HelixCorp research facility? That would be the most likely location."

"No one knows," Olivia said. "The main complex is located a few miles north of the city. The ones where the illegal stuff is carried out are in unmarked places. They could be anywhere."

"Terrific." He got up and headed for the hallway. "I want to try my own experiment. Stay here."

He hurried to his room and shut and locked the door. He closed his eyes and concentrated on the spectral figures. The ghosts constantly around him could be the key to helping him find the woman he loved. He took a deep breath and reached out with his thoughts. Some specter had to hear him.

"I need your help. A woman has been taken, and she's very important to me. Please. Help me find her."

A shadow detached itself from the wall and glided over to him. "It's not our place to interfere in the lives of mortals. We can't help you with this, Traveler. If you want the woman returned, you must do it on your own."

"You don't have anything useful?" Martin swiped the water forming on his forehead, flinging the droplets to the floor. "You float around me for months. When you get around to talking to me, it's to tell me a mysterious master wants me back. You call me 'Traveler,' and yet the one time I ask for help, you say no? All of you, and your master, can go straight to whatever hell you came from."

Martin stormed back to the computer room and flopped down in a chair. Kaz and Olivia stared at him. "It didn't work. Do what you have to. Try to find out where she's been taken. One way or the other, we'll get her home."

Chapter Eighteen

Three of the men in the lab lay against the wall. Felissina readied her power for the next batch of thugs to come through the door. She yanked off the ripped sleeve of her hospital gown and threw it to the floor. Anita walked in, and she backed away while the energy around her hands sparked brighter.

"My team and I fought you many times. I know what you're capable of, so you won't take me unaware," she said.

"Oh, please. Save the heroic speech. I've heard so many over the years, they bore me now." She glanced at the men sprawled on the floor. "This would've been much easier if you'd cooperated."

"Dream on, telepath. You may try to kill me, but I'll fight you until the end."

Anita grabbed her with her telekinesis and slammed her on the exam table. She fastened two bands around Felissina's biceps as she used the wrist cuffs to hold her arms down. "The bands are power dampers. I need to get some physical data from you, and it will be better if you don't blow up my lab. I apologize for the restraints. This is no way to treat a princess or a member of the vaunted Angels hero team."

Felissina tried to access her power and couldn't. "Damn you to whatever hell you believe in. When I get free, powers or no, you can believe I'll escape."

Shadowjack walked in and leaned against the wall. The look on his face confused her. He should be triumphant. He should be gloating over his capture of her. Why did he look worried? Could the traitorous wretch feel guilty about his crimes after all this time? He walked over to her, keeping Anita in sight the whole time.

"When we return to our dimension, I shall ask for your hand. The usurper will refuse, but I'll make him see it's the right path for him and you."

"I'll see to it he doesn't. You'll pay for all you've done to me, here and back home. Your days are numbered, Shadowjack. I promise you."

"Somehow, I don't think so." He stared at her, his gaze sad. "You have no idea what I've sacrificed for you."

Anita stood at a computer console. "This machine works like an x-ray and CAT scan combined. It will take pictures of your internal organs and skeletal structure so that I see the images on this computer. It won't damage you, but it does take a little longer than the usual procedures. After I collect this data, I'll compile it with the notes I've already taken on you."

A large machine descended from the ceiling. Felissina stared at it, wishing the whole time she could blast it into pieces. The machine hummed and rotated around the table. After what felt like an hour, the machine retracted. She heard Anita murmuring to herself, but from her voice she sounded pleased with what she saw.

A lab tech walked in and placed a tray on a table. He pushed it over, and the squeaking of one wheel amplified ten times in the sterile room. Anita picked up a needle and a small rubber tube. "Don't worry. I need to draw some blood. Tomorrow, we'll get in to how your powers work."

"I guarantee, you won't like how I demonstrate them to you," Felissina snarled.

Anita sighed and filled clear tubes with blood. "You're being tedious again. I know all about what you can do. I have some tests I need to run to determine the type of energy you use." She leaned close and whispered in Felissina's ear. "Then I will strip you of your incredible powers and transfer them to my boss."

"You can't." Felissina struggled against the straps even harder. "I won't let you."

Anita dropped the filled tubes in a plastic medical bag and sealed it. "I'll do whatever I please. Your wishes make no difference to me."

After Anita left, the blindfold covered Felissina's eyes again as they took her back to her cell. Thinking of her future sent unaccustomed dread racing through her veins. When Anita got what she wanted, she knew she'd be disposed of where no one would ever find her.

****

Ra-Vel stared at the girl on the examination table. Yes, he sensed traces of fairy magic in her. The adaptation of the formula went quicker than he expected. Now, the girl was on the schedule for the power transfer and termination within the next few days. He smiled as he breathed in the heady scent of her fear. His work with Anita, then Shadowjack, irritated him to say the least. Each one thought they held all the cards.

"Those two I've been forced to work with are naïve and foolish," he said. He smiled at the girl's look of confusion mixed with fear. "I wouldn't have to expend much effort to take over and run this operation myself. Even Benedict Trust will learn he isn't a match for my power. If only Kaz would join me in my plans. However, I won't bore you with my ramblings any longer."

He stalked from the room. Anita had called for another meeting, which would, once again, grate on his nerves. Listening to more of her nonsense about getting immediate results or Trust's disappointment set his teeth on edge. He'd put his own agendas on hold to work at HelixCorp. He had no desire to waste any more time at the research facility.

He pulled a small, clear glass ball from his jacket pocket. He passed his hand over it, and an image appeared. Well, well, well. His Kaz started a search for Felissina. The man and woman with her looked like those people Shadowjack hunted. Anita had wanted Martin Long picked up to be slated for one of her experiments.

"My dear Kaz," he said. "You have no idea what the future holds for you. I have to convince the fools I'm forced to partner with that the demise of your friend, Martin Long, is necessary. I know you'll cooperate with me then. After that, we'll see what happens."

****

Felissina had been taken prisoner several times in her hero past, but this time her fear bordered on terror. Martin. Concern for his safety must be the cause of this irrational fear filling every miniscule atom of her body. She shook her hands, trying, in vain, to stop the tremors gripping her limbs. What was Shadowjack planning to do to him, Olivia, and Kaz? She smiled a little. She'd not had too much contact with Kaz, but she somehow felt as close to her as she did to Olivia and Martin.

"Why didn't I consider the consequences of my actions when I left the underground?" She threw the pillow against the wall. "Because I've been as arrogant and overconfident as the heroes Martin and I discussed."

She stomped as she paced the small room. "I never considered Shadowjack would dare attack me during the day." She slammed her fist into her palm. "Grayson accompanied me. His presence should've been enough of a deterrent. Absolute desperation must have driven Shadowjack's actions. It's the only possible explanation."

She gazed around at her cell. "Anita Haines truly does mean to keep me here. Not a seam, not a crack, nothing to give me any kind of leverage to escape." She straightened her spine, glaring at the door. "Still, I've got to try. My friends are counting on me not give up." She huffed out a sigh. "And now I'm talking to myself. I thought that only started after a prolonged period of captivity."

Black energy leaked out of her fingers and coalesced around her hands. Her muscles strained, and pinprick tingles raced along her nerves. Never before had she tried to pull so much power out of herself. Her arms trembled while she focused her energy. Her chest heaved as sweat beaded on her forehead. When she couldn't contain it any longer, she unleashed the blast. Seconds ticked by before she dropped her arms, and her breath came hard from the exertion.

She used the bed for support as she waited for the

spots in front of her eyes to fade. She hurried over to the door. Not a scratch, not a dent, not a single scorch mark marred the surface. She frowned. And it was still sealed tight. She'd take another few minutes to recover, then try again. Maybe if she used part of the bed's metal frame, she could damage the lock.

Anita's voice slammed into her mind. *"Don't try it. You'll never get through the door. If you do, my troops will cut you down before you can blink."*

Felissina staggered to the bed and grabbed her head as she sank to the floor. "I can't believe how much that woman's telepathic contact hurts," she murmured as she pushed herself to her feet. "It appears she'll take no chances on me escaping while I'm her 'guest.' "

She began to pace. "Come on, Felissina, think," she muttered. "I've gotten out of tough situations before. This is no different. I can't give up because there's no obvious solution. I need to create a plan of escape. I know it can be done."

She walked over and leaned her head against the door. But how?

****

"You really believe this Martin Long is too dangerous to leave alive?" Vertigo asked.

Ra-Vel smoothed his slacks. "I'm afraid so. He commands a devastating power. However, you brought me in as an advisor. You may do as you wish." He nodded toward Shadowjack. "My compatriot believes him to be a liability. After I heard about his encounters, I must agree. We'd get more cooperation from his companions if he's removed."

Disappointment filled Anita and annoyed her at the same time. "I would've liked to have had him here so I can see exactly what it is he can do. However, I got to my present position by listening to people who are experts in their respective fields, so fine. Dispose of him. Then see if you can pick up the two women you claim are his allies. If they can't be used, they'll follow him to eternity." She turned to Shadowjack. "Can you handle this?"

He walked to the door. "As you say in this dimension, it will be a piece of cake."

Chapter Nineteen

Shadowjack prowled the streets, looking for Martin. Anita told him, no, insisted, he eliminate the man in Felissina's life. As soon as the human appeared, his time on this planet would be short. He bowed his head, praying for, but not expecting, forgiveness. His cell phone buzzed. Martin Long's location wasn't too far from his own. The shadows behind him beckoned, and he used them to teleport to the location where Long waited.

It made his job easier when he didn't have to search for, then chase, his prey. Martin hurried down the street, and Shadowjack suspected his destination. He must be on his way to see the witch, Kaz. Well, he couldn't let him get to his powerful magic user friend. Carrying out his assignment would be nearly impossible if he did. Time to make his presence known.

"And where are you off to in such a rush?"

Martin spun around and came face to face with Shadowjack. "Where's Felissina? I know you took her. Tell me where she is."

"I just needed one small favor from you. I asked you to talk to her. You went against my wishes, even after I told you of the importance of my mission. I won't be held responsible for what's about to happen."

Martin narrowed his eyes. "Have you forgotten what I can do? All I have to do is destroy you, bit by bit, and you'll tell me all I need to know."

Shadowjack laughed. "I don't think you can. I know your type. You wouldn't hurt anyone if you could help it. And if you injure me too much, I wouldn't be able to talk at all. That wouldn't serve your purpose, would it?"

"I guess not." Martin scowled and folded his arms. "So what do you want?"

Shadowjack gestured to crates stacked against a brick wall. "Have a seat. We'll talk for a moment, then you'll understand."

Martin hesitated, then eased down when Shadowjack laid a hand on his gun. "Okay. What do you want to talk about?"

"You. The people who hired me determined you've become a liability. There is a very small chance you could interfere with certain plans. We can't allow you to become a hindrance." Shadowjack shook his head. "I've been told to eliminate you. I'm sorry for what I'm forced to do. I didn't want it to go this far."

"I see." Martin stared at his opponent. "Who gave you this rather gruesome job of executioner?"

"Dr. Anita Haines. I believe you know her as Vertigo. Felissina is too concerned about you. It's been decided that to ensure her cooperation you need to be removed from the picture. If she has no hope, she'll have no resistance. I'm sorry this course of action has been deemed necessary."

"You have to know I won't go down without a fight."

"Somehow, I knew you respond like this. It's a shame you don't have my combat experience. Then it would be more of a challenge."

Shadowjack yanked his gun out and fired off a shot as Martin rolled off the crate and jumped to his feet. He reached out with his power and the gun began to dissolve. Shadowjack flung a rock from the ground at him and clipped his head. Martin staggered back and grabbed his temple. Shadowjack threw a small baton and took out his knee. He fell on his back grabbing at the injury as his eyes watered.

Martin stared at him. "I never thought I'd end up shot to death in a back alley."

"No one ever does."

Shadowjack pulled a smaller version of the gun he carried in his holster. Before his victim could recover, he squeezed the trigger. The laser blew through Martin's chest. He rolled to his side and clutched the wound. Shadowjack stood over him and shot him twice in the back. He pulled out his cell phone and took pictures of Martin's body.

"In case the princess needs proof." He took one last look at Martin lying on the ground, not moving. "I shall pray for you as you journey into the afterlife.

****

Olivia opened a portal and appeared in Kaz's office. "Has Martin come here?"

"No. Why?"

"He said he wanted to try and find out where the bad guys might be hiding Feli. He ran out before I could get more out of him. He promised he'd be back with her or info about her in about an hour. It's way past time he returned." She gnawed on a cuticle. "I know he's gone off like this before, but I'm really worried about him."

"You and I both know Martin never lets us in on

his destination. This isn't anything new," Kaz said.

"It's different this time. I know it." Olivia stood in front of Kaz's desk. "Before I came here, I sensed something in the air. I can't describe it, but it felt wrong. What if he got attacked by Shadowjack or someone from HelixCorp?"

"Liv, Martin's a very powerful...some kind of person. No one can take him down."

"Yes, he is, but he doesn't leave the underground. His fighting experience is barely a step above mine. Shadowjack has some serious skills. We need to find Martin. I just know he's in trouble."

Kaz walked around her desk. "Let me send out some feelers. That way, we'll have a better idea of what we'll walk into."

Olivia nodded before she collapsed on the couch. Kaz headed for the door, then stopped and stared at her. "Since when can you open portals?"

"I wanted to surprise you." Olivia gave her a weak smile. "Surprise?"

Kaz glared at her. "When this is done, you and I will have a serious talk, missy."

After Kaz left, tears flowed, leaving hot trails down Olivia's cheeks. Panic clutched her stomach, and nausea rose in her throat. Martin and Felissina had to be okay. She believed they were with her whole heart. Her team couldn't survive without Martin there to keep everyone calm in emergencies. Their leader did a good job with keeping everyone steady, but the others trusted Martin more.

And Felissina. How would the Angels get along without her? Olivia had done some research on the team. Each member claimed some special talent, and

Felissina knew the complicated sciences. Her dimension's science and technology had advanced far beyond Earth's. She'd helped her team in more ways than one on numerous occasions.

"Please," she prayed. "Please let them be okay."

****

"Okay. I can't pick him up my usual witchy way." Kaz mumbled as she rubbed her temples. "So if I can't find him with magic, I'll do it the old fashioned way."

She opened a portal and stepped through into the underground. Every room had the heavy air of emptiness, and the complete silence muffled her steps. Where could everyone have gone? The whole team never up and disappeared all at once. She closed her eyes and sent out a tiny ball of light. It zinged through the hallways and rooms, then zipped back to her hands.

Images appeared in her mind. The team had scattered throughout their home. She got the sense Martin told them to be prepared in case an invader came down. At least they were all safe. Shadowjack's target had to be Martin, and he obviously hadn't returned. Which led to the question, where had her friend gone? She gated herself back topside.

A cold wind slammed into her, and she zipped her jacket all the way up. None of the passersby looked like they felt the swirling, icy breeze. The hair on the back of her neck rose. This had either been summoned by magic or it came from the spectral realm. Hard tremors made her teeth chatter at the thought of the realm of the dead. If true, this ill wind didn't blow good for her or her friend.

She did have one more way to find out. Kaz hunched deeper into her jacket and hurried to a narrow alley, dreading the spell she needed to cast. Taking a deep breath, she pulled her wand and murmured a silent prayer for any color but white. White meant the death of someone close to her. She cast a quick spell, and light flowed out and filled the area around her. It glowed bright, ethereal white.

Kaz sent out a small bird charm and spent anxious minutes as she waited for it to return. As often as she used it, the time she'd spent to infuse the tiny charm with a tracker spell made it time well spent. It made it easier for her to find Martin when he got himself hurt, which had started to become more frequent recently. She raised her hand up, and the bird landed on her palm.

Her blood ran cold as the tracker revealed Martin on the ground, unmoving. If she lost her best friend, she didn't think she could go on. Could he only be unconscious? The tracker spell gave her the location, and she gated to where Martin lay. Her hands covered her mouth as she stared at the holes in his back.

She dropped to her knees beside him, brought her hands together, and then drew them apart. She sensed no life in her friend. For the first time in years, tears flowed down her cheeks. She eased him onto his back, no longer afraid of touching him. The laser burn in his chest still smoked.

Martin had crossed over into the realm of the dead.

****

Shadowjack returned to HelixCorp and walked straight to Anita's office. She and Ra-Vel were there, studying the file on her desk. Again, he cursed the circumstances forcing him to work with the two of them. Would this interminable assignment never end?

"I've brought you the princess and now have taken care of the other problem we discussed," Shadowjack said. "Martin Long has been eliminated. I don't care what kind of power he has. No one walks away from three point-blank shots."

Anita smiled, her eyes filled with predatory glee. "Wonderful. I'll see you get a bonus for this. I'm sorry I doubted you."

He inclined his head to her. "Apology accepted. I don't need any bonus. The taking of a life should never be rewarded." When she stared at him, he cleared his throat and changed the subject. "Have your other various projects progressed well?"

"As well as can be expected. Ra-Vel and I have almost completed our work on my test subject. As soon as we're done, I'll be able to give my full concentration to the Angel. Mr. Trust is anxious to begin the transfer of her powers as soon as possible."

Shadowjack stalked forward and leaned on her desk. "You never mentioned you would take her powers. You stated you wanted information from her and nothing more."

Anita stood and glared at him. "Are you really that gullible? Mr. Trust has paid a lot of money for her. You'll get her once she's stripped of her powers. Now get out."

Shadowjack turned to go, his hands curled into tight fists as he tried to hide his anger.

"Wait a moment," Ra-Vel said. "Your assistance is still required. I wish to employ you to help me get rid of the witch, Kaz."

"I don't much care to work for you."

"Believe me. It will be worth your time." Ra-Vel

bowed to Vertigo. "If you would excuse us for a moment?"

"Of course. I need to go see the Angel. Take all the time you need."

After she left, Ra-Vel turned to him. "There is a girl, Kaz's protégé. If we take her, Kaz will have no choice but to come for her. Then I'll be able to destroy both of them. Kaz has stepped on a few too many important toes. My leaders want her taken care of in a rather permanent fashion."

Maybe if he helped Ra-Vel with his plan he might be able to get Felissina out before Anita and Trust damaged her. It wouldn't hurt to give her two new subjects to "play" with, so maybe she'd ignore Felissina. He would bide his time to get what he needed from the mage. He'd done this same type of ruse before in his own dimension when he let the usurper think he owned the general. Shadowjack sat in the chair and propped his feet up on Vertigo's desk.

"Okay. Talk to me."

Chapter Twenty

Martin studied the land he'd appeared in. He knew he'd been shot by Shadowjack, and he'd felt his life drain away. Each tiny rock, pebble, and grain of dirt dug into his skin while he lay on the cold concrete. As soon as he arrived in this strange place, the silver mist surrounded him again and covered him like wispy armor. He inhaled a long forgotten musty scent, reminding him of a wet basement.

Peace, familiar and calming, filled him, giving him a level of comfort he hadn't had since he was a child in his mom's kitchen. He knew the large tree in the distance. Flashes of memory shot through his mind. Or did he? He vaguely remembered talking to someone there. Possibly another soldier, like him. Martin shook his head. He hadn't ever been a soldier. Not in his known life, anyway.

He walked toward the tree, then stopped. If he turned right, he'd find a large house in the distance. Someone he thought he should know, someone important, lived there. Where did all these thoughts and hazy memories come from? Did he belong here like the specters kept telling him? He squeezed his eyes shut, wanting to wake up in his underground room. He opened his eyes, not surprised to see the misty land still stretched out around him.

As he stared at the far-reaching landscape, he

realized he didn't hurt anymore. The laser shots in his chest and back were gone. But he'd ended up in a place looking like it should house all the great horror movie icons. Everything was black and white as far as he could see. No blues, reds, greens, yellows, or any other color.

Shades of gray made up the rest of what the black and white didn't. Misty figures floated in the distance. He started walking into the fog and frowned when it parted before him like the Red Sea. He half expected his own body to be as filmy as the figures surrounding him. He poked his chest. He was as solid as ever, but was covered in a strange, silver ethereal glow.

A hooded, robed figure glided toward him. "Welcome, Traveler. It's good to have you home."

"Stop right there." Martin held his hand up, stopping the specter. He did a double take as the mist solidified into a blade. "I don't want to hear any of your garbage again. Unless you have some helpful information, get away from me. I can't get used to the fact I'm dead."

The figure rasped out a wheezy laugh. "You can't die, Traveler. You're one of the immortals. Have you forgotten so much of your home?"

"What home? You mean this place? I know where I'm from, and this isn't even close."

"You're in the spectral realm. This is where you lived before the Great War took you from us." The figure threw its arms around him, soaking his clothes through the misty armor as it held him close. "You've been missed, my friend."

Martin had no chance to back away before the specter embraced him. His spine stiffened at the contact. It figured the first person to be able to touch him would be a dead guy. While the specter held him, there were no visions. No death or darkness. No dismal future. When the figure stepped back, Martin stumbled away from it. The mist around him and the sword vanished as he put more distance between them.

"Why didn't I see any future for you when you grabbed me? I mean, I know you're dead, but this never happens. When I touch someone, anyone, I always see death for them."

The specter cocked his head and studied him. "You shouldn't be able to command such a high-level power. The master and his core legion have those powers and no one else. You've evolved from traveler to scion. What has changed you?"

"How the hell should I know?" Martin shouted. "All I get are ridiculous statements and riddles from you. So, unless you know my origin, send me back to my body. I'm done with you and this whole bizarre situation. I have to rescue someone I love."

"Love?" The figure stumbled backward. "Our kind does not love. To feel love for another means you must possess a soul. Denizens of this realm do not have souls."

"Bull." Martin stabbed the figure in the chest with his finger, making small drops of water spurt out. "I love a woman of great strength and beauty. I don't care if you think it's possible or not. I'm out of here. When you have a little more straightforward information to divulge, you know where to find me."

Martin concentrated on his body. The shadow land faded from view, and he became aware of Kaz as she knelt next to him. He could hear her murmur in a strange language and realized she tried to cast a spell to save him. Well, he'd saved himself without help from her or anyone else.

"Ow," he murmured.

"Martin! You're alive." She jumped to her feet. "If I could touch you, you would be so squeezed right now."

He pushed up on some nearby boxes, not surprised to find the laser burns gone from his body. "Yeah, yeah, yeah. Get us out of here before Shadowjack comes back to see if I'm still dead."

She summoned a portal and took them back to The Center. Olivia ran over to him and stopped before she touched him. "Martin. I'm so glad you're okay."

"I'm not sure I am." He eased himself down on the couch while his friends stared at him. "Kaz, what do you know of creatures from the spectral realm called travelers or scions?"

"I've heard rumors and found just a couple of mentions of them. Why do you ask?"

He laid his head back and closed his eyes. "These spooky figures seem to think I'm one of them. While I was 'dead,' the specter I talked to said I can't die. I'm immortal, and I used to be one of these travelers. It seems I've evolved to scion. I changed jobs I didn't even know I had."

Kaz hurried to her bookcase and furiously started to flip through different tomes. Olivia stared at him. "What else did the specter say? What did it do? What happened?" she asked.

"I could touch it with no effects. It also said our kind doesn't love and doesn't have a soul. You want to hear the kicker?"

Kaz turned around, a thick volume cradled in her arms. "What's the kicker?"

"It mentioned the master again. Given where I've come from, I think the master is Death himself."

"And that's what scares me," Kaz mumbled. "I need to read more on this, but here's what I found so far." She flipped open a book and pointed to a specific page. "The spectral realm has a hierarchy, with Death at the top of the food chain. His direct 'generals' are the scions. Below them are the collectors. Below them are the travelers. The travelers command the spirit legions that are below everybody. I don't know what they all do, but if the specter called you a scion, you're one of the big shots."

Martin scrubbed his hands over his face. "And this day just keeps getting better."

****

Felissina paced in the small room. She'd blast the door, take a break, and then try to blast the door off its hinges again. All she'd tried yielded no results in her favor. Taking a deep breath, she let it out a little at a time. She feared she would be here until they let her go or worse. Were her friends safe? Every time she thought of them, muted panic would flare, making blood pound in her ears, and the sour taste of bile rise in her throat.

The door opened, and Anita walked in. "Thank you for the demonstration of your power." She pointed to the corner and a hidden camera. "You've given me a lot of footage. Once I begin my analysis, I'll know more about you than you know about yourself."

"You know I'll stop at nothing to destroy you," Felissina said. "You won't keep me here against my will."

Anita sighed. "Once again, you've bored me. Better heroes than you have tried to escape this place, and none succeeded. The procedure will go easier for you if you cooperate. You'll be back with your pathetic team in no time."

"I don't believe you. You forget, telepath, I know how you work. If you have the chance to terminate an opponent, you take it. You've destroyed many lives, and mine will not be one of them."

"Yours is already over. You don't know it yet." She pulled out her cell phone. "Yes, it's time. Please come down to the Angel's cell."

They waited a few minutes, glaring at each other the whole time. The door opened, and Shadowjack walked in. Felissina didn't like the look the two of them shared. She backed up until her legs hit the bed. The smug look on Anita's face testified to some terrible deed they'd committed.

"What did you do?" she whispered.

"I regret to have to show you this." Shadowjack walked slowly over to her. "Your love, Martin Long, is dead. I killed him. Shot him three times. Once in the chest, twice in the back. I am so sorry, your highness," he said, his voice hushed.

Felissina dropped onto the bed. She clutched her chest, trying to keep her heart from pounding out of her chest. Her lungs ached as her breath came in staccato bursts. There didn't seem to be enough oxygen in the room for her and her tormentors. Tremors started in her hands, working their way up her arms to spike through the rest of her body. Her world shrank to the bed she sat on and the cold floor under her feet.

"You're wrong," she whispered. "Martin's alive. You're trying to trick me to giving up hope. I would've known instinctively if he were dead."

Shadowjack pulled out his phone and held it out. Her hands shook as she took it from him. He'd told her the truth. The gruesome pictures were worth more than thousands of words. Martin lay on the ground, smoking holes in his back. The next picture showed the gaping hole in his chest. The phone tumbled from her grasp and hit the floor with a quiet smack. Those images burned into her mind's eye forever.

Tears streamed down her face. How could Martin have died and she not feel it? They'd become so very close. The word "soulmates" echoed in her mind, tormenting her with the lost possibilities. This time when her body shook, it wasn't fear which gripped her, but rage. It built in her heart and leaked out in the ebony energy flaring from her hands. She raised her tear-filled glare to him.

"I'll kill you for this."

She launched herself at him and pulled back her arm to slam hard punches into his face. He threw her off and slapped her hard. Black energy shot from her hands to strike him in the chest and stomach. All the while, Felissina raged, screaming threats incoherently in his face. He grabbed her by the shoulders and threw her on the bed. She pushed up to stare down the barrel of his gun.

"If the two of you are done with your little fight, we have more work to do." Anita opened the door and looked over her shoulder. "Good night, Angel. You have no hope now."

The door shut, and the lights dimmed. Felissina lay

on the bed and wept into the pillow. Shadowjack killed Martin because of her. Grief consumed her heart, stole her breath, and took her strength. She'd always heard the most dangerous person was the one with nothing left to lose. In the space of a few moments, she'd become such a person. She'd fight until she or Anita lay dead. Without Martin, her life meant less than nothing.

****

Martin grew tired of the endless questions from Kaz and Olivia. He understood the need for information, but he only wanted to sleep. They wanted explanations he couldn't give. Irritation prickled his skin. He tried hard not to glare at them, but his anger refused to be denied. His heart raced and his hands curled into tight fists. His jaw ached, forcing him to unclench his teeth.

"Okay," Kaz said. "You've described the land as black and white. Did you see any vegetation? Any trees, bushes, fuzzy critters which belong in an animated movie to sing with a princess?"

"I don't know, and you need to back off," he said, his voice rising more and more. "Kaz, Shadowjack murdered me today. I need something to drink and some rest. Then I need to find out where he took Felissina. She's in danger. Anita Haines has her, and you know what happens to people that crazy telepath is done with. Now would you please cut me some slack?"

Martin stormed out of Kaz's office and found an empty exam room. He stretched out on the bed and laid an arm over his eyes. He needed a few minutes to get his thoughts together. Maybe he could come up with a plan to save Felissina and whoever else had been taken prisoner.

Sleep crept over him, and he dreamed of the spectral realm again. Sadness overwhelmed him while whispered questions peppered him. Why didn't he want to come home? Why would he want to save a life? How could he love when he didn't have a soul? Didn't he miss his comrades in arms? Why couldn't he understand how much he was missed?

He jerked awake and groaned as he sat up. Grit irritated his eyes, and the short nap hadn't given him enough time to recuperate. His body ached and, even though he may have slept, he didn't rest. Fatigue weighed down his limbs and his mind. The strange dream and whispered voices plagued him, whether he was wide awake or sound asleep.

He glanced at the pillow. A few more minutes wouldn't hurt. Visions of the spectral land filled him. And take a chance on hearing those creepy voices again? Yeah. No more sleep right now, thank you very much. When his powers escalated, why did the weirdness around him have to increase, too?

He pushed thoughts of specters out of his mind and concentrated on Felissina. He saw her clearly from her golden blonde hair to the fullness of her figure. He smiled when he thought of her bright, green eyes. He could still see the appreciation in them as they'd been together without ever having touched. The thought of them being soulmates gave him a level of comfort he hadn't known for a long time.

He gripped the edge of the bed and hung his head. "I've failed to keep you safe, Feli. How can I ever face you again, knowing I couldn't stop Shadowjack from taking you?"

A strange, damp softness filled his palm. He

looked down and realized the silver mist coalesced around his hands. Strength filled him as it seeped into his skin and formed a thin layer over his body. For the love of Pete, what now? The strange mist formed around him with more frequency now, in response to his emotional state. Again, he wondered why Olivia stopped him from using the gun all those years ago.

Of course, with what he'd been told in the spectral realm, it wouldn't have done any good. If he were a true immortal, he couldn't end his pathetic life. No matter which way he turned, he couldn't find a way out of his tormented existence. He'd never wanted to throw something as much as he did right now.

"Martin, are you all right?" Kaz asked softly as she stood in the doorway.

He shook his hands and concentrated on banishing the mist. "Yeah, I'm all right. I needed to blow off some steam and grab a few minutes alone."

"Hey, you were murdered. I can see how you'd be a little upset."

Martin stood and pinched the bridge of his nose. "Do we have any clue on where Felissina might be?"

"I might have an idea on how we can find her, if it works." She waved him out the door and down to her office. "You had a clear vision of her when Shadowjack attacked her. Do you think you can do it again? We might be able to get a starting point."

"I can try."

Olivia shrugged into her jacket. "I'll go out to talk to some of our people. Someone may have gotten some news or can at least give us a location where to look."

Martin nodded. "Good idea, Liv. Promise you'll be careful. We know now Shadowjack has no problem with murder. Don't become his victim."

"I'll be careful. He doesn't know what I look like, so he could pass by me and not even know."

Kaz grabbed her in a tight hug. "He might have allies who do know you. Watch out and port back here the second you think you're in danger."

"I will."

Olivia gated out, and Kaz turned to Martin. "Let's talk about death, shall we?"

Chapter Twenty-One

Olivia hurried through the streets. The few people she thought might have some information didn't know anything. All of them told her to make contact with the old gnome who lived in a rundown apartment complex. He knew things no one else did and never minded helping those who asked politely. If he couldn't tell her what she needed to know, no one could. She picked up her pace. Two more blocks, and she'd be there.

She hurried around a corner and stopped dead. A tall, thin man with black hair stood in front of her. She recognized him as the escaped criminal Kaz warned her about. Kaz briefed her on his crimes and why he'd made the top ten list of the most dangerous mages alive. As far as Olivia knew, he should still be locked up.

"Ra-Vel," she said, barely succeeding in keeping her voice flat and unemotional. "Kaz told me all about you. She even uses your picture as a dart board in her office. How did you escape Dukar Prison?"

He studied his nails. "You'd be surprised at how easy it is to bribe someone who hates their job. Of course, after the guard got me out, I disposed of him. It's not good to leave witnesses alive, especially when you have no intention to pay them off."

"What do you want?"

He grabbed the front of Olivia's jacket and pulled her close. "You, dear girl, will make the witch, Kaz, come to me. She won't be able to resist the urge to rush to your rescue. And if I can't bend her to my will, I'll destroy her and you. I know all about you, too. I have many more contacts in this city than Kaz knows. I made it my business to find out every little detail about her and who her associates are."

Olivia called up her magic, which Ra-Vel blocked with ease. "I won't let you hurt Kaz," she growled. She cast another quick spell. When it bounced off the shield he'd erected, it became clear she'd gotten in way over her head.

"Those weak attempts are all she's taught you?" He gestured to someone behind her. "You don't have the power, skill, or experience to defeat me. Shadowjack, if you please?"

A solid blow hit the back of Olivia's head, and she slumped forward into Ra-Vel's arms. He threw her over his shoulder, turning a cold smile to Shadowjack. "Another part of the plan is now complete."

He opened a portal, and the three of them disappeared.

****

Anita stared at Olivia. "This girl looks too young to have any power I can use."

"Her magic will grow stronger over time. I didn't let her know, but her attack did cause me a small measure of discomfort," Ra-Vel said. "You can use her. I can help you drain her power. Then I have given Shadowjack the honor of ending her pathetic life."

"After I have her power, I don't care what the two of you do. Make sure she's ready by the time Mr. Trust arrives."

Ra-Vel moved closer to Anita, and she stood firm,

letting him close the distance between them. "Remember, he said I could have you when this project is done. I'm pleased we'll continue our association."

She telekinetically shoved him backward. "Don't try to intimidate, threaten, or frighten me. None of those tactics will work." She stomped toward the door. "And I have no desire to continue our association. It wasn't part of the original agreement, and I won't be forced into a situation not of my own design. Are we clear?"

"Crystal, but have no worries. Our partnership would be very lucrative for both of us. Think about it."

She left the lab area and went to Felissina's cell. She flung open the door and stared at the Angel. "Get up. I have more examinations to perform on you."

"No. It's exhausting to be kept a prisoner with no one to inform me what's going to happen to me." Felissina turned on her side. "Now, if you would, please leave."

"If I work, so do you."

Felissina sat up, blinking the sleep from her eyes. "You're even more unpleasant than usual. What's happened?"

"I…" Anita started, then stopped, and she scowled. "None of your business. You couldn't help me, even if you wanted to."

"I'd help you if you weren't on the other side of the law. Vertigo." Felissina stopped, then started again. "Anita, we're both out of our element here. Why are you so upset?"

Damn the Angel. She shouldn't show this much compassion for someone she detested. "It turns out the man for whom I've done every job he's asked of me treats me as if I'm worthless. He passes me around like some piece of equipment. Are you happy? Now you know how much I'm worth. Less than zero."

"I don't think so. I believe you have simply allied yourself with the wrong people."

"Why do you care so much?"

Felissina stood straight, looking her directly in her eyes. "I'm royalty. I'm supposed to put my prejudices aside and give advice to those who need it. Unfortunately, you're the one who needs me now. Therefore, I'm obligated to try to help."

"How very gracious of you," Anita said, her words laced with bitter sarcasm. "But I don't need your or anyone's help. I've taken revenge on people who've hurt me before. This time will be no different. I'm stronger than most people realize."

Felissina nodded, and Anita knew she'd said too much. She refused to relive her torturous past. Yes, she'd taken revenge on the people responsible for her father's massive heart attack when she'd been a senior in high school. Yes, she'd avoided the law ever since. But to say all of it out loud, and to a hero no less, she couldn't, or wouldn't, bring herself to do it.

"Go to sleep. I'll be back later when you don't irritate me so much."

Anita stalked out and slammed the door behind her. The Angel got to her. If she'd stayed in her presence much longer, the whole sordid story might have come pouring out. Time to go home and organize her thoughts. Trust would detect any weakness in her, and then her usefulness would be at an end.

****

As hard as she tried, Olivia couldn't stop the tremors gripping her body hard enough to make her teeth rattle. She'd tried to convince herself the cold from her cell got to her. After all, the room didn't exude any sort of warmth, by temperature or décor. Deep in her heart, she knew it couldn't be her barren cell.

This cold came from within and leeched outward to chill her skin. It oozed from her heart to congeal in her stomach. Fear froze her blood and tightened her muscles until she thought they would snap. Panic ate at her courage. It blocked her mind from devising any type of plan of escape. It leaked from her pores to soak her clothes with a cold sweat.

Worry and panic made her tenuous control over her magic begin to slip. The metal-framed bed shook as her abilities affected it. At least the walls were regular drywall or plaster or something not metal. She had some consolation the only other metal object nearby was the door. She took several deep breaths to slow her racing heart. She had to get a grip or she may end hurting herself before Ra-Vel even had a chance to do whatever it was he wanted to do.

"Why didn't I learn how to create portals sooner?" she muttered. "If so, I could've been out and gone by now." She jumped to her feet. "Martin, Grayson, and Kaz wouldn't panic like a child. I bet even Feli has figured how to escape by now. Kaz says I'm getting more powerful every day. I can do this." Her concentration slipped, and her portal closed before it was bigger than a dime. "I'll find another way out and warn everyone."

She walked to the door and ran her hands over the surface. Metal. Strong, beautiful metal. If she could keep a tight control on her magic, she could use it on the door to free herself. She backed away and wove her hands in an intricate pattern. Blue energy glowed and twined itself through her fingers. She closed her eyes and directed the energy into the lock mechanism. The handle began to twist, and a quiet groan could be heard. When all the energy disappeared inside the lock, Olivia snapped her fingers and the whole panel popped off to slide across the floor and stop at her feet.

"Ha. I knew I had it in me." She closed her eyes and murmured, "Stay in control and you can do this."

She poked her head out of the doorway. No one to the left or right. How long would the hallway stay empty? She took a deep breath and stepped into the corridor. Which way to go? She turned left, her steps light and quiet. A door opened, and she ducked back around the slight bend. Anita Haines. Olivia waited until the click of her heels faded, then hurried down to investigate.

She used a little magic to open the door and stepped inside. "Feli!" She ran to her and grabbed her in a fierce hug. "We've been so worried about you. I thought you would've gotten out by now."

"Olivia? How did you end up a prisoner, too?" Felissina hugged her back. "As you can see, I'm still here. The door seems impervious to my power."

"They brought me in a little while ago. I'm not sure how long but it feels like hours. Turns out, it's easy to pop off a metal lock when magic affects it adversely. I only had to use a little to open yours."

"You said your control had gotten better, and you're right." Felissina took her hands and gave them a quick squeeze. "Shadowjack gave me the news of Martin's death." She sat down on the bed. "I can't believe I'll never see him again."

The door banged open and Ra-Vel walked in. "I detected the use of magic nearby. I thought I'd find you here, girl. You're stronger than I thought. I'll have to find a better way to keep you contained." He motioned Shadowjack forward. "Take her to a new cell. If she tries to escape, shoot her." He grabbed Olivia's arm. "If you try anything like this again, I'll personally destroy your friend over there. Do we understand each other?"

Olivia nodded and bowed her head. "I understand."

As Shadowjack forced Olivia to leave with him, Ra-Vel turned to Felissina. "No one will come for either one of you." He stood in front of her. "By the time we get what we want from you, you'll both pray for death to be swift. Good night, princess."

Chapter Twenty-Two

"Kaz, you've stared off into space for the past ten minutes," Martin said. "I know Liv is late. I know you're worried. Are you working out a rescue plan, or have you traveled to the Twilight Zone on me?"

She shrugged. "Maybe a little of both." She held a hand up, stopping his retort before he could respond. "I need clarity to be able to concentrate on the task at hand. Sometimes it means I have to daydream for a bit so I can focus."

Martin flopped down in a chair. "I'll never understand your thought processes."

"Which makes two of us." She got up and paced. "We know Olivia went to see someone from the fairy realm. If we can retrace her steps, maybe someone saw where she went."

"It's a mighty big 'if,' my friend. We have to consider she's been picked up by the bad guys. If so, it's possible she and Felissina might be at the same location, wherever it may be."

"I hate to say it, but you're probably right. All we have to do is find it."

Martin got up. "And save Felissina and Olivia. And beat the bad guys. And find out what's the deal with me and my freaky title."

Kaz chuckled. "Sounds to me like you're afraid of a little hard work."

"Sounds to me like you're a glutton for punishment." He opened the door and bowed. "After you, madam."

"Thank you, sir." She slid the Wand of Oros into her boot holster and paused when Martin stared at her. "Yes, I know it's not mine. It's got a weird vibe and I don't like it, but I think we might need the Wand. It packs a bigger punch than mine. Time to get our walking shoes on."

"Are you sure about this?"

She grinned. "Am I ever sure? Let's go."

They headed to the entrance and the ogre, Larry, blocked the door. He held a note out. "This came for you, Kaz."

She scanned it quickly, then read it slowly a second time and frowned. She folded it in half and tucked it in her back pocket. "Let's go." She laid her hand on the ogre's arm. "You know what to do if we don't come back, right?"

He nodded once. "I know the plan. I'll inform George, and we'll be ready at a moment's notice."

Kaz and Martin hurried out to the street before he turned to her. "You want to tell me what Larry meant? I mean, I know your contingency plan to evacuate everyone to the underground. Why would you want it to be implemented now?"

"It's as we figured." She handed him the note. "Ra-Vel has Olivia. He'll release her if I surrender to him. He also says Shadowjack will release Felissina, since you're dead and all."

Martin scanned the note. "You know you can't agree to this. He's had it in for you ever since the dagger incident with The Family. Who do you think set

185

the vampires on you?"

"Yeah, yeah, yeah. It's all ancient history, or so I thought. It appears someone wants to hold on to a major grudge."

In spite of the seriousness of their current predicament, Martin had to chuckle. "Kaz. Dear, sweet, darling Kaz. You planted evidence against him and had him locked up in Dukar Prison. Incarceration tends to upset a person."

"So what? Ra-Vel, the stupid idiot, decided to involve vampires in my business. I told him I had the whole ugly situation under control. He didn't believe me and planted The Family's ancient dagger in my home. I merely returned the favor. But I'm not bitter toward him for trying to frame me first, am I?"

"Of course you are."

Kaz's shoulders sagged a little. "So what if I am? Besides, if I meet him, you're my ace in the hole. Both he and Shadowjack think you're dead. I know you'll have my back."

"I'll always have your back."

They jogged down the street to Olivia's last known location. People who knew her said she'd been told to talk to the old gnome in a rundown neighborhood. Martin and Kaz looked at each other. The gnome was considered ancient by fairy standards. By human standards, he should've been dead for a couple of centuries. Martin knew Kaz had run-ins with him before and couldn't be called his biggest fan. As a matter of fact, except for Gizel, Kaz didn't like any gnomes.

Martin glanced sideways at Kaz. "I'm getting a bad feeling about you talking to the gnome in question."

She snorted. "I can be nice."

He grinned. "Kaz, you don't get along well with gnomes. Or just about any other supernatural creature." When she glared at him, he cleared his throat and changed the subject before she zapped him. "Where and when do they want to meet?"

"The note says for me to call him when I'm ready." They stopped in front of a rundown apartment building. "This is where Liv came for information. Let's see if she made it this far."

They were stopped at the doorway by a short, squat, greasy creature with black eyes in a piggy face. "You can't come in," the goblin said, glaring at them with hate and distrust.

Kaz leaned close. "You want to bet? We need to see the gnome who lives here. A friend of ours wanted to see him when an enemy took her."

"Who do you seek?"

"Olivia Greene. The mage, Ra-Vel, has taken her prisoner. We have to talk to the gnome. He may know how to help us find her."

The goblin stood in front of them, barring the doorway. When several long moments passed, he pointed to Kaz. "You come in. Death must wait outside. We don't like his kind in here."

Martin started forward, but Kaz stopped him. "It's okay. I'll deal with him while you hang out here. This shouldn't take long."

"What did he mean 'death must wait outside?' I'm as alive as you."

"We'll figure it out later." She leaned as close as she dared and whispered, "Stop with the emotional landslide. You know how much goblins hate it. Don't provoke him."

"Yeah, well, don't piss off the gnome. You know how vindictive old gnomes can be. If you need me, give a yell and, goblin or no, I'll come running."

"I'll be all right. Be cool and wait for me. I'll be back before you know it, hopefully with something useful about Liv."

She disappeared inside, and he stared at the closed door. He didn't worry about Kaz. She had enough power to take out anyone who'd be dumb enough to ambush her. The creature's insult rankled him, but it did give him another clue to his origins. The goblin called him "Death," but why? How did the creature know more about him than he knew himself?

He kicked a rock on the ground. All the riddles about him were enough to give him a serious drinking problem. If it weren't for his friends, he would've traveled down that road a long time ago. Movement out of the corner of his eye grabbed his attention. He stalked over to the shadows and folded his arms. A spectral figure stood there and beckoned him over. As he got closer, water again beaded on his forehead. He swiped at it and flung the drops on the ground.

"I don't want to hear what you have to say," Martin growled. "It's always complete gibberish."

"But the master wants you returned. Please, come home. You are sorely missed by your legions. They need you." The specter held its hands out to him. "Come with me now and forget your ridiculous notion about love. Our kind doesn't love."

"Your kind doesn't. Mine does. I'm human, nothing more. Don't you think I'd remember if I were a minion of Death?" Martin turned his back. "I need to find my soulmate. Don't bother to come back unless you're ready to reveal who or what I am."

Martin stalked back over to the front of the building. He wanted to be inside with Kaz to find out what she learned. The building itself looked like every other rundown edifice in need of major renovations in the city. The bricks showed their age, the mortar between them cracked, showing deep pockmarks. If creatures from the fairy realm lived here, they'd use magic to make sure the city ignored them and let them live in peace.

Time to see what he could find. He had never tried to contact someone's mind before. He didn't know if he could or even how to do it. He closed his eyes, took a deep breath, and concentrated on Felissina. Where could she have been taken? He pictured her in his mind and, quicker than he thought, he could see her as clearly as if she stood in front of him.

He "saw" a featureless room but couldn't discern where she was being held. He guessed if she didn't know her location, it wouldn't be in her mind. He took a deep, steady breath to halt the panic in his chest before it blossomed even larger. She still lived and hadn't been harmed. He took another deep breath and tried to calm down. He heard the door bang open and looked up.

Kaz stomped down the steps, her hands curled into fists. She must have had a premonition about getting angry today. How else could he explain why she'd chosen to wear a deep maroon, satin shirt? Her heavy boots must have been in case she felt someone needed to be punted. He didn't see any blood, so he guessed she held her temper until she made it outside. One should never think about giving a kick to gnomes, not when they hired goblins for bodyguards. She stalked by him, and he fell into step next to her.

He waited a moment, then asked, "I take it the talk didn't go well?"

She glanced at him. "Ain't you one hell of a detective? I hate any gnome who isn't Gizel. Stupid, stuck up, know-it-alls." She stopped, whirled around, and stabbed her finger toward the apartments. "The little bastard in there wouldn't even talk to me," she shouted. "When I convinced him to say any words at all, he talked in riddles. A lot of riddles. I swear, I thought only the Conclave and politicians could talk in so many incomprehensible circles."

"I didn't get much either," Martin said. "I tried to sense Felissina's location. I found her, but not where she's held. Even she doesn't know where she is."

"Damn all of them." Kaz kicked a nearby trashcan. "I hate to have to meet with Ra-Vel, but he's our best solution for answers right now." She stared at the sky and sighed. "Why does the universe hate us?"

"The universe doesn't hate us." When she glanced at him, he shrugged one shoulder. "Just karma, the cosmos, and the huge expanse of space hate us."

"Oh, ha, ha, ha. You're quite the comedian, aren't you?" They walked on for a few minutes. "You've changed since you met Felissina."

"Liv said the same thing. I think it's because we're meant to be together. The specter told me I don't have a soul. If what he said is true, how could Felissina and I be soulmates?"

"Who knows?" She stopped short, making him glance at her. "If you don't have a soul, it could be the reason the scans caused you so much pain."

"Kaz," he said slowly, "maybe it's because I do have a soul and shouldn't?"

"Giving us one more complicated question for another day." She pulled out her cell phone. "Ra-Vel gave me a number to call when I made my decision to meet him. No time like the present. I really hate having to call him. I know he's going to try something I'm really not going to like."

"I'll make myself scarce. If he gates in and Shadowjack decides to tag along, it will blow our surprise."

They headed over to the next block and found an alley wide enough for one person. There weren't any people around either, which made the upcoming confrontation easier to handle. Would the bad guys show after her call? If so, could Kaz get them to reveal the location of their friends? He hoped so. If not, he'd never see Felissina or Olivia again.

Chapter Twenty-Three

Felissina punched the lab tech in the face, dropping him to the floor. "I've had more than enough. I refuse to be poked and prodded any longer. If you want to know the full extent of my abilities, send in Shadowjack. He'll get a taste of my powers and can give you a full report."

"Not necessary," Anita said. "I believe I have all the data I need. Your powers seem to be a mix of anti-matter and plasma. I wish I had time to run more tests, but I'm on a tight schedule." She handed the clipboard to her assistant. "Call transport. The Angel is ready to be taken to the main facility." She turned back to Felissina. "There, you'll be stripped of your powers. When the transfer is complete, you'll be terminated. I'm sorry it worked out this way, CT."

"The tone of your voice doesn't sound very apologetic. You know I'll fight until the very end. You may take my power, but you won't have an easy time of it."

"We'll have to see, won't we?" Anita stood to the side and let two techs in with a stretcher. "Make sure she's sedated. You don't want to deal with her. She's my problem."

"Yes, ma'am."

Felissina dodged the outstretched hands of the man beside her. She slapped the man in front of her in the face, making him take a couple of steps back. A third clipped her knee from behind, dropping her to the floor. Two of the men held her down while the other jabbed her with a needle. She kicked out, satisfied when one of the men grunted.

Her limbs grew heavy, and her struggles weakened. The air around her had turned into a heavy, lead blanket settling on her limbs. Damn, she hated sedatives. She tried to tell the men their obscene comments about her body weren't appreciated, but her mouth refused to form the words. As she slipped into oblivion, her limbs trembled, but from fear of the future or the drug, she didn't know.

****

"Once again, are you sure about this?" Martin said.

Kaz nodded. "This is the only option left to us. I know neither one of us likes it, but what choice did we have?" She scowled. "If they've hurt Liv or Felissina, I will *not* be happy. I don't think they'll like to see me unhappy. You'd better get scarce. They could be here any time now."

Martin hurried to the narrow alley and flattened himself against the wall. Their adversaries pulled up in a modest sedan. Well, that was an unexpected way for them to arrive. He had expected another portal to open. Kaz stood ready and waiting, her outward appearance steady. He was always amazed at how calm and composed she looked, even when worried or, more often than not, angry.

Had he looked that calm and composed in the past few days? He didn't think so. Ever since Felissina went missing, his lungs refused to take in enough air. A strangling tightness engulfed his chest. Ice coursed through his veins at the thought she might be hurt at any moment. The longer they remained separated, the more his heart ached and his focus faltered. He took a deep breath and tried to steady his hands. Now was not the time for twitchy nerves.

Please, Kaz, get the information we need.

When the two men got out, Martin recognized Shadowjack. The black utility suit, red beret, and wide, silver belt were a dead giveaway. The tall man with black hair and the tailored suit must be Ra-Vel. He sensed an inherent darkness surrounding the mage, ebbing outward in expanding circles. This guy kidnapped his friend? Liv must have been terrified. Even though he was a good distance away, he could still hear everything being said.

Kaz glared at the mage towering over her. "You've taken two people dear to me, Ra-Vel. Give them back. Now."

Ra-Vel placed his fingers under her chin and smiled as he tilted her head back. "Dear Kaz. You're as beautiful and fiery as ever. I gave you the chance to join me, but you chose to have me incarcerated instead. It's hard to forgive such a heinous betrayal."

"Are you crazy? You started it, you freak." Kaz slapped his hand away. "We weren't partners, friends, or whatever weird fantasy you built up in your delusional mind. Where are Olivia and Felissina?"

"I'll be happy to take you to them. They hope you'll come rescue them, but I'm sorry. You won't be able to accomplish your particular goal."

Kaz moved closer, maybe an inch from Ra-Vel's long nose. "You want to bet? I can accomplish a lot of goals before you'd blink twice. If you give me my people, you and your friend may get out of this alive. If you don't, I make no guarantees."

The mage laughed. "You can't and won't kill me. You know the laws of healer magic as well as I do. If you intentionally harm another, your skills become diminished. Not to mention you'd come under the scrutiny of the Conclave. You can't afford to be called before them again, not so close to your recent infractions. They've already reserved a cell for you in Dukar."

"You're so lucky there aren't any innocent people around to be hurt. As seriously as I take my oath as a healer, I believe the greater good could be served if you were removed from all our lives. I'd gladly suffer any consequence to be rid of you." She placed her hands on her hips. "You know that, right?"

Martin grimaced. When Kaz stood that close with her hands on her hips, it signified her temper climbing from simmer to boil to nuclear. He didn't want to reveal himself, but if she didn't get this wrapped up, he may have no choice. From the looks of things, Ra-Vel knew how to push all her buttons.

"What do you say, Kaz? Come, pledge your loyalty to me. Then, and not before, will I return to you what you demand."

"Not a chance, scumbag."

She flicked her fingers. In seconds, she summoned the wand to her hand and pointed it at Ra-Vel. Silver light shot from the wand and struck him in the chest. He flew backward a good ten feet before he slowed enough to roll out of it to his feet. His eyes widened as he stared at the onyx wand she held.

"How did you come in possession of the Wand of

Oros? Its magic is forbidden."

She advanced toward him. "Which should show you how desperate I've become."

Shadowjack pulled his gun and aimed it at Kaz's head. "Enough of this. Ra-Vel, disarm her. Dr. Haines is impatient for this next delivery. We can't be late, or we'll miss the transport truck."

"You are correct." Gold light shot from Ra-Vel's fingers and wrapped around the black wand and Kaz's wrist. "Your games are over, little witch." He yanked her into his arms and held her tight. "Now that I have you in my possession, your mind, your body, and your soul will be mine."

"Ugh. Gross, with an added side of cliché. By the elder gods, don't you read any current books?"

Martin started toward the group but stopped when Kaz glanced at him. She gave a small shake of her head. He took a step again and she scowled as she mouthed for him to stay put. He nodded once and stepped back into the shadows. Someone had to be on the outside to free them. Right now, it was up to him to be such a person. He suspected Kaz had intended to be on the inside, to lend aid and assistance if she could. They may take his friend, but they wouldn't keep her, or anyone else, prisoner.

He reached out a hand to her, and she gave him a slight nod. Ra-Vel shoved her into the back of their car and sat a little too close. Before Shadowjack pulled out, Martin saw a bright orange light flare from the backseat, and he smiled. Ra-Vel must have tried to take some inappropriate liberties. From all the years they'd been friends, he had no doubt Kaz could handle herself.

****

Martin made his way back to the underground. Now what? His soulmate, not to mention both of his closest friends, were taken prisoner. How would he find them? He hurried to the phone and called Grayson. He needed advice and information. His friend should be able to provide both.

"What's up, Martin?" Grayson said after the first ring.

"Let me say, I've never been this alone in my life."

"That doesn't sound good. How can I help?"

Martin sat and pulled a pad of paper and a pen closer to him. "You were there when Felissina was taken by Shadowjack. Now some two-bit mage called Ra-Vel has taken Kaz and Olivia. I have to find out where he's taken them."

Grayson whistled. "Wow. These guys have been busy. Did they give any clue as to their plans?"

"Well, we already know Anita Haines and Benedict Trust are involved. Shadowjack mentioned they needed to get back so they didn't miss a transport. But transported to where?"

Grayson's silence stretched out for several minutes. "Trust is the head of HelixCorp, and Haines is his main go-to person. It's likely they've taken our people to a secret facility. Transport means they'll be moved to the main facility right outside the city limits. Haines has better resources there, more techs, and her bigger lab is also located there."

"Great. I can get the address from the internet."

"Do you want some help? I can call in some friends who live for this kind of work."

Fear loosened its grip a little from Martin's heart, allowing his breath to come easier. "No. I got this. I have an advantage over the bad guys. They think I'm dead."

"Are you? I mean, were you?"

Martin chuckled. "Just for a little while. I'm better now. Thanks again, Grayson. So far, you're the one person I get any help from. If I need you, I'll call."

Martin hung up and tapped the pen against the desk. He needed to take full advantage of their ignorance of his return to life. But how? It'd be nice if the ghosts around him were useful.

"We are useful," said a whispery voice behind him. "You're a scion, a leader of all spectral legions. We're yours to command."

Martin turned to the specter. "Even if you don't like it? Even though you tell me I can't love and have no soul?"

"Yes, my lord. The master commands we serve you since you have been found. He waits for you to be ready to come home. He watches over you. He doesn't wish for you to be lost to him again."

Martin shuddered. How did his life turn into such a bizarre horror movie? "Uh, thanks?" Moisture began to run down his face. "You need to get out of here before you wreck all our computers."

The specter vanished, and he pulled up the HelixCorp website to get the location. He noted how far he had to travel. He could take the tunnels part of the way. Then he'd need another way to get there. He'd go in at night. If he got lucky for a change, there wouldn't be too many people around. He knew Shadowjack and Ra-Vel would be his biggest problem, not the workers. Not unless they gave him a reason for concern.

He'd have to go now. He only had to go about ten

miles in the city and ten miles outside the city to get to HelixCorp. However, he didn't have transportation. He drew a quick map to point him in the right direction. Time to go. He stood and headed for one of the tunnels he knew led away from the city. He sensed the specter at his back, following him. For the first time since his ghostly follower appeared, he didn't mind the cold mist flowing around him, plastering his shirt to his back.

Chapter Twenty-Four

Kaz sat next to Olivia in the transport truck. "You know, it's a double-edged sword. I was relieved when Ra-Vel took the Wand of Oros, but I really need to get it back. Forbidden magic tempts too many mages. I don't want to become one of them, but I wish I had the damn thing right about now."

Her leg began to bounce. "The elven lords expect the wand to be returned by the next full moon. I've already pissed off the vampires. I can't afford a fight with another supernatural faction. My list of friends grows shorter every day."

"Yeah, that's all true, but you know you'll always have me and Martin." Olivia paused. "Are you sure you're okay?"

"I'm just frigging dandy," she mumbled. "Where's Felissina? Have you seen her?"

"I broke out of my cell the first night I arrived. I found her, and she hasn't been hurt. Ra-Vel told me there would be bad consequences for her if I broke out again. I didn't get chance to tell her about Martin. She's grief stricken over him."

Kaz nudged her with her knee. "I'm glad you didn't. Right now, they don't know he's alive. We've got to keep quiet about him. He'll find us and, when he does, I'm pretty sure sparks will fly far and wide."

She took a deep breath and closed her eyes. Martin

had better get here pretty damn quick. Death waited for all of them at the end of this road. If Felissina had already been brought here, her time could be a lot shorter than theirs. Could she stall their demise long enough to give Martin time to arrive? She lightly thumped the back of her head against the truck's wall. And where the hell were the bad guys taking them anyway?

****

Felissina's pulse throbbed in time to the headache pounding in her skull. Bright, fluorescent lights buzzed overhead, and she squeezed her eyes to slits to reduce the glare. She tried to sit up and couldn't. Her powers didn't respond either. What happened to her while she had lain unconscious? Did those thugs violate her?

"You haven't been harmed, Angel," Anita said. "I rode with you to protect you from my men. I can't have you damaged yet."

"I can't believe I almost felt sympathy for you," Felissina said. "I should've realized sooner you were a lost cause. Whatever your plans may be, get on with them. The sooner you try to hurt me, the sooner I can destroy you. If I die, so be it. This world has become ordinary and far too empty."

Anita stood over her. "This is quite a change of attitude. Would you care to tell me the reason?"

"You were there when Shadowjack showed me proof of Martin Long's death. You can't hurt me any more than you've already done. I'll fight to avenge him. Afterward, I don't care what happens. If it's my turn to die, fine. I don't wish to live without Martin." She narrowed her eyes. "As long as I take you down with me."

"Have it your way." Anita walked to the door and waved in two assistants. "Take her to the transfer lab. She's scheduled to have her powers stripped tonight."

While her gurney remained parked in the hallway, Felissina's thoughts turned to Martin and the odd love they'd shared. She closed her eyes and pictured his face. If she couldn't see him again, she had no reason to continue. She'd never conceded defeat until now. With his death, she'd have her final fight.

If the people who held her didn't kill her, she'd end her own life. A tear rolled down her cheek. She lifted her shoulder to dry it but couldn't. Martin deserved her tears, but she refused to cry or whimper for herself. As the daughter of a warrior king, she had her father's strength running through her veins. She'd fight until the end, as she always knew she would. Then, and not before, they could take her life.

The men came back, and Felissina started the journey to her final fight. Would she see Martin on the other side? She hoped so as the men parked her gurney in a small room. It didn't matter what world, dimension, or realm they lived in. As long as they were together, their lives would be perfect.

Anita walked over. "The machine needs a little time to warm up. It will lock on to the unique power signature in your DNA. After that, it will syphon out those abilities and store them in the collection tank in the back of the machine. Then, it's just a matter of completing the transfer process." She checked the controls and made some minor adjustments. "I believe Mr. Trust wants to speak with you before we begin. Once he sees I've done all he asked, he'll rethink his treatment of me."

"I hope you're right, Anita," Felissina said in a low voice. "I truly hope you're right."

"I believe I am, all thanks to your capture."

Felissina listened to her heels click against the tiles and closed her eyes. In a few more hours, she would try to take down this evil organization. In a few more hours, she'd no longer have to bear the pain in her heart. In a few more hours, her soul would join Martin's in the afterlife.

****

Kaz rolled her eyes when Ra-Vel entered her cell. "Great," she said. "Isn't it enough I'm stuck here waiting for you to implement some idiotic revenge scheme? Do I have to look and listen to you, too?"

"There are other better uses for your smart mouth, Kaz."

She gave an exaggerated shudder. "Once again, I have to say gross. Listen, Ra-Vel. I'm not sure how this will play out, but you need to remember something. If I survive this situation, I'll hunt you down until I see you dead at my feet. I don't care anymore what this will do to my powers or what the Conclave thinks. You've hurt me more than you know, and you'll pay dearly for everything you've done."

He laughed outright. "The problem with your revenge scheme, little witch, is you won't survive this. You're doomed. Accept it and move on."

Kaz scowled at his back as he walked away. "I hate him so much."

"You aren't supposed to hate. It messes up your karma," Olivia said. Kaz's dark look turned black when she grinned. "However, at this point in time, I don't think you care."

"You're right. I don't care." Kaz plopped down next to Olivia. "Our ace better show up soon. I don't think we have a lot of time left."

****

"You promised the princess would be returned to me when you finished your experimentation," Shadowjack said. "I don't like people who go back on their word."

Anita glared at him. "You'll get your princess. It's unfortunate she won't be alive for you to take home."

Shadowjack pulled his gun. "Then I'll take her now, and your experiment be damned."

Anita slammed him against the wall with her telekinesis and disarmed him with ease. "I'm sorry, but no. As a matter of fact, I forgot to tell you another piece of my plan." She walked over and glared at him. "I've also selected you to be part of the project. You were safe from me until you completed your mission. You've done all you said. Now it's time for you to be scanned and have whatever power you possess taken and transferred to Mr. Trust."

Her telekinesis held him in the air as she floated him down the hall behind her. She flung him into an empty cell. "Enjoy what time you have left. It will be a relief to be rid of you."

He smiled as she slammed the door shut. "How about that, doctor. We finally have something in common."

The telepath's arrogance knew no bounds. She'd left him with most of his equipment. He only had to open the wormhole, and he'd be home free. However, the usurper insisted he return with the princess. He slammed his fist against the wall. He'd also promised her parents.

He pulled a small tool from his utility belt and began to work on the lock. "At least I made it to the coordinates to get us home," he muttered. "Princess, I hope you appreciate all I've done for you in this hellish dimension."

The locking mechanism turned out to be more complicated than he anticipated. As he worked, his thoughts ran rampant. Maybe he shouldn't have killed Martin. He sat back on his heels and hung his head. Damn Anita, Ra-Vel, and everything else about this assignment.

Now he'd placed himself in a no-win situation. For the first time since his early days as a mere soldier, he'd neglected to consider the future ramifications of his actions. Now, he feared he'd have to free the two witches, Felissina, and himself. Since he'd taken Martin out of the picture, he'd need the assistance of Martin's compatriots.

He may be the best of his king's guards, but there were times, like now, when he needed help. The wisest man knew when the odds were against him, and he counted himself as pretty wise. He worked on the lock again and grinned. He did have one small consolation. At least Anita still couldn't read his mind.

Chapter Twenty-Five

Martin wiped moisture from his forehead. He looked back over his shoulder and scowled at the specter behind him. "Can you cut back on the mist a little?"

"I'm sorry, my lord, but no. I'm a water specter. Water will always accompany me and affect all who come into contact with me."

Terrific. Martin rolled his eyes. "Tell me this, Drippy. Do I only get you, or can I call more?"

"As a scion, you have as many specters as you need at your disposal." The spirit hesitated. "What does this 'Drippy' name mean?"

"It means I have to give you some kind of a name or it will be difficult to keep track of you once the action starts."

Knowing he could call ghosts to him gave him the bare bones of a plan. He needed to figure out how to summon them. Better to wait until he got closer to HelixCorp. Drippy's help made it easier, guiding him to different tunnels when he left his own area.

"How much farther do I have to go? It feels like I've walked for hours."

"Not too much more, my lord. You've traveled between worlds. The trip would've been three times as long on foot if you hadn't utilized your power."

Martin wiped more water from his eyes. "Will you

stop with the 'my lord' stuff? And how did I walk between worlds? I have a hard time with 90 percent of what you say."

Drippy gave an imitation of a shrug. "It appears you did it without conscious thought. I thought you knew your capabilities."

"What have I ever done or said to give you the impression I know anything about what you tell me?" he grumbled. "Let's just go save my people."

Martin stomped along the tunnels and thought about how to rescue Felissina and the others. Did Anita Haines torture her? Would he be in time to save her? What about Olivia and Kaz? Were they still unharmed, or did Shadowjack and Ra-Vel already get rid of them?

Kaz would do some damage to them, but Olivia had less experience in fighting than he did. Would she keep her head or panic? He ran his hand along the wall, absorbing the silent voices as they whispered their long-forgotten stories.

"We are here, my lord." Drippy pointed to a small utility door. "You can get out that way."

Martin exited the tunnel behind a row of English box hedges. He whistled quietly. A whole lot of fence, at least eight feet tall, stood in his way around the expansive grounds. Good thing he only had to reduce a small section to ash. He said a silent prayer there weren't any alarms wired to it.

The HelixCorp logo glowed green as the sun descended and the shadows lengthened. The main building dwarfed the smaller, outer campuses. It rose ten stories high, and who knew how deep the lower levels went. How would he find three women hidden in the monstrosity in front of him? The overused metaphor about needles and haystacks filled his mind.

Martin turned to the specter, no longer bothered by the water as it soaked his clothes. "How do I call the other ghosts?"

"You think about them, and they will appear."

"Really?" Martin rubbed his chin. "I thought the whole process would be a little more complicated."

He closed his eyes and thought about the specters at his side. He didn't need many, just about ten or so. When he opened his eyes, he stood in the middle of a circle of specters. Their hollow eyes stared at him while they waited for his orders. Okay. It might take a little time, but he could get used to the specters following him.

A memory flashed behind his eyes. He'd summoned legions of specters in the past and fought in their ranks with them. He'd stood on a small hill, swinging a sword at…whom? Other specters like the ones around him? No, that wasn't right. A static scene in his mind showed him vanquishing something that looked like a demon. The sensation of being victorious in a fight crawled through him. It felt odd, but familiar, on a deep, primal level.

He turned to his small army. "There are three women in there I need to find. I want some of you to scout and tell me where they are. When I know where they're held, we'll come up with a plan on how to save them."

He concentrated on his friends and hoped his "army" picked up on who he wanted. The specters dispersed, and he waited with Drippy, who floated next to him. In moments, they returned and showed him where Felissina, Kaz, and Olivia were held. From one of them, he picked up Felissina planned to fight, but then wanted to die. She thought Shadowjack ended his life and no longer wished to live without him.

"Okay. Here's the plan, and Drippy? You'll be very important to our success."

****

"So, you are the Angel called CT," Benedict Trust said. He stood by Felissina's gurney and stared at her. "I expected someone a little more impressive."

Felissina scowled at him. "Once I get free, you'll see how impressive I can be. It doesn't matter what you wish to do, but I promise you this. I'll see to it I end your life with my own bare hands."

He grabbed her chin and forced her to look at him. "Maybe it's good you're scheduled for termination. I don't know how I'd be able to get on with my life if you were to become a constant menace." He leaned close to her face. "You can hear how worried I am about your pathetic threat, right?"

Her eyes flashed as her hands curled. "If all you plan to do is insult me in my final hours, I would thank you to leave."

"Does she have to be disposed of when you're finished with her?" Trust turned to Anita. "She could keep me amused for a long time."

"No. Termination isn't necessary." Anita glanced down at Felissina. "But a live subject runs the risk of discovery."

Felissina tried to move away from Trust's touch as he stroked her hair. "I believe she'd be worth the risk. Strip her powers, then prepare her for transport to my penthouse. I have enough safeguards in place so her team will never find her."

"Anita, I would prefer you to kill me now than spend another moment in this so-called man's presence," Felissina spat. "I won't be kept a prisoner."

Trust leaned close to her and whispered in her ear. "You don't have any choice in the matter. I'm eager for your company in my home."

After Trust left, Felissina stared at Anita. "Why would you ever want approval from him? Haven't you felt something, I don't know, evil in him?"

Anita paused. "He gave me a chance when no one else would. He deserves my loyalty, unless circumstances dictate otherwise." She checked the gauges on the machine. "I'm sorry, Angel. You're my ticket to the top."

After they left, soft ticking reached Felissina. Every tick, tick, tick, stole another precious second of her life. The lights flickered, and she frowned. Would she be spared by a power failure? Stranger things had happened in her hero life. A slight, cold breeze swirled around her, and the restraints popped open. She sat up and rubbed her wrist. A mist flowed around her, and silence enveloped her. What happened to the strange ticking noise?

The mist flowed into the seam around the door. Several seconds later, the lock disengaged and the door swung open. She tiptoed over and checked the hallway. The mist formed itself into a vague humanoid shape. It raised a transparent arm and pointed to her left.

She'd never been one to refuse a rescue, even though she wanted to die after she discovered Martin's fate. This mysterious specter wanted her to live, so she would. She'd live and take revenge on all who hurt her and the love of her life.

She kept her steps slow and silent as she trod down the hall behind the specter. If it could get her out, then she would be grateful to it and all future specters she would meet. Now wasn't that a strange thought. And here was another one. Why wasn't she afraid of it? Why did the specter's presence give her a measure of comfort? Another question for another day.

She checked the walls as she progressed. She had no desire to trip any alarms, hidden or obvious. "Thank you, Kristin, for all the exercises making me learn how to escape places without the use of my powers," she whispered.

Her transparent rescuer stopped at the head of a long hallway lined with doors. It pointed to the doors on both sides as it passed by. She nodded her head and followed.

"If I read your gestures right, you want me to free the other prisoners." The specter bowed its head. "I've been so selfish," she murmured. "Pitying myself when so many others need my help. How could Martin have ever wanted to be with me?"

She studied the lock and shook her head. "I need a key card to open these. If I force them, it will set off an alarm, which I believe we'd like to avoid."

Another specter hovered over her shoulder and dropped the required key card in her hand. "Thank you. I appreciate all your help."

She opened the door and saw several teens inside. "I've come to free you. I'm from the superhero team, The Angels. My name is CT. I need you all to follow the specters. They've given me the means to help you all escape." She turned to the specters behind her. "Lead these people to the outside, please. Keep them safe."

She did the same procedure at the other doors she opened. She came to the last two doors. She opened the one on her left, and her eyes widened before she rushed in. "Olivia. Thank the gods you're unharmed." She turned to the red-haired woman with her. "Kaz. I didn't realize they captured you also. You haven't been hurt, have you?"

"Not in the least. Glad to see they didn't poke you yet either." Kaz gave her hand a firm shake. "How do we get out of here?"

"Specters helped me escape and then helped me free you. I have one more cell to open, and we can go."

She took two steps to the last door, when it opened. "Shadowjack. I see you've joined the ranks of the imprisoned. Didn't Anita Haines like your work? And how did you open your cell?"

"I still have a few tricks up my sleeve. Haines said you were scheduled for termination. I objected. She took me for one of her experiments." He held his hand out to her. "Come with me now, princess. I have the means to get us back to our home dimension."

"I can't leave. Not yet. HelixCorp needs to be exposed for the criminals it houses."

He walked toward her. "Let this dimension's hero population deal with this. We belong in our own. There's so much you don't know and so much I need to tell you. I do know your parents are well and miss you very much. Please, your highness," he pleaded. "Let's go home."

Water began to run down the wall in tiny rivulets. Kaz tapped Felissina on the shoulder. "We need to go now. I can sense some heavy-duty events about to happen."

"Shadowjack…" Felissina started.

"Back away from her, Shadowjack. Now."

They all turned to the new arrival. Martin stood there with a crowd of spirits around him. His body shimmered behind the silvery gray mist covering him. He raised his arm, and electronics began to spark as water wound its way into the circuits.

"Martin," Felissina whispered. "You're alive."

Chapter Twenty-Six

"I mean it, mercenary," Martin growled. "Back away. I won't let her go anywhere with you."

"I should've known you'd have some power to keep death from your door." Shadowjack stalked toward him. "What's your plan to stop me? I told you before, she must return to her home. It's very important she be there now. She's desperately needed."

"I have an unlimited army at my beck and call." Martin nodded to his friends. "Add in my friends and their abilities, and you're grossly outnumbered."

An alarm blared, the sound bouncing around them. They jumped as they looked up and down the hallway. Time to go before the security guards showed up to make this great rescue a total failure.

Martin turned to the specters. "Get the prisoners out of here. One of you, try to get the authorities to come."

"I will do so, my lord," Drippy said, then vanished.

"Stop calling me that," Martin shouted to the empty space where the specter hovered moments before.

A crowd of agents came around the corner, Ra-Vel in the lead. He stared at Martin and his group and smiled. "Why am I not surprised to see you still live? It's nice to see you've done me the courtesy of staying in one spot. Your pathetic rescue is over. I'm so glad I knew this would happen." He drew the Wand of Oros and aimed it at Kaz. "Now I get to be rid of you and watch the life leave your body."

"You can try," Kaz said in a singsong voice. "But you have to catch me first." She glanced at Martin, who nodded, then grabbed Olivia's hand and ran after the prisoners.

****

Kaz and Olivia turned down hallway after hallway, but still couldn't shake Ra-Vel. "Damn," Kaz muttered. "He's like a dog with a bone."

They darted around another corner, expecting he'd be there in seconds. "Kaz, please tell me you have some kind of a plan. I'll even take a bad one," Olivia said as she leaned against the wall, her chest heaving as she sucked air into her lungs.

"I don't know, maybe?" Kaz peeked around the corner. The mage stood there as he twirled the Wand of Oros around his fingers. "He's starting to get on my nerves. Liv, we've got to get the wand back. The elves will kill me if I lose it."

"I know. I remember the warning they gave you. I don't think you want to work in the dwarves' mines 'til the end of your days.' What do we do?"

"Follow my lead. I wish some of Martin's spooky friends were here to help."

As she spoke, three specters appeared around them. "Wow. Talk about ask and you shall receive. Here's the plan."

She stepped out in front of Ra-Vel. "Give me back the Wand of Oros. I want this to end peacefully. However, it's all on you. I don't want to have to make you sorry for crossing me. Don't force a fight you don't have a prayer of winning."

"You can't ignore the light within you, Kaz. I know your principles won't let you kill me." He held up the wand and studied it. "I've always wanted an artifact of great power, and now I have it."

"Ra-Vel, don't you ever get tired of acting like you're in a really bad fantasy movie? The elves will come for the wand and you. Are you sure you want to take your chances with them?"

He pointed it at Kaz's heart. "No, little witch. They'll look for you first. By the time they realize you don't have it, I'll be long gone to where they'll never find me."

Olivia's magic stirred Kaz's hair, and she allowed herself a small smile. Her chance arrived on an Arctic breeze as it fluttered across her back, sending tiny shivers up her spine. Ra-Vel's ego overrode his judgement. Or maybe he didn't care about how powerful she'd become and the allies she'd made. Kaz knew the strength of Liv's magic, even if she didn't have too much field experience wielding it yet. Ra-Vel was in for one heck of a surprise.

Kaz grinned. "As much as I hate clichéd phrases, I've just got to say, you'll never get away with this."

The arrogant fool stood there and laughed at her. She spoke quiet words of a low-level spell of clumsiness. Olivia darted out with her own spell as she created a sheet of thin ice on the floor. Ra-Vel's feet began to slip and slide, while he struggled to regain his balance. The specters zipped down the hallway, the wind in their wake toppling him over.

Kaz ran down the hallway as Olivia erased the ice in front of her. She dropped onto Ra-Vel's chest and yanked the wand from his grasp. "Thanks for taking care of this for me, but I want it back now. Oh, and Ra-Vel?" She punched him in the face and smiled when she heard a distinctive pop. "Don't threaten me anymore. It's kind of a bummer."

She walked back to Olivia as she clutched the wand in a tight grip. "Simple, easy, and direct. The best way to beat anyone."

"Kaz, look out!"

Kaz turned and ducked under the knife Ra-Vel swung at her. She grabbed his arm and swung him around. He slammed headfirst into the wall and crumpled to the floor. When it became apparent he wouldn't get up any time soon, Kaz took his knife and slipped into her belt.

"I did not see that coming. He's more of a zap first and stab later kind of guy. Thanks for the heads up." She lightly punched Olivia's shoulder. "We'll make a fighter mage out of you yet."

Olivia glanced down the hallway. "Should we go find Martin and Felissina?"

"No. He'll find us when he's ready. He expects us to have gotten out. Let's go. I'm sure our spooky rescuers have freaked out the freed prisoners by now."

****

Martin wiped the moisture from his face as Felissina started toward him. Shadowjack grabbed her arm and pulled her tight against his body. Martin walked closer to them and halted when the mercenary held his hand up.

"Stop right there. We both know you can't take her from me. My mission in this dimension was to find her and bring her back. As soon as I open the wormhole, I will have accomplished my goal. The revolution can't begin until she is there to lead the assault. Let me take her home."

"No. I'm sorry, but Felissina belongs with me. She stays."

Shadowjack laughed. "And how will you stop me? Your only power is to dissolve different items. It's a very dangerous, but a mostly useless, power."

Martin watched him hold Felissina tighter as he opened a panel on his belt and slapped a button. A black dot appeared behind him, then started to grow. Rainbows of color shot through it and electricity crackled. The hairs on his arms stood up as static shot through the hallway.

As Shadowjack dragged Felissina toward it, her hair whipped around her face. Martin stared, feeling helpless, as she tried to twist free from the mercenary's grip. He ran toward them and knew the only path to save her was the one he feared more than anything. She turned tear-filled eyes to him and reached out her hand.

"Martin, help me. Don't let him take me."

If he stood by, she'd be gone. To take her hand, to save his soulmate, to see her future, would torture him for the rest of his immortal life. They inched closer to the wormhole as Felissina fought and dragged her feet in order to slow her process. He couldn't let her go. He couldn't live without her, even if he knew what her future held. He lunged forward and grabbed her hands.

Images bombarded his mind. He became one with her newborn self. A cute, chubby little girl with blonde, curly hair. The man and woman smiling at her made her feel safe. He saw everyday items through her infant's eyes and wondered at the newness of the world.

Scenes flashed through his mind as he grew into a toddler with her. They were one as she ran through her palace home. Her laugh became his while she hid from her governess, before she tottered down the hallway. Pure, simple glee consumed him, and he couldn't stop the laugh escaping him. Her love for her parents grew as she did, filling his heart until he thought it would burst.

Time sped by, and he grew with her into her pre-teens. Kindness and concern for the palace staff filled him as he interacted with them through her. He started training when she did, and short swords became her specialty and her favorite weapon. Her muscles strained as she learned more complicated maneuvers with the blade. Her exertion leached into his arms, making them shake. He frowned with her when her instructors insisted she practice harder in hand to hand combat.

When her powers manifested, tingles of energy zinged through his blood. Black energy formed around her hands as her abilities grew strong and fast. Her fear consumed him at her almost non-existent control. Her father's voice rang in his ears as he taught her the strict self-discipline she needed. She took no days off, determined to practice until she mastered every lesson he taught her.

Excitement built in him as preparations began for her eighteenth birthday celebration. She'd grown into a beautiful woman, and her father's pride filled him. She played the perfect hostess as she chatted with all the guests and made sure everyone had fun and enough to eat and drink. Her dance steps made him tap his feet, and she caught the eye of a particular gentleman. He regained some of himself as jealousy spiked in his heart when he shared her thoughts that this man could be the one.

The images fast forwarded to the attack on the palace. His vision blurred for a moment when she jerked awake, before fear rose and choked off his breath. In the throne room, her father pressed his medallion into her hand and told a servant to get her to safety. Through her eyes, he saw Shadowjack come in behind the usurper. His fear ramped up in concert with hers as he ran with her through the dark tunnels. She and the servant ended up at the science building.

Her apprehension made him squeeze her hands as he watched the wormhole open through her eyes. The generator functioned normally when she first jumped through, but then pain slammed into her, bleeding into him. Martin gripped her hands tighter as he tried to remain upright. Rainbows of light wrapped around her and flashed. Tendrils of darkness shot past and she tumbled headlong out of the tunnel of light to end up in the middle of a small park. Her fear bled into him, and bile rose in his throat.

Her relief became his after she'd been taken to Angel Haven. He smiled as he trained with her and the Angels, her skills improving at a rapid pace. The images slowed with Shadowjack's attack on her in the alley. He knew when she'd been told of his death. Her grief almost swallowed him whole before the fight in her rose again.

The images stopped there. No future. No darkness. No death. Shadowjack gave a hard yank, and her scream shocked him back to real time. Had he been in her memories for hours or minutes? The scenes had played out in rapid order. It must have been only a few seconds. Nothing in the hallway had changed or moved.

Martin tugged her more toward him. He drew his arm back, landing a solid right cross on Shadowjack's jaw. The mercenary's grip on her loosened, and Martin jerked her free. He slammed his shoulder into Shadowjack's midsection and pushed him into the wormhole. The portal shrank, then closed itself.

Martin held Felissina close while she cried. "It's okay. It's all over. I've got you."

"You're alive. You haven't been taken from me." She sniffed and gazed up at him. "You're holding me."

He smiled and nodded. "Yes, I am."

"You're touching me. How is this possible?"

He tipped her head back so he could see her eyes. He wiped away the tears on her cheeks with his thumbs. "I don't know, and right now I don't care."

He lowered his mouth, reveling in the feel of her warm breath on his lips. They could talk all they wanted to later. He gently touched his lips to hers. Her warm, pliant body pressed closer to him. This couldn't be a dream, could it? The velvety softness of her lips matched his to perfection. Her breath became his as she deepened the kiss. He pulled her tighter to him, reveling in the kiss he'd wanted for so long.

No dream. Not this time. The heat from her body bled into his. His heart pounded in concert to hers as she held him tight enough to choke off his breath. He didn't care. He could hold her. He could touch her. Every longing, every tormented night he spent, poured into the kiss they'd both desired.

She matched his desperation, and he could feel her fingers press hard into his shoulders. Why didn't they break apart? They were in danger. Then she moved closer to him, and he no longer cared. His princess, his superhero, his Angel held him prisoner with the softness of her mouth and the strength of her body.

He trembled as her arms circled his neck and held him as close as she could. Her fingers tangled in his hair, and she tugged his head closer. Goosebumps rose up on his arms, and he pulled her tighter against his chest. He buried his face in her neck while she murmured his name over and over. His first physical contact in years had been a tender kiss from the most beautiful woman in two dimensions.

And it was worth the wait.

Chapter Twenty-Seven

Anita jumped up when the alarms screamed. She ran to the transference lab, not surprised to find her prisoner gone. She frowned as she ran her hand around the edge of the door. Water? The sprinklers hadn't gone off. Where did the water come from?

No matter. Trust would blame her for the hero's disappearance, even though he'd seen she'd had the situation under control. She used her mind scan to see if one of the Angel's teammates found her. After all, the only other people who knew Shadowjack grabbed her were either dead or taken prisoner themselves.

She couldn't find any trace of the hero team, but a strange thought pattern invaded her mind. The thoughts were a dead zone, like it didn't exist. She shook off an involuntary shudder, refusing to be cowed by a foreign entity. There. Around the next corner. Her steps slowed as, once again, the eerie internal chill gripped her mind and heart.

Darkness filled the stranger's mind. The dead zone she sensed ran through her, turning her blood to ice. She forced herself to break the link before she became consumed by the emptiness. She turned the corner and saw Felissina in the arms of a tall man.

The Angel's rescuer. The darkness she detected poured from his mind as it sought her out, trying to devour her. His psychic energy felt different from any person she'd ever scanned. His mind, his aura, his very self, carried the psychic signature of death.

Goosebumps covered her arms and raised the hair on the back of her neck. She shivered and wrapped her arms around her waist to hold the fear in. She took several steps back but knew no distance would be far enough while he remained in the building.

"What are you?" she whispered.

"I don't know, but I can tell you this. I've come to take Felissina with me. You can't stop us."

"I don't want to stop you. I want you gone." Anita shrank from him. "Get out. Leave. Take your Angel and go away. I don't know what you are, but it's not natural."

"You are so right." He stepped closer to her, and she backed away. "I'll know if you pick up where you left off. Do us both a favor and just don't. Do we understand each other?"

"Understood. Just stay away from me."

She watched gray, misty figures surround him as he walked away, his arm around Felissina's waist. She sagged against the wall and didn't move for several minutes. She kept a hand to her chest and took deep breaths to stop her rising panic. The familiar tap of footsteps reached her. She pushed away and smoothed her hair back. Benedict could be dealt with easily, unlike the man who took Felissina away.

"We've been beaten again, Anita." Trust motioned some people forward. "Escort her to my office. I think we need to have a very serious chat."

Two of Trust's bodyguards came forward and stood on either side of her. Yes, Mr. Trust, she thought. We'll have a chat all right. Her eyes narrowed, and a small smile curved her lips. *But how it goes depends entirely on you. If you're willing to be reasonable, everything will be fine.* There was no point reading his mind. She'd find out soon enough.

What would he say though? Could it be time to give up on her dream of being the executive in charge of all research at HelixCorp? This lab and all the experiments she'd participated in had become her life. She wouldn't give it up without a fight. She had to make Trust see he still needed her. She still had so much to contribute to the company. If he'd listen, she might still be safe from his wrath.

****

"Please hold me," Felissina whispered.

He held out his arms to her, grateful when she snuggled tight against him. He'd waited for a moment like this for such a long time. Now his dream had come true and they would be together now and forever. Gazing in her eyes, he knew she felt the same about him.

Drippy told him the rescued prisoners had been picked up by the authorities. Now he could turn his full attention to the woman who stood in front of him. He wanted to be with Felissina and have her hands on him. So many years passed since he'd attempted any type of physical connection. He couldn't stop touching her face, her hair, or any other part of her.

Martin caressed her cheek. "I'll hold you and never let you go for as long as you want."

He stared at their hands as their fingers intertwined. He kissed each fingertip before he pressed her hand to his face. He closed his eyes and smiled. A touch. A real touch without the horrible visions he saw. She pulled him toward her room, kicking the door shut when they entered. He had an idea what would come next.

"Do you remember several days ago when we were together?" she asked.

"Yes. How could I forget? It's been on my mind ever since."

He cupped her cheek as he placed light kisses on her lips and down her neck. She pulled his shirt off and traced the lines of his chest. Her hands drifted lower, and he trembled as her fingers danced over his abs. He reached behind her and untied the hospital gown she still wore. First she exposed one shoulder, then the other.

"We get to have our moment at last," he whispered. "I hope I'm ready for this, because I think I'm more than a little terrified."

"I'll be with you the whole time," she said. "There's no reason to fear."

She let the gown drop, and his breath caught. She wore no garments underneath, and she looked even more glorious than before. He picked her up and laid her on the bed. When she tugged on his jeans, he smiled and stepped out of them. She patted the bed, and he took his place next to her.

Her smooth skin had the slick feel of silk against his calloused fingers. The heat of her body warmed his hand as he let it roam over her. He trembled when his palm covered her breast, and he lingered there. She arched into his touch, and he swallowed hard, trying, and not succeeding, to stop his hands from shaking. When his mouth replaced his hand, she moaned and grabbed his shoulders.

He knew it would be right to be with her, but he

didn't know how right. He found her ready for him and remembered he'd told her what he'd do next. He stroked her until her body trembled from his touch.

"I need you now, Martin," she panted. "I know we acted this out so it took more time, but I can't wait any longer."

"I feel the same way." He nudged her legs apart. "Open your eyes. I want to you to see me."

He smiled when she gazed at him. When he entered her, light exploded behind his eyes, but not white and bright. It looked more like a purple-black, regal and strong as gold light traced out her family crest. A strange shape rose with the light. It appeared to be a hooded figure, cloaked and gray, as silver mist trailed behind it. He felt her legs lock around him, and the time for thought ceased.

Her breath quickened and he kissed her when their release hit hard. She did say she didn't even want his words to escape her. Their hearts returned to normal, and she stroked his cheek.

"I've never had such a wonderful experience." She paused. "Did you see a bright, purple light?"

He nodded. "And a gray figure. I think those were our souls. Grayson told me a little bit about how soul bonding looks." He kissed her nose. "There's no force on any world to break us apart."

She stroked his cheek. "Did you know your eyes change color to match your mood?"

"They do? I never knew."

"When you came to rescue me, they turned completely silver." She ran her hand down his chest. "When we're together, they're solid green. The first time I saw you, they were half green and half gray. You are unique, my love."

"So are you, sweetheart. I suppose I should let you up."

She held him tighter. "I believe I like you right where you are. From the sensations I feel, I don't think we're done yet, and your eyes have turned a darker shade of green."

"You could be right, princess. Let's put it to the test."

And as she predicted, they got no rest for the remainder of the night.

****

Martin stood in the kitchen and fixed a snack for himself and Felissina. She wouldn't return to Angel Haven now. They'd become soulmates in every sense of the word. He stared at his hands. He thought he'd always be alone and yet he'd found the one woman he could touch without consequences.

He turned when Olivia came in. "Hey, Liv. Are you okay after your first real experience with fighting bad guys?"

"I'm fine, but what about you? Since when can you control ghosts and spirits and stuff? You haven't come out of your room since we got home."

"I've been with Felissina."

"Does that mean what I think it means?" She stared hard at his neck and erupted in laughter. "You've got a hickey. How can you touch her?"

"I don't know. After my murder, I changed. I don't know why I can touch her and no one else." He thought about the way he'd touched her for the past day and a half. "If you'll excuse me, I have lunch to deliver."

He picked up the tray and carried it back to the

room he shared with the woman of his dreams. She sat up in bed, the covers pulled up over her chest. He set the tray on the small night table before he perched on the edge of the bed.

"I'm glad you came back quickly," she said. "I find I'm quite famished."

"I made sandwiches."

He smiled as she pushed the covers down. "I don't want sandwiches right now." She leaned forward to run her hand along the inside of his thigh. "Can you suggest an alternative?"

He trembled a little and reveled in the feel of her fingers on his leg. "I think I can help you out."

He took his jeans off and climbed in next to her, the food forgotten. He'd never get enough of her. He should be glad of his immortality. He paused until she nibbled on his neck. He would live forever, but she wouldn't. How would he keep his soulmate with him for the rest of eternity?

****

Olivia sat in Kaz's office. "I tell you it's true. They've been sleeping together since the rescue. He's got a hickey."

Kaz leaned back in her chair and propped her feet up on the desk. "Good for him. Not sure how or why it happened, but he deserves some happiness in his life."

"I'm worried about him." Olivia sat forward. "His powers have never evolved so quickly before, and now he can summon ghosts? Why did the one call him 'my lord?' Do you have any thoughts about this?"

"Right now, he's got his freak on with our princess, superhero person. They've got to stop sometime soon. When they do, we'll have a sit down and see if we all can't figure out what happened." Kaz jumped up. "I've got a wand to return. Word is the Conclave started to question the surge of forbidden magic, and I don't want to get caught with it. Also, the elven lords are antsy to get it back, toot frigging sweet." She stabbed her finger at Olivia. "You don't know about the wand or the elves or anything else I've done lately, got it?"

Olivia grinned and saluted her. "Yes, ma'am. I've got to get back to the underground. There's still work I need to get done."

Kaz waited until Olivia left then lifted the heavy tome she'd been reading back onto her desk. Martin said he'd been called a traveler first, then a scion. She'd researched on what those titles meant. Her friend commanded a lot more power than he knew. The fact the residents of the spectral realm were soulless concerned her. If true, Martin and Felissina couldn't be soulmates.

Kaz slammed the book shut and leaned on it. She and Martin discussed this already. She went to the exam room and grabbed the case with the Wand of Oros. First she had to get rid of this forbidden magical albatross. If she hadn't been so desperate to help Martin, she never would've gotten the damn wand at all. The elven lords could have it and were more than welcome to keep it from her sight for the rest of her life.

She'd started to wonder about how to get to the spectral realm. All of her questions might be answered there. However, all magic users were banned from contact with the land of the dead. She didn't know anyone who even wanted to be around the spectral realm. The magic users who did ended up in Dukar Prison. No wonder Martin always wanted to bang his head against the wall. Dead ends could frustrate a person.

She opened a portal and stepped through. She hoped Captain Happy Pants would come out of his room soon. There were still a bunch of loose ends to tie up. Like, what happened to Ra-Vel, and should she be worried about the trouble he'd stir up?

Chapter Twenty-Eight

Ra-Vel made his escape when HelixCorp erupted in chaos. He stood on a nearby hill and watched as law enforcement and medical vans pulled up. Shame about the girl he'd been working on with Anita. He would've enjoyed the discovery of her hidden potential and then exploit it. She might have even been a decent apprentice. The fact he'd lost Anita upset him, but not as much as he thought it would. He'd begun to make extensive plans for her. Oh well. Easy come. Easy go.

He scowled. Kaz should've been dead by now. He'd held the Wand of Oros. It should've been easy to end her life. But she'd summoned phantoms from the spectral realm. It shouldn't have been possible. Her magic dealt with life, not with spirits. His magic could be considered more compatible with the dead.

He gated himself to the Conclave's headquarters. The monthly conference of mages was about to convene, and he'd never missed a meeting. Just because Kaz was on his mind didn't mean he would jeopardize his position within the Conclave. The red-haired witch would have to wait.

****

Four days since they'd broken out of HelixCorp and Kaz's patience reached its breaking point. Olivia told her Martin and Felissina only came out to shower, which they did together, and to eat. Well, she'd used up most of her patience and now didn't have a shred of it left. One way or the other, she'd get them out of bed to do some work.

She pounded on the closed bedroom door. "Martin Long, you get your oversexed ass out here, right frigging now."

She listened to scurried movement and gave him another minute, then pounded again. "You know I can get in there, door or no door, so hurry up."

Martin walked out as he pulled his T-shirt down. "You're in a foul mood today."

"Whatever." Her eyes narrowed as she stared at his neck. "You do have a hickey." A hard laugh burst from her when color crept up his neck. "Come on. We still have work to do and questions to answer."

Martin glanced back at Felissina, who looked decidedly un-regal at the moment. When he took a step toward the room, Kaz gated him to the living room, where Olivia was waiting. She frowned at Felissina. "You, too, missy. Get yourself up and dressed. Pronto."

Kaz had no time for googly eyed romance or people who couldn't keep their hands to themselves. When Felissina hurried in, she sighed. She hated being the one to force them out of their love nest, but they'd given her no choice. Kaz really couldn't blame him for not wanting to come out. He'd lived in complete isolation for such a long time, it must've been a heavy burden. He could be forgiven for a little overindulgence. For now.

"Okay, gang. Time to focus," she said. "There are still questions we need to answer."

"Like what?" Martin asked.

"How about how you can summon ghosts? Why

did one of them call you 'my lord?' Why would HelixCorp want all those supers? Why did Ra-Vel work there?"

"Kaz is right," Felissina said. "There is still so much we don't know. My team has been investigating HelixCorp behind the scenes with the help of Grayson's partners. From what we learned, the upper floors are all legitimate research labs. The lower levels, where we were held, are the part no one knows about."

"Could Anita Haines have found out about you and hired Ra-Vel to kidnap you, Kaz?" Olivia asked. "He seemed very interested in your demise."

"And what happened to Anita?" Martin said. "She caught up to me and Felissina but then she backed off. She looked scared of me."

Kaz paced. "What happened to Shadowjack?"

"I can answer your question," Felissina said. "He opened a wormhole. When he tried to pull me through, Martin saved me. He's been transported back to our dimension."

Kaz threw her hands up. "Yippee. Out of all the millions of questions, we have at least one answer."

"Calm down, girl," Martin said. "As much as you want to, you can't solve every problem in one night."

"Are you challenging me?" She glared at Martin. "You're the next puzzle. Stand up and come over here."

He did as she asked and backed up when she held her hand out. "You can touch Felissina. Take my hand. Let's see if 'my lord' is fixed."

He jammed his hands in his pockets. "I've thought about this a lot." He glanced back at Felissina. "I think I can touch her because she's from a dimension the opposite of ours. We're matter. She's anti-matter. When

I grabbed her to get her away from Shadowjack, I saw her past up to the exact moment we were at in time. I couldn't see her future. I don't think I'm fixed. I think it's because she's from a different dimension."

Kaz dropped her hands. "Of course it is. Do you try to complicate my life on purpose? First, I have to wait days for you two to quit your 'rabbits in heat' act. Now you tell me there's one person, *one,* you can touch. There are times, like these, when I wish I had never left the stupid wizard ranch." She opened a portal. "You two may as well go back to bed. I want to go home. Don't call me. I'll call you."

Before she could step through, a floor to ceiling doorway of mist and shadow opened. A figure close to eight feet tall stepped through. A large hood hid the face, and the robes swirled around in the winds blowing in from wherever it came from. A skeletal left hand grasped a scythe, taller than the figure by several inches.

No one in the room could speak or move. The hood turned to each of them before it stayed the longest on Martin. The creature raised its right arm. A teeth-grinding creak, louder than a rusted, squeaky gate, echoed through the underground. The skeletal index finger pointed straight at him. The winds continued to howl, and held every person frozen in their seats. Kaz's portal snapped shut, and she tried to back away but couldn't make her feet move.

"Martin Long," a deep voice intoned, echoing around the room. "I have waited long enough for you to return. I have come for thee."

Tendrils of mist sprung forward and wrapped around him. The figure turned back to the doorway as the mist dragged Martin behind him.

The doorway closed, releasing them from the paralysis which gripped them. The three women blinked and stared at each other for a few minutes before they could speak.

"What happened?" Olivia asked.

Felissina looked at her friends. "Do you know the identity of the figure? His gaze terrified me."

Kaz stumbled to a chair and flopped down. "Ladies, I think we've been visited by Death himself." She looked at the spot where the doorway disappeared. "And he took Martin."

****

Anita stood in front of Trust's desk. For the first time since he hired her, she wished he'd shut up. The man should have gone into politics. He could talk and talk and not say one sentence with any relevance.

"Have you been paying attention to me, Anita? You're in enough trouble without the added problem of disrespect."

"I'm sorry, Mr. Trust," she said, trying her best to sound sincere. "Where do we go from here?"

He leaned against his desk and folded his arms. "I haven't quite decided yet. All of your test subjects have escaped, and I'm not sure what to do with you. We're in the middle of an incredibly bad situation. If any of those supers talk, they could ruin our whole operation."

She stood rigid, her arms at her sides. "You've seen how the calmest of situations can spiral out of control. This is what I always seem to deal with, but it's never happened here. It happens out in the field more often than not."

"I never realized how much one or two renegade

heroes can upset the balance." He walked around his desk and sat on the edge. "I've gotten a lead on a new scientist who will be able to help you with your research. He might be able to help you beef up security, also. He'll be waiting for your call on where to meet. His cell number is in the file."

"If you believe it's necessary, then of course, you have my complete cooperation." She took the folder he handed to her. She scanned the contents and smiled. "I know this researcher. I've worked with him before."

"I take it you're pleased with my new acquisition?"

"Yes, sir. I'm glad you're allowing me to continue to work here. What else do you need from me?"

"At the moment, I need you to mobilize your team. Pull back to one of the smaller facilities for right now. This whole section needs to be sealed off so the various hero teams or law enforcement agencies can't find it."

Anita nodded. "I'll make the arrangements. Will you be staying in town or at one of your other locations?"

"I'm still the CEO of HelixCorp and need to be available for the Board. You can reach me at my penthouse if anything important comes up." He stood and shoved several files into his briefcase. "Remember, as head researcher, you're also an important figure to the Board. Make sure you come to the monthly meeting to make your report."

She turned to the door. "I'll be there."

****

Anita hurried to her office. She began cleaning out her desk. As she removed the picture of her father, her lead assistant came in. She motioned him closer.

"I've been told to shut down this facility."

"What do you need from the team?"

"Tell them to copy all the computer files onto the portable drives. Then wipe and destroy all the computers we need to leave here. Box up any and all paper files and get them loaded onto one of the transport trucks. This whole section needs to be sealed off against the authorities. Benedict Trust is expecting us to take care of shutting everything down." She glanced around the room. "It's a shame. I really liked this office."

Her assistant shook her hand. "I'll make sure it's all done properly, Dr. Haines."

"There's one more thing. We have a new researcher coming on board soon. Make him feel welcome. I'll call him as soon as we're settled."

He smiled and nodded. "You'll have the team's complete cooperation."

When he left her office, she grabbed a few more items. From the bottom drawer, she pulled out a thick folder and tapped her nails against it. Trust had been gracious with the loss of all their test subjects, but he wouldn't be so forgiving forever. The folder still held important information, even though most of the heroes it mentioned had escaped.

She still had the trials' results, scans, and blood samples. He'd be happy with her foresight of holding onto the files.

Chapter Twenty-Nine

Felissina ducked as Kaz threw book after book over her shoulder onto the floor. "Is there anything I can do to help?"

"Thanks, Feli, but no. I know what I want. I just can't remember where I saw it. It might be in my main library. This one here is more for quick reference."

Olivia walked in. "George thinks you're nuts to want to open a gate to the spectral realm, but he may have someone who can help us."

Kaz lay flat on the floor and rubbed her knees. "Wonderful. Tell me what he said while I try to get some sensation back in my legs."

Felissina walked over and extended her hand. "Come on, Kaz. Martin would say you're becoming overly dramatic. Let's hear what we have to do if we want to find him."

The three of them headed for the conference area. Felissina marveled at the size of The Center. "Your clinic is quite spacious. I had no idea."

"It's all done with magic," Kaz said. "It's a simple compression spell. Rooms are small until they're needed. When a person passes by, they expand. It's kind of like motion sensor lights."

"Very ingenious. This world should appreciate its magic users more."

"It'd be nice, but it doesn't even appreciate its

Annette Miller

heroes. Magic users have faced prejudice for a hell of a lot longer. Heroes will catch up to the disrespect train soon, though."

When they were seated, Olivia spoke. "George says there's a woman who walks between worlds. We might be able to persuade her to gate Felissina to the spectral realm."

Felissina jumped to her feet. "What are we waiting for? Let's go and find this person."

"Hang on, Feli." Olivia tapped her fingers on the table and wouldn't look at her friends. "I know where she is and who she is. Kaz, you know her, too. She commands a very high price. I don't know if we can pay it."

"Don't worry about the cost. Whatever she wants, whatever she asks, I'll give it to her."

"You don't understand, Feli," Kaz said. "Magic users don't want money because they have no need for it. Most times, they demand something personal from the person who wants the favor. I'm not sure what she'll ask for, but I know you shouldn't give it, no matter what it might be."

Felissina stood. "Speculation about what this person may or may not want doesn't do us any good. Let's go find her and ask her, face to face, her price to return Martin."

Kaz shrugged and stood. "Can't argue with her logic. Let's go, Liv."

Olivia hesitantly told them their destination and the person they needed to see. Kaz balked and almost refused to take them. Felissina couldn't understand her reluctance. Wouldn't she want to do whatever it took to retrieve her friend? She knew she would pay the person's price, no matter how high, to get Martin back. They were bonded beyond the physical. Their relationship became what some would call spiritual. She agreed with the assessment with her whole heart. After asking if they were sure for the tenth time, Kaz finally gave in and opened a gateway.

They stepped out of the portal onto a barren plain. No animal noises greeted them, and no wind blew. Even the sun's brightness appeared muted in a washed out, greenish-orange sky. The trio shivered and looked at each other. No one wanted to be the first to move. The arid air turned their throats as dry as the surrounding landscape. Dust motes swirled before their eyes.

Felissina peered through the thick, iron bars of the locked gate. A dingy, granite wall, a minimum of at least ten feet high, was topped by thick, iron spikes. Behind the wall, a massive, black, stone edifice crouched like some mythical monster. A stagnant moat circled the base of the structure, and small rocks stuck out of the scoured ground.

"Where are we?" Felissina asked, her voice hushed.

"This is Dukar Prison. Magic users check in, but they don't check out. The guards here are as much prisoners as those who are incarcerated." Kaz glanced at Felissina. "The landscape is kept barren so that if someone should get out they'll have no cover. There's traps and runes inlaid into the ground. We can walk across the ground to the prison, but you can't get out without a special password to disarm the other hidden booby-traps. This is not a nice place."

Felissina swallowed hard, the tremors in her voice

matching the ones gripping her body. "And the woman we need to see is inside?"

"Yep."

She lifted her head, refusing to cower in the miasma of the prison's depressing atmosphere, and squared her shoulders. Standing out in the open where she was sure they were being watched wasn't the place to show fear. If she could convince her flight response to behave, she might get through the meeting with the mysterious woman they'd come to see.

She glanced at Kaz and smiled. "Then let's go meet with her. Time's wasting, as my teammates would say."

Olivia took a deep breath and walked up to the gate. She tapped a small box with her wand. "We seek an audience with Selena."

Tense minutes passed before the gate swung open on creaky hinges. The trio walked purposefully up the dust covered path. Felissina followed Kaz's example and stared straight ahead. From what her friends told her of the prison's reputation, she truly believed it was designed to suck life and hope out of all who entered.

I'm a hero and a member of a royal family. I've come to get help finding my soulmate, she repeated in her mind, hoping the mantra would give her strength.

Once inside, Kaz and Olivia surrendered their wands. The guard stared at Felissina for a moment, then let her pass. Another guard motioned for them to follow him. The witches stared straight ahead, but Felissina stole glances at the walls. Portraits of former wardens graced the hallway to glare down at the visitors, intimidating all passersby with their judging eyes and silent condescension.

This Selena woman must be powerful to make Kaz and Olivia so apprehensive. Felissina stood taller. Strangers had never cowed her before, and she refused to let this woman, whom she'd never met, be the first. She would ask for her help. If she thought Selena's price too high, they would find another way to save Martin. She hoped a trade could be worked out. Her skills as a negotiator had always been highly praised by her parents.

The guard stopped them before a huge oak door covered with odd signs. He motioned for them to wait. He knocked three times before pulling the door open with a spine shuddering groan. He shut the door behind him, leaving the three to stare at the barrier, wondering if they would be allowed entrance.

Felissina studied the carvings. "These are very intricate. What are they?"

"They're runes and wards of protection to stop the prisoners from getting in," Kaz whispered. "Selena is the current warden."

"Why are you afraid of her?"

Kaz stared at her. "I'm not afraid of her. Much. We were in school together and kind of parted on a bad note."

Felissina laid her hand on Kaz's arm. "I hate to ask when I'm dependent on your assistance, but is there anyone whom you haven't upset?"

"Right now, you, Liv, and Martin." She shrugged. "Maybe a couple of other people. Who keeps count anymore?"

The guard returned, holding the door open for them to enter. "We may be in more trouble than I first believed," Felissina muttered as the door closed with a soft bang.

They walked to the large dais in the middle of the room. The woman at the desk ignored them. Felissina didn't think she looked at all frightening. She'd pulled her dark hair back in a tight bun. Small, wire-framed glasses perched on the end of her nose, made her thin face look long and angular. The quiet scratch of a pen reached them, and they waited in silence while Selena finished her work.

She stood and walked down the few steps to the floor where they stood. She stopped right in front of Kaz. "And now you come to me for help. Not quite as high and mighty as you used to be, are you?"

"It's been a lot of years, Selena," Kaz said. "Act like an adult and not a spoiled brat."

Selena smiled, and her face softened. "I've missed you, Kaz. The years have been kind to you."

"How did you end up with such a crappy job?" Kaz spread her arms wide. "This gig is for witches they don't know what to do with."

"Right again." Selena turned her back to them and walked away. "I've stepped on a few too many toes of the Conclave. This is my punishment. Why are you here?"

Felissina stepped forward. "Kaz is here on my behalf. I need passage to the spectral realm."

"Impossible." Selena stalked back over to them. "Why do you think I'm here? The Conclave discovered my last trip there and let me know they weren't happy about it."

"My soulmate has been taken by Death," Felissina continued. "I want him back."

"No one returns from the spectral realm. Dead is

dead."

Kaz spoke up. "So here's our problem. He's not dead. Death came and took him. He's got some strange ties to the spectral realm. Specters called him a scion. We want to get him back."

Selena backed up until she hit the dais. "If Death has come for one of his scions, all of you need to stay out of it. He won't take kindly to your interference. All the specters in his realm are his to command." She stared at Felissina. "Especially the scions."

Felissina ran to her and took her hands. "I won't leave him there. He's my soulmate. See for yourself. We're joined."

Selena murmured a quick spell as she stared at Felissina. "Impossible. Scions have no souls. How can you be soul bonded to someone with no soul?"

"I don't know, but we did, all the same. Therefore, it's not as impossible as you seem to think it to be."

Selena stared at her for a moment, then said, "Come with me."

She strode out of the chamber while the three friends followed close behind. They trotted to keep up with her before she stopped in front of a small door at the end of a deserted hallway. Selena glanced over her shoulder as she produced a small, ornate gold key. She turned the lock and stood back while they went in. She followed them and locked the door behind her.

"I've spelled this room to make it soundproof. I'll open the gateway and let you through. You won't be able to call me when you're ready to return. You'll have to find your own way home."

Felissina nodded. "I understand."

"Do you still wish to go?"

"I do. I can't bear to be without my soulmate for another minute." She stared at the witch. "What's the price for your help?"

Selena stared at Kaz and Olivia. "Never come to me again. If you do, I'll have you locked away forever." She turned back to Felissina. "The Conclave already has a cell prepared for Kaz. I really don't want to see her occupy it." She winked. "Not yet, anyway."

"Agreed," Kaz said.

"The price is agreed on and paid." Selena pulled up an area rug. Etched into the floor were odd markings. "These were here when I took over the position as warden. I don't know what the previous wardens did, but they carved gateway runes into the floor. I've been told, in no uncertain terms, this gate is never to be used. I'm in danger by helping you."

"Thank you," Felissina said. "I won't forget your kindness."

Felissina looked at Kaz, who stared wide eyed at the design. Olivia clutched Kaz's arm, and the two of them backed away. Felissina didn't know what the markings meant, but they terrified her friends. Selena chanted and red light zipped through the runes as they began to pulse and the magic gave them power.

Felissina hugged her friends. "I'll find a way to get us both home. I swear. Take care."

Selena nodded to her. "Go now. I can keep it open for a few moments. Any longer and the Conclave will detect it."

Felissina took a deep breath and walked into the circle. Wind whipped around her, and she took a few more steps. She looked back and saw Kaz and Olivia wave to her as the gateway spiraled down to a pinpoint of light. The wind stopped as soon as the doorway shut. She gazed around the landscape and sighed. How would she ever find Martin? A low fog obscured her vision. Well, she had to pick a direction some time. A journey always started with a single step.

Gray overtones gave the landscape a washed out look. Low silver-gray clouds hung on the horizon. The trees were bare, the branches still as no breeze blew. The heavy silence muffled any sound she made. Felissina glanced down and noticed all of her color had dulled to almost white. Moisture beaded on her forehead, and she wiped it away.

More collected, and her clothing clung to her like a second skin. She wiped the excess water from her face and frowned. No rain fell, and the air felt dry. How could she be soaked through? A spirit appeared next to her. She stared at the blue tinge around what would be its face and hands.

"I know you." She narrowed her eyes. "You aided my escape from HelixCorp. Who are you?"

"The scion has named me Drippy. I am a spirit of the water. You shouldn't be here. This land is for the dead."

Felissina stepped closer to it and wiped more water from her face. "The scion is my soulmate. I'm here to fetch him home. If you won't help me, I suggest you stay out of my way. I intend to free him from this place."

Drippy floated quietly in front of her for a moment. "I will guide you to your beloved. Stay close. It is easy to get turned around here."

She followed Drippy as he floated away. "I *will* find you, Martin. Whether we stay here or somehow make it back to Earth, it won't matter. We'll be together, and I won't let anyone take you from me again."

Chapter Thirty

Martin landed in an undignified heap on an Oriental carpet in a lavish study. The hooded figure shrank in size and leaned against the desk. The scythe disappeared as soon as they arrived. The figure crossed his arms and still didn't speak. Emily Dickenson said it best. Death not only stopped for him but gave him an express ride to the land of the dead.

Martin stood and dusted off his pants. "You must be 'the master' Drippy referred to. I guess you're Death?"

The figure dropped his cloak. Martin couldn't hide his shock when Death looked like anyone else. He appeared as an older gentleman, gray hair and a short, neatly trimmed, gray beard. There weren't any wrinkles on the man's face, and he dressed in black jeans and a dark green pullover shirt. He noticed Death's eyes were silver-gray, like his own turned when he became angry.

Martin pointed to Death's feet. "I didn't expect Death to wear high-top, green tennis shoes. Did you have a good reason to forcefully invite me here?"

"I brought you here, scion, because this is your home," Death said. "You are my right hand. I've given only you almost all my powers to help keep balance in the realms."

"My name is Martin, and my powers aren't controllable. I'm pretty sure you don't have those kinds of problems."

"Let's sit down, shall we?" Death tugged on a bell pull. When a servant appeared, he ordered tea and food. "The whole theatrical act takes a lot out of me. I hope you're hungry. My servant can travel to any restaurant and bring back whatever you like."

"I could eat just about anything. Sandwiches would be good." Martin stared at him. "When will you tell me why you kidnapped me?"

"Kidnapped?" Death thought for a moment. "I returned you to your home. This is where you belong. Your realm is here, not the human world."

"Don't take this wrong, but I don't remember you, this land, or the ghosts. How do all of you know who I am?"

Death stroked his chin. "I expected you would have some memory problems. You've been gone for eons. I'd hoped you'd remember everything yourself when you came back here."

"Eons?" Martin staggered to a high, wingback chair and sat with a thump. "It isn't possible."

When the tea and food arrived, Death took a cup and settled back in the chair opposite him. Martin took the other cup and a sandwich. When it became obvious Death wouldn't speak until after he'd eaten, Martin ate the sandwich he held. Soon, only crumbs lay on the platter. Death snapped his fingers, and the fireplace sprang to life. The crackling flames gave him some normalcy in an abnormal place.

"It's hard to picture you as an ordinary person," Martin said. "I thought the whole skeleton image was your true self."

Death shook his head. "Humans expect the Reaper

of Souls to appear in that persona. I don't mind. I've always liked to play to the crowd." He settled himself more comfortably in the chair. "Now, you have questions. I have answers. Let's begin."

"Have I ever been human? If not, how did I end up in a human body? And what do you mean I haven't been here for eons? Where have I been?"

"Hungry for knowledge I see." Death smiled. "Let me answer your first question. It will answer a lot of the others you rapidly fired at me. It's a kind of history lesson."

Martin rubbed the back of his neck. "Hang on a second. My life is a history lesson?"

"It would appear." Death picked up a book from the table next to him and held it in his lap. "I decided to read our histories the other day, as the mortal world measures time. Eons ago, a huge battle raged between all the realms. Good, Evil, fairy, magic, humans, Life, and Death became locked in a war. Life and I tried our best to stay out of it. She nurtured new life, and I escorted the souls of the slain to the other side. We hoped to show the others how the realms could work together and live in peace."

"What happened?" Martin asked.

Death scowled. "Evil is what happened. Every time we'd get the worlds back on an even keel, Evil would stir the pot and the wars would begin again. We wanted to vanquish Evil out of existence, but you can't have Good without Evil and vice versa. Just like you can't have Life without Death or mundane without magic. There must always be balance. More's the pity."

"Sounds frustrating," Martin said. "Would you like to tell me my part in this great scheme of the cosmos?"

Death rose from his chair, laid the book aside, and walked to the bookcase. He ran his fingers along the spines and selected a thick volume. "You were my right hand. You were my favorite, and I trained you personally. Until you gained more experience, you held the title of Traveler."

Martin leaned forward, his knuckles white as he held the arms of the chair in a tight grip. "Stop. Just stop with the obscure names and titles. Drippy called me scion several times, and 'my lord.' I don't know what they mean and frankly, I'm not sure I even care anymore."

Death turned to him, his eyebrows raised almost to his hairline. "Drippy?"

Martin hesitated when the corners of Death's mouth twitched. "The water spirit who follows me around. I'm always dripping with water by the time he leaves."

"Drippy." Death chuckled. "A most appropriate name. A name worth remembering." He handed Martin the book he took down and returned to his chair. He waited while Martin thumbed through the pages. "The travelers are those among us who can travel between worlds, universes, and dimensions with ease. They are the lowest rank in my hierarchy. They call the collectors of souls to escort those who have passed to this realm. Then there are the scions. Scions preside over the collectors and the travelers. They report directly to me."

"The artwork in this is incredible."

He turned another page and stopped. A picture of a man with a sword raised in victory gleamed in the light. He traced the figure. As he did, his power triggered. He could hear the sounds of battle and feel the elation of believed-to-be vanquished enemies. He frowned. The book's past should be revealed to him, not the picture's past. Had his powers evolved again? He stared closer at the picture.

"This is me," he whispered. He looked up at Death. "How? I've never swung a sword in my life."

"You've never swung a sword in your *human* life. I expect after being kept away from me for a few millennia, you may have forgotten one or two bits from your 'life' here."

Martin snapped the book shut and stared at the other man. "Did you say 'millennia'? Earlier you said eons. How old am I?"

"We're immortals. Age is a construct of man. You're as old as you need to be." He stroked his beard. "I find the gray look to be most dashing and dignified, don't you think?"

"Yeah, sure. You look great." Martin frowned. "Now, can we get back to the history of me?"

"Of course. The picture you studied depicted your last battle. One of Evil's warlocks had cast a banishment spell, and you were caught in it. I couldn't find you when the battlefield cleared. I searched every century. I sent my travelers, collectors, and scions out to search for you but, alas, you were lost to us."

Martin glanced down and rubbed his chest. "So how did I end up in this body?"

Death closed his eyes and steepled his fingers. "Thirty seven human years ago, a human woman gave birth to a baby boy. There were problems, and the child didn't survive. I sent my collectors to retrieve the soul when, suddenly, the child began to cry. The child's spirit called to me so I knew he passed to my realm."

Martin leaned forward. "My mother told me the doctors declared me a stillborn. When I started to cry, it confused everyone. They knew the child died, but I started kicking and screaming."

"My theory is this. When you were banished, you were lost and your spirit wandered. I suspect your memory problems began then. Evil then found you and took you prisoner. After who knows how long, they placed you in the dead child and hoped it would kill you. It didn't, but you've had to deal with powers strong enough to consume you. When you were made human, all your abilities should have dissipated."

Martin stared at his hands. "But they didn't. For a long time, I could only read the past of objects. Then I touched a woman and her son who died in a plane crash. My powers started to change and evolve after that."

"Which brings me to my next theory. So much death filled you, it jumpstarted your actual abilities. Of course, they shouldn't have been so out of control. I think your human body tried to protect you from power it couldn't handle. Humans are marvelous creatures."

"They do keep you on your toes," Martin agreed. "How do I get control of these abilities? Will I continue to see death every time I touch someone?"

Death stood and placed his hands on Martin's shoulders. "You've come back home. Your powers should align themselves now." He poured two glasses of red wine and handed one to Martin. "As soon as we free you from the human shell you're in."

"I like the human shell I'm in," Martin said. "Can't you fix me the way I am? I can't be a spectral creature any longer. I have a soulmate, and she needs me."

Death stood still and silent for endless minutes. Martin pushed out of the chair and walked over to him. "Sir? Are you okay?"

"Spirits, scions, collectors, travelers, all in my realm do not have souls. We gave them up to be able to stay neutral in every way."

Martin frowned. "You gave up your souls? It explains why Drippy got so indignant when I told him about Felissina." When Death stared at him and raised an eyebrow, he clarified. "My soulmate."

"This is unheard of, but not impossible." He turned to Martin. "I believe you may be more powerful than I knew. I believe you are the link I need to join me back to Life. We haven't seen too much of each other over the past century or two."

"So why do I have a soul when no one else here does?"

"Life imbues all creatures with souls. When you took the human body, she must have sensed it and gave you a soul, even though technically you should've remained soulless." He grabbed Martin in a tight hug. "I am very proud of you, my son. You are the bridge for which we've been waiting."

"Hang on a second." Martin pushed out of his embrace. "Did you call me your son?"

"Yes, I believe I did. Sit down. There's more to tell. While the realms waged war, I and my specters met with Life and her nature spirits." Death gave Martin a sly wink. "What can I say? A beautiful lady, a handsome gentleman, and a little too much honeydew wine at lunch. One thing led to another, and we were given the gift of a son. We knew Evil would find out about you. Realizing how important a prisoner you would be, I took you to a mutual acquaintance in another realm. As you grew, you were taught how to use a sword and other battle skills. I came to you often to teach you about your powers."

Martin staggered back to his chair and stared at the iconic figure. Wow. His natural, or should he say supernatural, father. "This is a little much to take in. My human parents aren't my true parents. I'm the son of Life and Death?"

Death shrugged. "I suppose I should say 'surprise.' When you disappeared after the last great battle, Life's heart was broken when we couldn't find you. She couldn't take being near me. I reminded her too much of you."

"This is unbelievable." Kaz and Olivia were in for a huge shock. How could he tell Felissina? "When I get home, my friends won't believe this. I don't think my witch friend would've figured out my origin no matter how many scans she tried."

Death stared at him. "Why do you want to return to Earth? You'll have all you'll ever need here."

The door burst open, and Felissina stalked inside. Water dripped from her clothes to puddle on the floor. "You *shall* return Martin Long to me, specter." She spread her fingers, letting her power flow through them in ebony waves. "Or you'll face the wrath of Princess Felissina Markhov of the Erlymere Province."

"Kind of a dramatic entrance." Martin walked over and took her in his arms. "I'd like you to meet my soulmate, Felissina Markhov. Felissina, this is my father, Death. She's the reason I want to go back." He wiped more water from her face. "I think Drippy led her here."

"I see. Pleased to meet you, Felissina," Death said as he kissed her hand. "Martin has told me about you. This complicates matters a bit. I can't let the two of you go back. Once you enter my lands of your own free will, you're bound to this realm."

She looked back and forth at the two of them. "I need a drink."

Chapter Thirty-One

Felissina gulped down a glass of wine. "Martin, is this true?"

He knelt by her chair, lightly tracing her knuckles. "It's true. I've gotten a history lesson about my life. It's been one heck of a revelation." Martin turned to Death. "However, you never said we wouldn't be able to leave. We have to go back. How would her team know what's happened to her? And why doesn't she have any color?"

"You're free to come and go as you please." Death nodded toward Felissina. "She entered the world of the dead willingly. She gave up her life when she crossed into my lands. Color comes from being alive, and she isn't any longer. There's a reason humans aren't allowed here."

Martin glanced at her before turning his attention to Death. "But she isn't human. She's not from Earth. She's from an anti-matter dimension."

Death considered this information. He gestured for Felissina to approach him. She did and he gazed deep into her eyes for several long minutes. He stepped back and nodded. "She may not be human, but she's not from any of the other supernatural realms either. She stays. Can we get back to your questions please?"

Martin took a deep breath. As much as he wanted to argue with the older man, he decided to use discretion as the better part of valor at this point. "As a scion, what are my actual powers?"

"Walk between worlds, summon spirits, call down the wrath of the dead. Typical spectral realm stuff."

"With all these abilities, is there any way I'll be able to control them? I've lived an isolated life as a human." Martin paused, holding Felissina tighter to his side. "Which still sounds strange to say. We can't stay here. I need to stay on Earth with Felissina. Can you make it happen?"

Felissina jumped to her feet and stalked over to Death. "I won't be kept a prisoner in the land of the dead. A witch who came and went on a regular basis sent me. If she could return to the living world, I should be able to also." She glared at him. "You're Death. You should have the power to grant me this."

"The witch you speak of came to some harm when she visited here. She tempted her fate one time too many. I won't allow such a situation to happen again." Death stared at Martin as he pulled Felissina back to his side. "And you. You're determined to hold on to your human self so much, you've gone and found yourself a soulmate. I don't understand you young people today. You give them the answers they seek, tell them what they want to know, and still they're determined to stay human." He sighed in resignation. "I'll do what I can to give you what you need."

Martin squeezed Felissina's hand. "Thanks."

"Know this." Death stood inches from Martin. "If I grant you this request, you must return to me often. You have to learn control over your powers. I'd like to be able to find and train you. Your soulmate will be important for the plan I have in mind. Let's go somewhere a little more comfortable."

Felissina shrank against Martin's chest. "He's Death. How do I know he won't try to take my soul so you'll have to return here permanently?"

"What kind of lies do they tell about me on Earth?" Death stared at her as his eyes glowed with ethereal, blue light. "Come, children. We have work to do."

A tall woman burst into the study, warm light radiating from her. Martin stared at her, but Felissina was forced to shade her eyes. A long gown of pastel green flowed around her as she walked, pooling around her bare feet when she stopped. Her tan skin offset her white-blonde hair, her eyes the color of new, green grass. Now, they were narrowed as she glared at Death.

"I sensed what you want to do, Death, and I won't tolerate it." She stepped closer to him, the scent of roses in her wake. "You know any occasion to do with life is my domain, even if they are here with you."

Death grabbed her and pulled her into a tight embrace and kissed her hard. "I have missed you, Life. You never returned my request for your company at the last saturnalia."

She traced his jaw and smiled. "You needed a rest after the previous one. I thought I'd give you a little more time to recover." A throat cleared behind her, and she turned. "Who are your guests?"

"The young woman is Felissina. She is Martin's soulmate."

Life took her hands. "Ah, yes. I can sense it now. She glows bright with the power of true love." She gazed at Martin and laid a finger on her lips. "You're immortal. Your life force feels familiar to me."

Martin swallowed hard, then wet his lips. "It

should. From what Death said, I'm your son."

Life smiled, and light and joy exploded in Martin's and Felissina's chests. "I'm so happy to have you returned to us." She placed her fingers under his chin and turned his head left, then right. "His eyes hold the colors of both gray and green. Very unusual and very reminiscent of both of us. I see he got my good looks, but I'm afraid he's stuck with your nose."

Death chuckled as he ran a finger down the length of his nose. "Not too bad, since I've been told it looks aristocratic."

Life harrumphed and glided to a chair. "I've often wondered what happened to you after the war between the realms. Death and I searched for you for millennia, but you couldn't be found."

"Death thinks I may have been held against my will by Evil. I don't remember. I do know I was born and grew up in a Boston suburb with weird powers which change and evolve all the time."

"I believe I remember your human birth. The child shouldn't have survived but did. When I sensed him, I was honor bound by the ruler of Good to bestow a soul in any new life." She glanced at Death. "Could that be why we couldn't find him? We searched for a scion of the spectral realm and not a human."

"So I'm a ghost? But ghosts don't have souls," Martin said. "At least, Drippy is very insistent about that point every time I talk to him."

Life frowned. "Drippy?"

Death assisted her to stand. "Don't ask. It's a long story. I planned to strengthen the bond between Martin and his soulmate. Even though she passed to the realm of the dead, we might be able to use Martin's power to make her immortal. If luck is with us, joining them will give Martin better control over his powers and he'll no longer be isolated."

Life smoothed Martin's hair back. "Have you been so alone, my darling one?"

"Yes." He glanced at Felissina. "Until now. I used to see people's deaths all the time. When I grabbed Felissina to save her, I never saw her death. I could see her life up to the present moment."

"Interesting." Life placed her hand in Death's. "Let's see if your father's plan will work. You must understand there may be consequences. Your power might be more out of control at first."

"Or he might have complete control. He'll be fine," Felissina said. "I'll protect him and keep him safe from any undue occurrence."

Death's laugh boomed through the room. "Well said. I believe you'll make a great addition to our family."

Chapter Thirty-Two

As they walked down through the corridors, Martin wiped the last of the moisture from her forehead. "What happened to you? How did you get here?"

"The witch I mentioned before. Kaz and Olivia knew where to find her. She opened a gateway to send me here. When I arrived, I had no idea which way to go. The landscape all looks the same in every direction, so I began to walk. I feared I would never find you. Drippy showed me the way."

"I'm glad you came."

She laid her head on his shoulder. "I began to get turned around, even though I walked in a straight line. The home of your father is difficult to navigate."

"I think he does it on purpose."

Death looked over his shoulder and smiled. "Of course I do. Even I get solicitors in the afterlife. A simple invisibility spell with a little misdirection thrown in keeps them away. Ah. Here we are."

He pushed open a door and led them inside. Two couches faced each other. The thick, deep green, velvet upholstery gave it a warm, inviting look. A fire crackled and danced in the huge marble fireplace. Dark brown, wood paneling covered the walls. A huge portrait of Life hung over the mantel. A pale gray area rug covered most of the hardwood floor. A small desk sat next to the wall to his right.

Martin looked at him. "I didn't expect a kind of drawing room. This is where you want to do whatever it is you want to do?"

Death closed his eyes and sighed. "What kind of a monster do you think I am? I don't have a mad scientist's lab in here. These couches will have to do, and they're more comfortable than the chairs in my study. Lie down, please."

Life stepped up and eased Death out of the way. "I believe I'll take over now."

Martin and Felissina each lay on a couch. Life joined their hands and closed her eyes. The unfamiliar words she spoke were laced with a strange, ancient, musical quality. Light glowed from her palms as she continued to weave a spell around them. It grew brighter and surrounded them. She held her hand out to Death.

"You're as much a part of Martin as I am. I need your power to help regain the balance he's lost in himself."

Death joined Life, and a bolt of deep gold light burst forth from them. Martin squeezed his eyes shut tighter. He worried about Felissina. Would she be able to contain the force Life wanted to use? More power than he'd ever felt in his life filled him. Would her body be able to handle it?

His mind shattered the restrictions it placed on his power. When he bonded with Felissina, his soul had started its journey of healing. With the restrictions of humanity completely shattered, he felt whole for the first time in his human life. Soon the light faded and the room came back into focus.

Life leaned against Death and pressed a hand to her

forehead. "I'm finished. Take a moment. You might be a little dizzy from the magic." She smiled at the two of them. "As Felissina has helped align your soul, so you have given her a part of you. She is now immortal. You no longer need to fear losing her."

Martin glanced at Felissina. She was no longer pale. All her color had returned, brighter and richer. He eased himself up carefully, and she followed his example. He stared at her. Her soul shone brightly, encasing her in its deep purple light. From the look on her face, she saw him the same way.

"I'm guessing it worked?" Martin said.

"One way to find out. I'll send for you soon, son. Felissina, I enjoyed meeting you. I must warn you I may employ you as a scion in the future." Death pulled Life tight against his chest. "Right now, Life and I need to catch up on some unfinished business."

He snapped his fingers, and the two of them ended up back in Martin's room in the underground. Martin opened the door and stepped into the hallway. They checked all through his home and couldn't find anyone. He led them back to his room and shut the door.

"I take it you saw my soul during the procedure?" He took her hand when she nodded, smiling when her trembling matched his own. "I guess my father gave us this one night before we let everyone know we're back."

"The let's make the most of it."

Twining her arms around his neck, she kissed him hard. He'd never been so glad to get home.

****

Olivia stood in the kitchen the next morning and made a light breakfast. Such a mundane task when two of her friends were still who knew where. When would they return, and could they return? Martin walked in and kissed her cheek, as though her thoughts conjured him up.

"Good morning, sunshine."

She stared at him, and her mouth hung open. "When did you get back? Did Felissina find you? Is she back with you?" She stopped and laid a hand on her cheek. "You kissed me. You can touch people now? How?"

He grabbed her toast and took a bite. "I'd rather wait until Kaz is here. I don't want to go through it twice. See you in a little bit."

Olivia ran to her office and dumped the communication potion in the bowl. "Kaz, you need to come right away."

"It's the middle of the night," she groaned. "Nobody does any kind of work in the middle of the night."

"It's nine in the morning. Trust me. You need to come now."

Olivia emptied the bowl before Kaz could object again. She straightened her already neat office, then cleaned the already sparkling kitchen. A portal opened and Kaz stepped through. She must have rushed to get ready. Her lavender, silk shirt hung outside her pants, buttoned wrong, and her vest hung open. Who knew her mane of red hair had so much frizz?

"I'm here." She yawned. "Kind of dressed and even less coherent. What's the big emergency?"

Olivia took her to the living area and shoved her in a chair. "Stay here. Okay. Close your eyes." She got Martin and Felissina and positioned him behind the chair. "Okay. Keep them closed."

Kaz huffed but did it anyway. "Games? Are you even serious right now? Do you know the incredibly hot dream you ruined when you called?"

Martin leaned over and covered her eyes. "Guess who?"

"Martin." She jumped up and spun around. "Martin! You guys made it back. You touched me. What the hell happened to you?"

"It's a long story so, for right now, I'll give you the condensed version. I'm a scion of the spectral realm and the son of Death and Life. I'm also immortal and so is Feli."

"Wait, what?"

"My parents fixed my powers. I can touch people now." He kissed Felissina's cheek. "Turns out, my soulmate here helped to solve my problems."

Kaz narrowed her eyes. "I thought you said spectral folk didn't have souls."

"So people keep telling me," Martin said. "Death said it must have been when Life sensed a new life. She bestowed a soul in me as a newborn."

"It's too early for you to confuse me." Kaz walked away and rubbed the back of her neck. "I don't know how to react. This is all new to me."

"Me, too," Martin said. "Felissina and I have to leave for a bit. Since I know I can walk between worlds and travel to other dimensions, we plan to free her family. Shouldn't take long." Mist formed around his hand. "I'm anxious to try out my new abilities."

"How long isn't too long?" Olivia asked. "We just got you back."

"I'm sure the usurper has grown complacent in my

absence," Felissina said. "I don't believe it will take long to dethrone him with the people's help. We should return within the next few weeks, maybe sooner."

Olivia shifted from foot to foot. "When do you plan to leave?"

"In the next day or two." Felissina took the young witch's hands. "I have to tell my team and make preparations. I promise, Martin and I will return in one piece."

"Let's get to Angel Haven," Martin said. "The sooner we go, the sooner we get home."

****

Martin waited in the family room while Felissina conferred with her teammates. Grayson walked in and stopped short. "Hey, stranger. What brought you out of your cave?" He peered out the window. "I don't see a car. How'd you get here?"

"My powers have evolved to their full potential," Martin said. He stood and walked over to his friend. He grabbed Grayson's hand in a firm grip. "I have full control now. No more visions."

"I'm glad to hear it. You don't see death anymore?"

Martin hesitated. "I do, but not the way you mean. I've learned some facts about myself." He stepped back and held his arms straight out. "Say hello to the son of Death and Life."

Grayson walked straight to the kitchen and grabbed a beer from the refrigerator. He drank it without stopping, while Martin watched and smiled the whole time. "You want to repeat what you just said?"

"I'm the son of Life and Death. Felissina reacted the same way you did when she heard. I gated us here, so no car needed."

"I guess it's not that strange after all. We've got a wizard who opens portals and hangs out with a priest who's also a wizard, a cyborg, a human/gargoyle hybrid, and me, the male harpy. I'm the most normal one here."

Martin laughed as they headed back to the family room. "Grayson, there's no one in this house who classifies as normal."

"When we add you, we'll also have the son of Death. The residents of Angel Haven will love this. Why'd you stop by?"

"I have to gate myself and Felissina to her dimension. She needs to fight the usurper and put her parents back in power. Since I learned I can also walk between worlds, I'm taking her home to help her out."

"You know, she asked me if you two were soulmates. It's nice to know you are. She deserves a decent guy." Grayson clapped Martin on the shoulder. "Bad luck she's stuck with you."

"And I'm very happy to be stuck with him, Grayson," Felissina said from the doorway. "I discussed our plans with my team. Their advice is we should rest today and leave tomorrow."

"Okay. Do you want to stay here tonight?"

"If you wouldn't mind. I haven't seen my friends for what feels like a long time. I'd like you to get to know them."

"It's strange being among people again. Stranger still to be topside and not mind. I think you were a big part of my change in attitude." He kissed the top of her head. "Tomorrow, we make another situation right."

Chapter Thirty-Three

Shadowjack stumbled through the wormhole at the science building on the palace grounds. He couldn't meet the stares of the scientists at first. The expectation on their faces said they wanted to know why the princess wasn't with him. The usurper wouldn't be happy he'd returned without her. To tell the truth, he wasn't too happy about it himself.

"I'm sorry our plan didn't work," Shadowjack murmured. They all began to talk amongst themselves. "She's alive and healthy. Events moved too fast for me to tell her the truth of what happened back here. It appears we're still on our own."

The head scientist walked over to him. "We all suspected that possibility. I don't think the people will rally without her leadership. It would help if we could free the king and queen."

"It won't happen. Even though they're not in the dungeon, they're still watched day and night. I'm not even allowed to see them."

"But you have been to them, right?"

Shadowjack nodded. "What the usurper doesn't know won't hurt him. I have some loyal men amongst the usurper's troops. Even his own guards are tired of him and want to see him ousted. We need to pick the right moment."

The scientist grabbed his hand in a firm grip.

"He'll have sensed the wormhole and will expect you to report to him right away. Good luck, Alden."

Shadowjack dropped the bulky stabilizer belt on the floor. It served its purpose, keeping him alive on Earth and doubling as a utility belt. No longer having to wear the heavy thing counted as a major blessing. He stalked across the grounds and into the palace. May as well get this over with sooner rather than later. He ignored the looks from the guards and stormed into the throne room.

The usurper had discarded the original simply designed thrones in favor of the current single large monstrosity. Shadowjack preferred the old set with their intricate carvings in the light wood. Royal purple velvet had covered the cushions on the seat and back, the dark color a nice contrast to the light, wood grain. Elegant in their design, the original thrones sat in the same place on the raised dais since the first king.

He lived for the day he could destroy the gaudy throne the usurper had insisted be built. The gold inlay itself cost a small fortune. The jewels set across the top were a testament to the extravagance of the false king. Deep red cushions spoke of his thirst for the blood, sweat, and tears of the people. Shadowjack hated the throne and man who sat on it more every day.

"You've returned, General Primeau," the usurper said. "Yet I don't see my bride with you. I've longed for our wedding night."

Shadowjack suppressed a shudder every time he thought about the usurper's hands on Felissina. "She found herself a suitor on her other world and he bested me in combat, your majesty."

"You shall have to return and try again. I will have

the princess as my wife." He rubbed his hands together. "And as my lover. Until she is here, you will get no reward."

Shadowjack's tone grew cold, and his eyes narrowed. "You've forced my compliance before with threats to the royal family and imprisonment of my family. You're lucky I don't do the people of Erlymere a favor by ending you myself. Keep your damn reward. I didn't accept your blood money before and have no desire to take it now."

The usurper's face turned red as he half rose from the throne. "Watch how you speak to me. Those threats are still in force. You will return and come back with the princess. Now, get out of my sight."

"Gladly."

Shadowjack stormed out of the throne room, glad to be out of the usurper's presence. He changed direction and headed for the tower steps. He took them two at a time, in a hurry to see the royal family at the top. He hesitated in the shadows.

Who guarded the king and queen at this time of day? He breathed a sigh of relief when he saw one of his own men. Anyone else would've made him have to change his plans, and he didn't have time for such foolishness. He knocked once and entered. Felissina's father stared at him as he shut the door.

"Did you find her, Alden?" King Markhov said. "Is our daughter, even now, in the greedy paws of the usurper?"

"No, your majesty," Shadowjack said. He knelt and bowed his head. "She remains safe. She has made strong allies in the dimension where she lives. I've come to beg your forgiveness once again. I never should have let that joke of a ruler force my compliance. I shall do my best to free you. I'll take any punishment you wish to give me. I am so sorry."

The king and queen looked at each other. "We confirmed your story the first time you told us. We knew we still held your loyalty. You aren't to be blamed, Alden, and no punishment shall come to you. You have apologized many times over the years. Do what you can to try and free us. Together, we can defeat the usurper and his troops."

Shadowjack rose. "I'll try to come back and see you soon. I'll come up with some kind of plan to put you back on the throne."

He hurried down the stone steps, grateful for the forgiving nature of his king. It helped that his troops vouched for him and corroborated his story. Time to head to the barracks and talk to his men. They should be able to come up with some type of plan to get rid of the current idiot who warmed his fat ass on the throne.

"Any idea is better than none," he mumbled.

****

Martin and Felissina appeared on the other side of a small town and tried to blend in. Martin wore a baseball hat pulled down low over his eyes, and Felissina borrowed a teammate's fedora. They each wore plain T-shirts, jeans, and hiking boots. He doubted the Earth look would help, but she assured him they'd be fine. When they arrived, they looked like everyone else. They fit right in, except for his baseball hat.

He took in the homes and shops in disrepair, the defeated look in the people's eyes. A heavy, musty aroma swirled around him. He'd noticed it in the spectral realm. He recognized it now as the scent of death. Specters moved in his peripheral vision. These poor spirits didn't know how to move on to the next realm. He wondered how they weren't shown the way to the afterlife. What happened to make them get missed?

"Travelers, collectors, and scions all have been here," he said. "There are still lost specters around. I need to help them move on when this is over." People shambled by, silent, their heads down. "I swear this looks like a movie set of a dystopian future. It doesn't look like what you described."

"I know," she said, her voice solemn. Martin draped his arm around her shoulders and pulled her close. "My poor people. My poor town. I should have found some way to come back sooner."

They stared at what used to be a vibrant village. Boards were nailed over the few unbroken windows. Trash lined the gutters of the streets, and most of the large flowerpots were broken. Large dirt rings showed where some used to sit. Torn and faded canopies hung limply from rusted metal frameworks. The buildings looked as forgotten and beaten down as the people who avoided them.

"It's all changed so much. I spent a lot of my time here. Most of the shop owners knew me. I don't know if any of them are left, let alone alive. How could one man do so much damage in fifteen short years?"

"Looks like with very little difficulty. Come on. Let's go find someone in power to talk to."

Felissina led him to a two story, white stone building. "This is where the magistrate has his office. He may be able to help us."

Martin called the lost specters to him. He sent them

to scout the province and let him know what they were up against. At the moment, the situation didn't look good. If the people were this beaten down, he and Felissina may not have any help. As the son of Death, he thought of himself as a blessing in disguise. He could call all the help he needed from the spectral realm.

They entered on the ground floor and jogged up the short staircase, their footsteps echoing through empty corridors. Most of the doors were boarded up. A hunched over cleaning woman swept the hall. There were little to no fibers left in her broom. The few it still possessed scratched softly against the broken tile floor. With the amount of dust and dirt piled against the walls, she didn't realize she'd already lost the cleaning battle.

Office doors sagged on rusted hinges, some with the glass broken out. Most of the desks lay on their sides or in pieces on the floor. Dirt and grime covered every piece of furniture and window around them. Worst of all, the heavy smell of disuse and abandonment clung cloyingly to all it could, including Martin and Felissina.

"Excuse me," Felissina said as they approached. "Is the magistrate available? We need to see him on a matter of grave importance."

"Where have you been?" The old woman stared at them. "There hasn't been a magistrate or anyone else in charge for years. The invaders ransacked his office and took all his work, all his papers. Everything is broken or gone. Our town is naught but a shell these days."

Felissina glanced at Martin. "If there's no magistrate, who attends to the needs of the town?"

"The needs of the town?" the old woman cackled.

"That pig of a king don't care about nobody. When he dissolved all the city councils, he promised he'd take care of the town. All he takes care of is himself. Even his personal guards are sick of him."

Martin felt Felissina's body tense as he put his arm around her shoulders. "I'm about to change the situation here," she said. "I won't let my homeland be abused like this any longer. Martin, we need to go to the palace. It's time to start our revolution."

"Feli, we don't have any troops," he said. "You need an army to start a revolution."

She drew herself up and whipped off her hat. "Nonsense. We both have our powers, plus your army from the spectral realm. I'm absolutely determined to take back the throne and free my parents."

The old woman dropped the broom with a loud clatter and covered her mouth. "Princess Felissina? We feared you lost forever." She wiped away the tears running down her cheeks. "We have waited so long for you to come home. I'll spread the word you've returned, and you'll have your army."

"Spread the word quietly," Martin said. "We don't want to tip off the bad guys."

The old woman winked. "Have you made contact with our loyalist in the palace?"

Felissina frowned. "A loyalist? I didn't know we had any loyal men left. Please tell me who it is, and I'll try to find him."

The woman lowered her voice and looked around, even though there were no other people in the hallway. "General Alden Primeau. He had no choice but to betray our king. He works to dethrone the usurper."

"I'll…try…to find him," Felissina stammered.

The woman pressed a finger to her lips and nodded. She gestured them to follow her, and she showed them the back way out. Felissina shoved her hat back on her head. It wouldn't do to get caught when they were so close to their goal. Martin checked the street before they stepped out, and they hurried away from the town hall. They had no desire to put the cleaning woman in danger when she'd given them important information.

All in all, not a bad start, given the circumstances.

Chapter Thirty-Four

Martin stared at her. "This is your world. What now?"

She headed down the street at a trot. "We should check the armory. Once we rally the people, they'll need weapons."

Behind what used to be the constable's office stood a sad, neglected building. Thick weeds grew around the cracked foundation, and paint peeled from the walls. A heavy bolt sealed the door shut and a large, rusty padlock hung from it. A notice nailed to the door stated any person not a member of the royal guards could no longer own any type of weapon. Any person found with a weapon in their possession would be executed on the spot. This law would be in effect until further notice.

Martin grabbed her around the waist and gated them inside. Dust motes floated in the pale light trying to force its way through the layers of grime on the windows. An even layer of dust coated the shelves and cabinets, a testament to the weapons lying dormant for years. The armory contained everything from guns to swords. Other melee weapons, like knives, long bows, and crossbows lined the shelves or hung from pegs. A tag hung from each weapon with a name and an identification number written on it.

"The usurper is at least organized, if not cleanliness." Martin ran his finger through the thick layer of dust. "Every piece in here is cataloged." He walked over to a large cabinet and took down a key from the peg next to it. "Hey, he's got quite a variety in here. Some of these guns look like they came from Earth." He pulled out a bulky gun. "This is the same as Shadowjack's gun. It's a type of energy weapon, right?"

"Yes. It fires a contained plasma burst." Felissina took it from him. "I can't believe Shadowjack has actually been working against the usurper all this time. He tried to tell me on Earth, but I wouldn't listen." She took a deep breath. "All of these will need to be cleaned and loaded. The energy batteries on the others will need to be primed and charged. How can we get these to the people?"

"First, we've got to get you to the people. Then we'll figure out how to arm them."

Martin walked over to a rack of short swords on the back wall. He took one down and cut an arc through the air. The grip felt comfortable in his hand. As he held it, memories flooded his mind. The picture of the battle in his father's book sprung to his mind. He stared at the blade in his hand. He'd been a soldier in the big war between the realms. He closed his eyes and remembered how it felt to fight for a cause.

How could he have forgotten what it felt like to hold steel in his hand? He swung it a few more times as old skills came flooding back. The sword's grip felt as comfortable as an old friend. He ran his thumb over the edge and shook his head. Duller than dirt. He'd need a whet stone to hone it. He saw, again, the picture of himself in the book. Talk about coming full circle.

"The edged weapons need to be sharpened." He

paused. "With how advanced your science is, I'm surprised to see swords and other hand weapons here."

Felissina took one down for herself. "Swords don't have to be reloaded."

"True. Let's head to the palace. We should be able to get some help from someone up there, right?"

She nodded. "I know some of the guards will still be loyal to my family. The problem will be how to speak to them without the usurper's knowledge."

Once again, he wrapped his arm around her waist and gated them inside the palace walls. He held his hand up and checked the courtyard. He nodded to her once, and they scurried across the open ground. Felissina led him to the science building where she'd made her escape years before. They descended the steps to the lab. She took a deep breath and opened the door.

"Princess," one of the scientists exclaimed. He ran over and pulled her into a tight hug. "General Primeau told us you didn't return with him."

"No, I didn't. I've returned with this man. His name is Martin Long." She stood close to him and laid her hand on his chest. "I've taken him as my consort."

"When the wormhole's control panel got destroyed, we feared you lost forever." The scientists all nodded and smiled. "We're happy to have you home, your highness. I'm glad your consort has come with you. Have you raised the army as the king asked?"

"I'm afraid we're all there is." She glanced at Martin. "For now."

Martin spoke up. "We went to a small town before we came here. The people look like they've had the life drained out of them."

"A profound observation, young man. The usurper

has drained the life out of the whole province. The other provinces aren't faring much better under his men. If we can re-take Erlymere, the other provinces will rise up and dethrone the rulers the usurper placed in charge. You can count on our help. We'll do whatever we can to assist."

Martin grinned. "Well, a revolution has got to start somewhere. See if you can get word to the people around here your princess is back. She's not happy with the condition of the province. We'll need all the help we can get to dethrone the usurper successfully." He glanced at Felissina. "Where to next?"

"I must find my parents and free them. They must be told I am alive and have come home."

"Not an easy task," a voice said behind them. They turned, and Shadowjack stood there. He raised his hands when they took a step toward him. "Take it easy. I'm here to help."

Mist swirled around Martin. "I don't trust you."

"Martin, it's all right. Remember what the old woman told us. He's the loyalist we were supposed to contact."

Shadowjack knelt before her and bowed his head. "I'll do what I can to help you, your highness."

"Why?"

He gazed up at her. "I didn't get a chance on Earth to tell you the whole story. The invaders forced my cooperation. Threats were made to my family, as well as you and your family. If I didn't help the usurper take over, the king and queen would have been butchered while he would make you watch. Then you would've been forced into marriage to him. I couldn't let that happen. Not to the king and queen, and not to you.

Your family has always held my loyalty, whether you believe me or not."

"Then why attack me on Earth? Why hand me over to a known villain? You could have tried to tell me what you were up to."

He shrugged. "We had no time to talk. I knew you'd attack as soon as you saw me. Circumstances forced my cooperation with Anita Haines. I could find the strongest signal for the wormhole generator in her lab. I didn't want to hurt you."

Felissina paused for a moment. "I believe I understand. As a superhero in my adopted dimension, my former hurts have been much more grievous than the injury you caused. I can't believe what I'm about to say, but for now, you have my trust." She and Martin shared a look. "We plan to take back the palace. Rally any of my father's faithful guards who are left. The usurper's time is over."

"As you command, your highness."

When Shadowjack left, Martin pulled her into his arms. "You're sexy when you give orders and lead armies and act all royal."

"I'm sexy all the time," she retorted. "You're just as sexy when you command the dead."

"I am, aren't I? Let's go wrap this up." He gave her a quick kiss. "You've got a concert in a couple of weeks."

As they stood in the doorway, she smiled. "The concert slipped my mind."

They were about to step out into the courtyard when the specters returned. Martin stood there to let them surround him. He nodded and they faded away. "We have to go back to the town. Somehow, the king expects you to come to him. I don't know how he found out you were here, and I really don't care. We need a plan before we confront him."

She nodded, and they gated back to the town. They hurried down the street and found an empty store with most of the windows covered. Martin gated them inside, and they hurried to the stockroom. If the usurper's men searched for them, there would be no sign they were there.

"So, Ms. Princess, do you have a plan?" he said.

"I believe I might." She frowned at him. "No wonder Kaz always yells at you. Don't think to call me 'Ms. Princess' again."

"How about Mrs. Long?" He grinned. "I mean if we live through this and all."

"Did you propose marriage to me?" She wrapped her arms around his waist. "Of course we'll live through this. Your father has decreed we are immortal."

"True." He laid her back on the floor and kissed her hard. "What do you think of the whole marriage idea?"

"I think I'll say yes. I also think we have too many clothes on at the moment. Your eyes are green again. This may be our last chance for some time, so let's take advantage of the relative quiet."

"As you command, princess."

They spent the next hour in each other's arms.

****

Martin pulled his T-shirt down and Felissina finished dressing. Streetlamps glowed and flickered in the dark. Lights headed in their direction, swinging back and forth, forcing them to hurry back to the stockroom. The front door rattled, a sure sign the usurper's troops searched for them. It could be Shadowjack's troops or their own people outside.

"Stay here," he whispered. "I'll find Shadowjack. We need his help with our plan."

She nodded, and he gated out. A few minutes later he came back with Shadowjack. They all returned to the stockroom and sat in a tight circle. Martin and Felissina took turns laying out the plan they'd devised.

Shadowjack glared at them. "Are you two crazy? There are so many ways your plan could go wrong. What if I can't get my men to be the ones we need in place? What if I can't free your parents to help us join the fight? What if the people can't get into the palace grounds?"

"What if you tried to look on the bright side?" Martin whispered harshly. "We know we have a lot of problems with this plan, but it's all we have. If you've got a better idea, tell me. I don't want Feli putting herself in danger any more than you do. I don't know what else to do. This whole plan hinges on you and the loyal guards finding us to take us to the usurper. We'll take care of the people. You take care of the palace side."

Shadowjack sighed and shook his head. "When do you want to be picked up?"

"Not for at least two days," Felissina said. "We need time to empty the armory, and the people need to prepare the weapons. Maintenance needs to be performed on every item we found."

"All right." Shadowjack glanced toward the front of the store. No lights shone. "Now is the time for you to go. Start on the outskirts of town. Take as many weapons as you can to the people. Find out if anyone still hides any type of weapon. I'm sure they do."

"Why are you sure they're already armed?" Martin asked.

Shadowjack tugged his beret down tighter on his head and grinned. "Who do you think armed them?"

Martin shook his head and gated him to the street. He turned to Felissina. "As much I hate to admit it, he's starting to grow on me."

Chapter Thirty-Five

"Everyone is armed and ready when you give the word, princess," Shadowjack said when they met up two days later.

Felissina paced. "Every weapon has been repaired? If there is even one small doubt, we won't go through with the plan."

"It'll be okay, Feli," Martin said. He pulled her into a gentle embrace. "You may be a hero on Earth, but you've never commanded an army before. You have every right to be nervous."

"I checked the weapons myself," Shadowjack said. "We're ready to do this when you are."

She took a deep breath and nodded. "Then let's put our plan into action and dethrone the foul usurper. The time has come to take back our land."

Shadowjack pulled her into a tight hug. "My men are yours to command. We've got your back."

"Thank you, Shadowjack." She smiled. "I mean General Primeau. As soon as this is over, you'll receive any reward you would care to name."

Martin looked at them. "It's time for you to 'find' us. We'll see you in an hour."

Shadowjack nodded once, and Martin gated him to his men. Soon, the door would be kicked in and they would be taken before the usurper. An old ploy, but it worked again and again, and it gained them the easiest access to the palace. Now if the usurper would play his part, the coup would end with little to no loss of life.

"Are you sure about this plan?" Martin said.

She shook her head. "No. I'm afraid too much could go horribly wrong. What if the worst happens? What if he decides to torture you? If the usurper discovers our plan and he gets his hands on me…"

"Stop it." He gave her a slight shake. "I won't let him touch you. There's nothing he can do to me or any place he can keep me prisoner. This plan will work, and I have a guardian I'll send with you."

Felissina felt moisture on her forehead and turned to Martin. "Has Drippy come with us?"

"Of course." He looked around. "Drippy, you nearby?"

The specter appeared, and Martin wiped his hands on his pants, happy to have a familiar 'face' with them. He looked at Felissina. "Feel better now?"

"Yes. It's a comfort to have a friend with me, even if he can't be seen all the time."

They spent the hour holding on to each other, waiting for Shadowjack to show up with his troops. Three light taps grabbed their attention. Time for the show to begin. Martin squeezed her hand, and they readied themselves to be "captured."

****

Shadowjack made a final trip to see the king and queen. He wanted to let them know the bare bones of the plan. They would be asked to stay put when the battle started. He'd made sure one of his men would be on guard duty. As he neared the tower where the king and queen were held, he slowed and kept to the shadows.

The usurper's right-hand man stood in front of the door. What the hell? Where could his man be? He started to slip away, trying to keep his presence hidden. If his teleport power worked here in his own dimension as well as it did on Earth, he'd have no problems.

"General Primeau, please come out," the guard called.

Before Shadowjack could move, multiple hands landed on his shoulders, and his wrists were bound behind his back. A hard shove made him stumble forward, almost impaling him on the weapons pointed at his chest. What went wrong? What did he miss? Did he trust the wrong people?

The guard approached him. "I can almost see the wheels turning in your mind. No one betrayed you. One of my men happened to overhear your plan conception. Tell me where the princess is, and you may yet live through this."

Shadowjack stayed silent. He promised he wouldn't betray Felissina, and he meant to keep his word. He pressed his lips together and refused to speak. The guard signaled the men to take him away. They dragged him down to the lower levels where he knew what would happen next. He'd keep his secret as long as possible, but in the end, all men talked.

****

The door to the shop burst open, and the palace guards rushed inside. Martin and Felissina held their hands up while the guards took their weapons. As they were marched out, she stared at the men who surrounded them.

"I don't know any of these men," she whispered.

Martin leaned close. "My question is, what

happened to Shadowjack?"

A guard shoved him from behind. "Be quiet."

They walked in silence and were taken to the throne room. The guards forced Martin to his knees while the usurper circled Felissina like a hungry shark, an oily smile curving his thick lips. Martin frowned as he watched the usurper approach. For a short man who looked like he weighed about three hundred pounds, he moved with a certain waddling grace.

"You have filled out in a very nice way, princess. I shall enjoy the exploration of your charms."

Felissina spat at his feet. "I shall enjoy it when I rip you open like the fat pig you are."

"So fiery." He gestured to his men. "Take her to my suite. I believe we'll have our wedding night first, then the ceremony. Tell her parents, if they're lucky, they'll be grandparents before long."

"You won't touch me," she growled.

The usurper grabbed her face. "You have no say in the matter. You will submit to me, or this man with you will be executed."

Martin gave her a small wink when she turned to him. The usurper couldn't make any threat against his life which would hold any weight. He'd gotten used to being the immortal son of Death quicker than he thought possible. He hoped the usurper and his men liked surprises. They were about to get a big one.

"My life isn't worth him touching you," he said. "Let them kill me. It would be better than having to have that fat ass anywhere near you."

"Such brave words," the usurper said. "Are those your feelings too, princess?"

"If they take your life, who will come save me, like

the heroes of old?" She turned to the usurper. "You must promise not to harm him if I do as you ask."

"Of course. Take him to the lower levels. Once my bride to be and I are alone, do not disturb us." His gaze raked over her body, and she shuddered. "She has her charms to show me."

Hands pulled him in one direction as the guards tugged Felissina in the other. He wasn't too worried about how their plan went off track a little. He'd be in a place where the guards would be lax in their attention. With luck, he'd find Shadowjack. He only needed to call the specters and send them out. Once they were involved, the whole fight would be over in moments. The people were poised to raid the palace as soon as Shadowjack gave the signal.

The new, improvised plan still worked. Granted, it diverged from their original plan, but as Felissina said, better to have a bad plan than none at all.

****

The usurper pushed her into his bedroom and locked the door. Felissina smiled. He made her part in their plan too easy. With the door bolted, his guards would never make it to him in time. Martin had no idea how badly she wanted to execute the usurper and put a permanent end to him. Moisture beaded on her forehead, and she knew Drippy stood beside her.

Sliminess oozed from the usurper as he stared at her chest. Her skin crawled as he reached his meaty hands toward her. She sidestepped him, and he swatted at empty air. He turned and stared at her.

Her mouth turned down in a deep scowl. "I'd ask if there was any way you could disgust me more, but I'm afraid you'd take it as a challenge."

"Such spirit." The usurper licked his lips. "I know you want me as your husband. I think I shall keep you locked in my rooms for a long time. You shall have to beg for everything, from clothes to cover you to food to nourish you."

"By all the gods, not another man trying to keep me prisoner. First Benedict Trust and now you. One thing you should know about me, pig. I don't ever beg." Felissina pulled out the thin blade she'd kept hidden. "But you shall have to beg for your life. Did you truly believe I would submit to you? You're a bigger fool than I knew you to be."

"You haven't considered my threat, princess. Did you not believe me when I said the man with you would be killed if you did not satisfy me?"

"He can take care of himself. Why do you think I let you bring me here?" She nodded toward the door. "You've given the order not to be disturbed, so I'm free to dispatch you as I see fit."

For the first time since she met the usurper, she saw real fear fill his eyes. He held his hands up and backed away. She stalked toward him as beads of water ran down her back. Drippy was wonderful backup. Having specters on your side could be considered a perfect advantage.

"I'll give you one chance to surrender. If I feel gracious, I'll grant you your pathetic life."

"I have not harmed your parents or anyone in the town. I have been a merciful ruler," he whined.

Her gaze hardened. "I've seen the town. You've destroyed it. The people, the town council, the shops are all mere shadows of what they once were." She poked his protruding belly with the thin blade. "You're a lazy, greedy king, and the people will be better for your demise. Unfortunately, as of right now, I need you alive."

****

As soon as the cell door clanged shut, Martin turned and smiled at the guards. "You know, you've all doomed yourselves. You can't keep me here if I don't want to stay."

The guards guffawed and clapped each other on the shoulder. "He's a magician. He'll escape the cell in a puff of smoke." The obvious leader turned to him. "Leave your cell, and you'll be cut to ribbons in seconds."

Martin watched both of them. "We'll see."

As soon as the guards left, he sat on the straw covering the floor. He spotted movement in the dark far corner, and Shadowjack stepped out. Through the torn shirt, Martin saw bruises on his chest peek out from the shredded fabric. His left eye had swollen shut and the skin turned dark purple. Dark, dried blood crusted under his nose. Three fingers on his right hand were twisted in an unnatural way, and he held his middle with his left arm.

"I wondered what happened to you. I guess the usurper discovered what we wanted to do," Martin said. "Will you be okay?"

"I'll recover." Shadowjack gestured to the cell. "Not the exact plan we devised, is it."

"No, but it still works. We're all inside and the people still wait for the signal to, as they say in the movies, storm the gates."

"Where's the princess?"

Martin glanced upward. "The usurper took her to

his room. He wanted the wedding night before the wedding."

"How could you let him take her?" Shadowjack demanded, then grimaced. "You were supposed to protect her."

"The usurper threatened to kill me. No one here knows I'm immortal. We ran with an impromptu plan. Since Felissina has him alone, she'll have no problem making him bow to her." Martin grinned. "And she has backup when she needs it."

"And your spectral army?"

Martin winked. "They can be here in a moment's notice."

"So how do we escape this godforsaken cell?"

"Did you already forget what I can do? Watch and learn."

Martin walked over to the cell door. He held his hand above the lock, and it rusted and fell away in a matter of seconds. He'd hated this power when it first showed up, but now he wouldn't take anything for it. Sometimes, destruction could be useful.

As they headed for the stone steps leading out of the lower level, the lead guard stepped in front of them. "You're out? How did you escape? It's impossible to get out of those cells."

Martin closed the distance between them and grabbed the guard by his tunic. "You said it yourself. I'm a magician. Abracadabra, asshole."

Chapter Thirty-Six

Martin drew his arm back, then smashed his fist into the man's face. He swung him into the wall and watched as he rolled down the steps and didn't get up

Shadowjack nodded. "Nice moves. I didn't think you had it in you."

"I guess my past has caught up to me. Turns out, I have a lot more offensive capability than I realized." He grinned. "And I have more in my arsenal than my powers."

They ran quickly and quietly up the stairs, avoiding the few guards in their path. Shadowjack laid a hand on Martin's arm. "I'm sorry I killed you when we were still on Earth. I didn't know what else to do. I let desperation override my common sense to make the princess come back to save our province."

"Since I'm not dead, I suppose I have to forgive you. Kind of a harsh way to force her cooperation, but I guess I understand why you did it." He paused then grinned. "Next time, maybe try a different way to get what you want?"

"Agreed. Now let's end this farce of a ruler."

They arrived in the kitchen area. Shadowjack nodded toward a far door. "That door leads to the back courtyard. I can get to the people from there. The king and queen are held in the topmost level of the east wing. Gate your way to them to bypass the guards. Tell them who you are and what remains of our original plan. They should be able to help or give you some suggestions on how to end this. I'll meet you in the throne room."

Martin grabbed Shadowjack's left hand in a firm handshake. "Good luck. Try not to get beat up any more."

"I'll do my best."

Martin waited until Shadowjack made it outside, then gated to where the king and queen were held. He stepped into a comfortable, but empty, sitting room. The sound of deep sobs reached him, and he crossed over to the far door. His heart ached as he listened to a woman weep. He took shallow breaths to ease the heartache bleeding into him. He knocked quietly and waited.

Steps approached and the door flung open. "Can you people not give us one moment's peace?" King Markhov bellowed, his wife standing just behind him.

Martin could see where Felissina got her looks from. The king was a tall man, broad chested and forceful, not showing any trace of fear. His hair and beard were a deep tan, his eyes green. The queen stood shorter, with the same honey gold hair as her daughter. Though tears still brimmed in her eyes, no fear showed on her face. Just anger and she directed it at him.

Martin bowed deep. "Your majesty, my name is Martin Long. I arrived here with your daughter, Felissina."

He grabbed Martin by the shoulders and dragged him into the room, then slammed the door shut. The queen dabbed her eyes with a white handkerchief, trimmed in delicate lace. They studied Martin for long minutes, then the king spoke.

"Know this. If you lie, I will need no weapon to kill you."

"I have no reason to lie to you. Shadowjack told me where you were being held."

The royal couple looked at each other before they turned to stare at Martin. "Who is Shadowjack?" the king asked.

"Sorry. I believe you know him as Alden Primeau. A lady we met in town told us he'd been spying for you while you were locked away."

"Is Alden safe?"

"He is now." Martin walked over and looked out the small window. A gentle mist floated in and swirled around him. He closed his eyes and nodded. "Alden has met with the people. They're ready whenever we give the word."

"But we have no army," the king said.

The queen stepped closer to Martin. "What is this strange fog which surrounds you?"

The mist solidified, and Martin chuckled. "He's a spirit from the spectral realm. Your majesty, the specters are your army. They'll help out the people when the battle starts. And ma'am? He doesn't like to be called a fog."

King Markhov stood straight and tall. He took his wife's hand and kissed her knuckles. "Then, Mr. Long, let us begin the final fight."

"Your majesties, I think you should remain out of harm's way for now. Because of how long you've been locked up, you may not have the strength to fight. I'll leave some of my specters here to watch over you. I promise you'll be safe with them."

"I do not wish to be out of the fight for my province," the king said, then sighed. "But you do make sense. We will wait here."

Martin bowed deep. "I'll send my right-hand specter for you when it's safe for you to come. His name is Drippy. You'll know when he's here."

"Go. Free our land. We have waited long enough for this day."

Martin nodded to the specter. As the mist zoomed away, he hoped whatever troops Shadowjack had armed were ready. The specter would tell him to begin the assault, then all hell would break loose.

****

Felissina smiled as shouts from below drifted through the closed door. Loud bangs and the clash of steel on steel echoed over the sound of lasers and gunfire. She agreed with Martin's earlier assessment. They did have quite the variety of weapons on her world. Her father always thought it best to be prepared for any situation, and the armory assured they always would be.

"Drippy, would you be so kind as to open the door?" The lock clicked, and the door swung open. "You're lucky I decided to grant you your life." She turned back to the specter. "Please ask your comrades to watch this fool while I go and help my people be rid of his influence."

A thick mist surrounded the usurper, and he cowered on the floor. Felissina flicked the crown he still wore to the floor and stood over him. "He needs to be brought to the throne room as soon as we have defeated his army. If his troops are as complacent as he has been, it should be over before it begins."

Felissina marched toward the sound of the fight, the thin knife held in a tight grip. At her first opportunity, she would arm herself with a different weapon. She needed a heavier blade to do more damage than this tiny dagger would be able to inflict. Black energy swirled around her hands. Again, she thanked the gods for her powers. This time, she wouldn't run from the invaders. This time, she would be strong enough to stand and defend her home.

Felissina rushed into the throne room, and her steps slowed. It appeared she missed the fight here. Men lay on the floor. Some moaned or didn't move at all. She glanced out one of the windows and saw most of the battle in the courtyard. If they wanted to fight outside, then she would oblige them.

She started for the open door. A hand grabbed her collar and halted her progress. She spun around, knocking away whoever dared touch her. Her eyes narrowed as she stared down the usurper's right-hand man. He'd drawn his sword and pointed it at her chest. She held her blade a little tighter and stepped back.

"Why couldn't you have let my king have you?" he growled. "He would've given you whatever you could possibly want."

"I want my province back and my parents freed. I don't believe he would have granted me such a request. Before you ask, no, I didn't kill him, but not because I didn't want to. He's under guard in his rooms."

"Such a small consolation from you when I feel you'll have him dispatched at the first opportunity." He gripped his sword tight. "You and I shall end our fight here and now."

The sounds of the battle grew closer, and Felissina

spared a glance over her shoulder. "I don't have time for you or your foolishness. My people need me."

She raised the knife and he laughed, as she expected him to. When he guarded against her small attack, she fired her black energy at him. He flew backward and rolled along the floor. He stood and saluted her with his sword.

"Good shot, your highness. You've excelled with your powers. I congratulate you." He stalked toward her. "But you're still not good enough to beat me."

As he charged, Felissina fired her personal energy at him again. He held the sword up, to block the attack. A thick mist flew by her, and she sensed the arrival of their spectral army. The specters encircled the man, and he screamed while they him pulled away into a dark corridor.

She blew out a sigh of relief. That went better, and quicker, than she expected. She glanced down and picked up the sword he dropped. She hefted it, then grinned. About time she had a decent blade to use. Time to see what she could do with it in battle.

Felissina hurried outside. It appeared the whole town crammed itself into the courtyard. They used the weapons from the armory or whatever they could pick up to fight the usurper's troops. She spotted Shadowjack down on one knee. His chest heaved as he tried to draw a decent breath. Fighting her way over, she blocked a blow from behind him. She dispatched the attacker then turned her attention to the man whom she used to consider her enemy.

"I believe you need some assistance," she said.

"I don't usually, but this time, I'm glad for it." Shadowjack draped an arm around her shoulders. "Let's end this."

"Agreed." She glanced around the crowd of bodies. "I can't find Martin. Do you know where he went?"

He pointed toward the gate. "He rounded up the runners and wanted to take care of the injured. We need you here, your highness. The people have started to stare at you. You've given them the hope they need to fight."

"Then they will have all the hope and strength I can give them." She raised the sword above her head. "It's time to end this." The people cheered, and she turned to Shadowjack. "Let's go."

Felissina fired her energy to clear a path to the gate. The need to find her true love gave her the strength and determination she craved. More than one man fell from her sword and her energy attack. She glanced to her left, proud to see Shadowjack fight with her. She fought her way to Martin. He may be immortal, but he could still be hurt.

Felissina stopped short when she made it outside the walls. A crowd of people stood behind Martin. His arms were straight out, his palms facing up. A wall of silvery mist shimmered in the sunlight behind him. A pewter glow emanated from him and wiped out any of the soldiers who tried to attack him. The short sword he held in his left hand looked like an extension of his arm. When an attacker broke through, Martin cut him down without a second thought.

"He's impressive," Shadowjack murmured.

"He certainly is," she said, her voice soft with reverence as she watched him defend the people under his care,

The usurper's troops gathered for a final charge.

The silver mist flowed out from behind him, enveloping the troops. Minutes later, the battle ended, hopefully for good. The invaders lay on the ground around him. Felissina ran to him, leaping over the prone men, and threw her arms around him.

"Were you worried about me?" he asked.

She looked up at him. "Why would I worry? You're immortal, aren't you? There's not much left to worry about when you can't be killed in battle."

He kissed the top of her head. "When you put it like that, I guess not."

"Your eyes have turned silver." She stroked his cheek and smiled. "I love the way they change."

Chapter Thirty-Seven

Felissina and Martin headed to the throne room and supported Shadowjack as he walked between them. Her parents stood on the dais where their thrones once sat. She ran to them and wrapped her arms around both. They held her tight, and she felt her mother's tears wet her hair. She missed the warmth of her mother's embrace and the strength of her father's arms.

She could feel the eyes of the assembled people on them while they held each other. The royal family should not engage in such behavior in front of everyone. At this moment, she didn't care. Everyone on their world could come and stare. So much time passed since she'd stood in her home.

They turned to address the crowd. Felissina stood in front while her parents flanked her. She raised her arms to quiet the people. "Our province is now free, and I am returned home."

The crowd's cheers made the prisoners cringe from the volume. One prisoner stood apart from the rest. The royal family glared at him. Felissina made her way down from the dais, her steps sure as she approached him. She stood in front of him, her silence as solid and hard as her stare, and he shrank away.

The crowd began to chant for his execution. She held her hands up and they quieted. "You hear how our people wish to deal with you. However, I don't believe the father of my beloved wants you in his realm either. You shall be banished from this world to a place where you can do no harm. Your men will go with you."

Martin walked up to her and stood by her side. "You met my father a few days ago and you already know him way too well."

"There is one more legal point we must adhere to." Felissina smiled at Martin, before grabbing the usurper's shirt in a tight grip. "Before these witnesses, you shall give up the throne you've stolen and reinstate the rightful king."

"I resign the throne and turn over rule of the province of Erlymere to King Markhov and his queen," he said in a shaky voice.

She beckoned Shadowjack forward. "General Primeau, see to it they leave our province. Then you will return to us so we may find out what this man did to you." Her gaze softened. "We shall make it right."

He limped forward and gave her a short bow. He grabbed the usurper by his neck and shoved him through the crowd as the people cheered. As Felissina watched him go, her shoulders sagged as the tension she'd carried eased. Arms circled her waist and she turned. Martin held her close and pulled her from the celebration.

"You really are a princess, you know that?" he said.

She laid her head back against his chest. "I believe I told you this before. I need time with my parents. Can you give me a little time to talk with them? I'd like to tell them about my life on Earth."

"Take all the time you need." He gave her lips a gentle brush. "I'll go help with the cleanup. Send

Drippy to find me when you're done."

Martin walked away, and she would never tire of the pleasure of watching him. His butt was made for jeans and deserved to be added to list on the refrigerator at Angel Haven. She turned to her parents. The three of them descended and headed for the small antechamber behind the dais.

****

Shadowjack and his troops escorted the usurper and his men to the science building. He led them around to the back of the structure. His men stood behind him and grinned while occasionally nudging each other.

"We are to leave your world, turncoat," the usurper growled. "Why do you keep us here?"

"Because we've got a different plan in mind." Shadowjack almost laughed at the hope on the fat, little man's face. "I hope you don't think you have your freedom."

The usurper's eyes widened as he understood. "The princess has decreed we were to be freed."

"What she doesn't know won't hurt her."

Shadowjack stepped out of the way. His men raised their weapons and fired on the troops from the invading army. He nodded to another squad in the trees. They came forward and buried the executed troops, erasing all signs they ever existed.

Chapter Thirty-Eight

Martin watched Felissina walk out on the stage and bow to the audience. He let his gaze travel around the crowd. It felt odd to be among this many people and not worry about someone triggering his power. This would take some time to get used to, but every day became easier than the one before.

In his darkest moments, he believed he'd never be around people again. As he worked side by side with the people in Felissina's dimension, his earlier jitters settled themselves the longer he'd been in contact with them. On Earth, Kaz and Olivia helped him ease back into crowded areas topside. He'd resigned himself to a life of loneliness and isolation. This was one time he didn't mind being wrong.

He patted his jacket pocket. A flyer for an upcoming fundraiser at a prominent Boston museum sat tucked against his chest. He smiled a little. When he showed it to Felissina, she had agreed they should go. After all, they had solved all their problems. Would it be so bad to want a little petty revenge on the man who fired him? Maybe, but he'd do it anyway.

Thick, velvet, maroon curtains were pulled to the sides, and the deep pleated one at the back of the stage rustled as vents circulated warm air. Banners hung to each side of the stage, the same design as the flyer he'd printed out. Felissina's face peered across the auditorium. Her expression looked like she welcomed everyone personally. The photographer captured her look with perfection.

Two pedestals, holding large flowerpots with colorful blooms, had been placed behind the grand piano. Its black lacquer gleamed in the bright lights. No music rested over the keyboard, but Martin knew Felissina would've memorized every piece. A perfectionist to the end. With all of his imperfections, he had no idea how it translated into her being his soulmate.

He gazed around the hall and noted the opulent red panels on the walls, decorated with a gold fleur de lis pattern. Dark wood frames outlined those with tulip sconces in between, their lights angled upward. The cushions on the folding seats were thicker than he would've thought they'd be.

Orange lights were placed along the black, plastic runner every few feet. He swallowed hard. He'd chosen to marry into this world of wealth and celebrity. He closed his eyes and pictured Felissina. As long as she stood with him, he could deal with whatever situation was thrown in his path.

Martin squirmed in his chair. He tugged at the tight collar of his shirt, hating the tuxedo more and more. He'd wanted so much to hear Felissina play, and the only shirt they could find just had to be one size too small. Not even this silk torture device created to strangle him before the concert even started could keep him away. Of course, once they were married, there would be a lot more tuxes in his future. He reached up to tug at the restrictive collar one more time and got his wrist slapped.

"Stop with all the fidgets," Kaz said in a harsh whisper. "You're worse than a kid."

"This collar is choking the life out of me," Martin retorted. "And I hate this ridiculous bow tie."

Kaz glared at him. "You may want to watch your turn of phrase from now on. I don't think Life would like to hear her son refer to her in such a way."

"You're the wrong person to dish out behavior advice."

Olivia leaned over Kaz and whispered, "Can't you two ever stop with the arguments? Now be quiet. Feli's about to start."

The house lights lowered to leave one golden spotlight on Felissina and the black grand piano on the stage. He trembled as he watched her and knew they'd be together as soon as her obligations were fulfilled. She began to play but Martin didn't hear the music. He focused his full attention on the woman at the keyboard. She'd piled her hair up on the back of her head with thin tendrils on either side of her face. Light glinted off the jeweled choker around her slim neck.

The dark blue, floor length, sleeveless, velvet dress showed her right leg up to the knee through a conservative split. He could see her slight smile while she played and felt his own mouth curl, too. The spotlight circled her, and he thought she looked like an angel from heaven. How did he get so lucky with such a beautiful woman? She loved him, faults and all.

Before long, the house lights came up and the audience surged to their feet in a standing ovation. Kaz nudged him when the audience's applause grew louder with whistles and cheers. When had the music stopped? Felissina stood and bowed to them. The brilliance of her smile lit up his soul and he clapped harder.

"I wish to thank you all for your attendance tonight to support our cause. Your generous donations will make a difference for those in need in our community." She waited while the audience applauded again. "If you don't mind, I'd like to call a very special person up on stage for you to meet. Martin, would you please indulge me?"

Martin turned a panicked gaze to Kaz and Olivia. They pulled him into the aisle and shoved him toward the stage. He walked forward to the front of the hall, keeping his focus on Felissina. His skin itched under the intense gaze of the audience. Yes, he'd slowly gotten used to crowds of people again, but all these stares sent his nerves jangling. Then he was beside Felissina, and she became the center of his universe.

"Martin and I have dated for some time now and have grown very close." She took a deep breath while her gaze turned tender. "I should like to marry you, Martin Long. Do you think it would be all right?"

"I think it sounds fine, my princess." He pulled her into his arms, leaned her back, and kissed her hard. "But didn't we already decide on this?" he murmured.

"The audience needed to hear the announcement," she whispered.

They broke apart and bowed, as the audience applauded harder and cheered louder. Flowers showered them and stagehands brought out two huge bouquets. Martin followed Felissina's actions and bowed when she did. He wiped moisture from his face and looked off stage to his right. Drippy stood there and Martin sensed his approval. When the specter bowed his head, Martin returned it.

The cheers, whistles, and applause continued for more than ten minutes. Felissina nudged him and they walked off, bouquets of flowers in their arms. They walked until they got to her dressing room. A stagehand took the flowers and told them he'd have them delivered to her home.

"You know he means Angel Haven, right?" Martin said.

She nodded. "It's fine. My friends love flowers, and I couldn't tell him how to deliver under the city, now could I?"

He pulled her close. "We'll never hear the end of this from Kaz. She's probably out there right now, complaining how we'll never leave the bedroom."

"I'm sure you're right, but Kaz understands. She'll give us all the time we need."

Martin pulled the pins from her hair and smiled. "There will never be enough time for the two of us."

"Then I am glad we're immortal."

He kissed her as he dragged down the zipper on the back of her dress. "Me too, princess. Me, too."

Chapter Thirty-Nine

Once again, the grounds of Angel Haven played host to a wedding. Felissina's teammates decorated the house and grounds with ivory ribbons, lace, and white and pink roses. Folding chairs were lined up in perfect, neat rows on top of the meticulously manicured lawn. Near the house, tables were set up with covered dishes for the reception. The day had plenty of sunshine and a rare warmth for being close to Christmas.

A portal opened, and Felissina's parents stepped through, Martin by their side. The tiny, gold leaves on the edges of their purple, velvet formal wear glinted in the sunlight. Under their garb, they wore the stabilizer belts. At Felissina's request, they left their crowns at home. An air of importance still surrounded them, and guests murmured as they passed.

"Thank you for your assistance with our travel," the king said.

"My pleasure," Martin said and, once again, tugged at his shirt collar. "I can show you where Felissina is, so you can have a few minutes together. I've got to go meet all my parents."

He dropped them off at Felissina's room and hurried back to the lawn. His human parents and siblings arrived with some of the other guests and were asking for him. His mother already dabbed at her eyes. His father grabbed his hand in a firm grip and gave it one hard shake. He greeted them and gave each a brief hug. He led them off to a quiet area where they wouldn't be overheard.

"Guys, when all of this settles down, we have a lot to discuss," Martin told them.

"What do you mean, honey?" his mother asked.

A gateway opened and Martin smiled. "This might explain it. Let me start with an introduction."

Death stepped through with Life. She wore a dress of pastel blue, and she'd woven daises through her pale hair. A slight smile lit her delicate features, and her feet were, once again, bare. Martin's breath caught as he saw his birth mother again. Would he ever get used to her immortal beauty? Death had decked himself out in a silver-gray tuxedo, almost the exact color as his hair. He still wore high top tennis shoes, but at least they were black. Martin waved them over.

"Mom, Dad, I'd like to you meet Death and Life. They're my birth parents. I want you all to sit together and get to know each other." His human parents stood still, and their mouths hung open. He looked toward the altar and Grayson waved at him. "There's no time to explain right now. I think the ceremony is ready to start."

He escorted his mothers, one on each arm, to their chairs and took his place by Grayson. Felissina's mother sat across the aisle and smiled at him. The music began and Felissina appeared, her arm looped through her father's as they slowly started their march down the aisle.

The most beautiful bride in the world walked toward him and soon would be all his. Their souls were already joined, so they held the wedding more for their friends than themselves. He didn't care. She'd wanted a wedding, so he'd given her one. When they told her friends, the whole lot of them burst into loud laughter. From what Grayson said, this happened to the Angels all the time.

As he heard the stories about how they met their own husbands, he got it. As they said, go on an adventure, come home with a husband. He still wanted to know about the significance of the list they'd taped to the refrigerator with all their husbands' names on it. Someone, and he suspected he knew who, added his name as well. He had officially joined the ranks of Men Not Going to Heaven Because What They Do to a Pair of Pants is a Sin.

Felissina's father lifted her veil and kissed her cheek. He placed her hand in Martin's then sat next to his wife in the front row. Martin's eyes never left the woman in front of him. He said what and when he should. The priest closed his book and announced them as husband and wife. He kissed his new wife, anxious to start on their honeymoon.

He led her to the makeshift dance floor, and the band played a waltz. "You look very beautiful today, Mrs. Long," he whispered.

"You're always beautiful, Mr. Long," she said before she laid her head on his chest. "Once again, your eyes have turned solid green. I'm beginning to know the significance of that particular color."

"You think so, huh? I believe this is the greatest day of our lives so far."

"And we'll have many more." She looked up at him and smiled. "If the son of Life and Death and a woman from an anti-matter dimension can't make their own heaven, then we must have taken a wrong path."

"And we're the perfect people to fix whatever the problem might be."

"True."

The sky faded to a violet twilight and torches were lit. Martin kissed Felissina and knew his messed up life had straightened out to a long and wonderful future. All thanks to the beautiful Angel princess in his arms.

A word about the author…

I graduated from Mercy High in Baltimore, MD in 1981 and got married to an Air Force man in 1982. We have two amazing boys who have grown into amazing young men. We spent sixteen years in southern New Jersey, four of them at McGuire AFB and the rest in Hammonton. We currently live in Memphis, TN where science fiction, wrestling, and hockey take up what time the cat doesn't. www.annettemillerauthor.com